JANE GILLEY was born in Nottingham and now lives on the beautiful island of Jersey with her husband, a rabbit and a Senegal parrot. Following a career in Interior Design, she now writes full-time.

By the same author

The Woman Who Kept Everything

The Afternoon Tea Club

JANE GILLEY

avon.

Published by AVON
A division of HarperCollins*Publishers* Ltd
1 London Bridge Street
London SE1 9GF

www.harpercollins.co.uk

This paperback edition 2020

First published in Great Britain by HarperCollins*Publishers* 2019

A catalogue copy of this book is available from the British Library.

ISBN: 978-0-00-830865-0

Typeset in Birka by Palimpsest Book Production Limited, Falkirk, Stirlingshire
Printed and bound in UK by CPI Group (UK) Ltd, Croydon CR0 4YY

MIX
Paper from
responsible sources
FSC™ C007454

This book is produced from independently certified FSC™ paper
to ensure responsible forest management.

For more information visit: www.harpercollins.co.uk/green

The
Afternoon
Tea Club

Chapter 1

It was a hot muggy Saturday afternoon towards the end of June, as the scrabble of elderly ladies, a couple of elderly gents and a few younger people ambled through the double doors of Borough Community Centre, looking around themselves at the bright, modern, carpeted reception. Some of them were moaning about missing their afternoon TV programmes; some were asking questions of each other; some stared wide-eyed at the unfamiliar building, probably wondering why their families had left them here, even though it was, supposedly, to have afternoon tea with like-minded people.

Families had dropped off ageing mothers and reluctant aunts. Some of the elderly women wanted their loved ones to come inside with them. However, Marjorie could see the families were keen to leave their aged relatives at the community centre entrance.

'Just go inside, Amelia,' said one family member, firmly, to a small wizened lady in a turquoise, hand-embroidered shawl.

'Goodness, Mum, you're going to have a lovely time in there. We'll see you later,' said another family member, slamming the car door – almost before they'd finished speaking.

Another lady was chatting to her elderly relative and then turned to leave. 'View it as a new adventure, Auntie Mavis! What've you got to lose? It could be great fun. I'll see you back here afterwards. Ta-ra!'

None of them stayed with their relatives to help them settle into their new experience, which was beckoning just beyond the entrance of the community centre doors.

Bit of time out for the families, Marjorie thought to herself, following the other people into the building. Gracie had offered to stay, after she dropped her mother off, but Marjorie had said no.

Being dropped off by her daughter reminded her of the day she'd taken Gracie to school for the first time. She'd been dreading it all night. Oliver had said he wasn't interested in 'all that' and said she could take Gracie by herself, which she'd preferred to do anyway. But she'd had a sinking feeling when she'd left Gracie whimpering at the school gates, her hand in that of a kindly teacher who'd said, 'Please don't worry, Mrs Sykes. She'll be safe and cared for here.'

Oh, Marjorie had known full well that Gracie would be much better off at school than in the awful atmosphere at home. But her worry, back then, had not only been due to the fact that she couldn't bear to be parted from her beloved only child all day and every day. More worrying to Marjorie had been the knowledge that because she didn't work and Oliver was at home all day long with back problems, she'd have to contend with his exacting rages *whenever* he felt like it!

'Hello, ladies, gents! Welcome to Borough Community Centre!' the young receptionist said cheerily and then proceeded to chat about the lovely weather they were having, as she guided the cautious groups of people down the corridor towards the main hall.

Perhaps they don't get out much either, thought Marjorie, walking alongside them. She spotted Mrs Lambert from the ground-floor flat, in the block where she lived with Gracie. She'd never considered that so many other elderly people would feel as lonely as her. She imagined old folk with grand-children to be amongst the luckiest people in the world. Mrs Lambert had grandchildren. Yet here she was at an afternoon tea party for the lonely; the fed-up; the neglected. At least, that's what Marjorie read into the leaflet that had flopped through the letterbox and was snatched up by Gracie.

A gleam had come into her daughter's eye.

'Talking of getting you out and about more, Mum ...' she'd begun in a tone she usually reserved for meaningful chats with the schoolchildren she taught. 'Here! Look at this!'

So Marjorie followed the receptionist, alongside a swarm of mainly bowed grey heads in drab or worn jackets or rain macs, even though it was a clammily hot day. Their questions subsided as they seemed to accept their forced afternoon out. Marjorie passed a young woman with a black and white cat brooch on her rather oversized bright yellow cardigan, with matching Alice band. She looked familiar but Marjorie couldn't think from where. Another lady was still wearing her sun hat, as they all shuffled into the hall towards a couple of nodding women, welcoming them with beaming smiles and wide-open arms. One of these women looked to be solidly middle-aged, wearing a pale blue cotton summer dress with capped sleeves and a badge in the middle of her chest that read: Eileen. The younger woman's badge said, Taynor.

'Ladies and, oh hello, gentlemen! Welcome! Welcome! Please come in and help yourselves to refreshments. Yes, come on in. Yes, just help yourselves. Then just take a seat at the tables, anywhere you fancy. Oh no, you don't have to worry about all that, it's totally free. No, you won't need your purses; you don't have to pay a penny! You're just here to enjoy yourselves!'

A long table down one side of the hall was covered with white cups upside down on saucers, dishes of sugar lumps, small porcelain jugs of cold milk, huge plates of Crawford's Rover biscuits and homemade Victoria sponge cakes with fondant icing. Three middle-aged women stood behind the table, wearing white aprons, asking the guests whether they wanted tea or coffee and encouraging them to help themselves to whichever biscuits or cake they wished. Marjorie couldn't remember the last time she'd seen anyone wearing an apron. Or was it on one of those cooking programmes?

Marjorie noticed how the sight of cakes and biscuits soon perked everyone up, including herself. They all chuckled and marvelled at the sight of so much free food! And this small indulgence then gave them reason enough to happily gabble to each other about what was on offer at the community

4

centre today and how nice the weather was and, 'Oh, I do like that necklace of yours!' or 'Well, isn't this lovely!' even though they didn't know each other.

Looking around her and wondering where to sit, Marjorie saw oblong tables set out for eight occupants. The chairs looked comfortable enough but the disposable paper table-cloths creased and moved as she tried to position herself at the table without spilling her tea or dropping her cake. *A little lacking*, Marjorie thought dimly.

Pleasant, soothing background music was filtering into the hall from somewhere, which created a lovely restful ambience. Yet as the guests were finishing off their refreshments, the commotion of chatter having died down, Marjorie could see they weren't entirely comfortable with their surroundings, even though it was a rather nice place. Marjorie hadn't made up her mind about this new environment yet. But to avoid confrontation with her daughter, earlier, she'd relented about coming along to sample the afternoon tea outing at Gracie's insistence. She'd do it the once, just to say she'd tried it. Plus, if it didn't work out, that would be the benchmark by which all other suggestions her daughter made would be met with *understandable* resistance. Marjorie wondered if the other old dears had arrived today under the same circumstances: unhappy with their lot but equally unhappy to have to make any positive changes for themselves, unless somebody else initiated that change for them.

As Marjorie sipped her second cup of hot tea, she could

see that most of the women looked quite thin or perhaps they didn't eat well enough. It was easy to think you didn't need to eat so much when you were elderly and sitting around most of the day. Or perhaps they couldn't afford to eat well. A few had walking frames or walking sticks and one younger lady was in a wheelchair. Apart from the youngish girl in the yellow cardigan and the cat brooch, who Marjorie couldn't place but who sat at her table, Marjorie felt sorry for these other women. 'Everyone has their crosses to bear,' her best friend, Lou, always said.

The servers were still coming around the tables, asking if anyone would like refills or more cake, when the two ladies who Marjorie believed to be the organisers stood at the front of the ensemble and coughed to clear their throats.

'Well, we must say we're absolutely delighted to see that so many of you have made the effort to come along to our afternoon tea party today. And we hope you're enjoying your refreshments. Mrs Spence, in charge of the servers at the back, there, made the cakes, which I'm sure you'll all agree are rather yummy!'

A few people looked up, realising someone was speaking.

'Eh? What did she say?' said someone.

'Shh! They're saying something!' hissed someone else.

'Right so, just to let you know, my name is Eileen and I work for a division of our local healthcare services. And the lady next to me, Taynor, is my amazing assistant. It was at my mother's suggestion that we organised this event because

6

she told me she is always loneliest in the afternoons when, she said, it can be soul-destroying with nothing useful or meaningful to do. Does anyone else, here, ever feel like this sometimes?' Eileen asked, pausing to glance around at her audience.

Some of the people in the room were fidgeting now or still chatting; some were burrowing around in their bags, some were half listening but more anxious to finish their cake. It seemed to dawn on them – rather slowly – that something was being asked of them. Eileen waited patiently. A few people murmured inaudible responses.

'Well, folks,' Eileen tried again. 'I'm just telling you about my situation at home with my mother. I must say, I never suspected that my mother was bored, or fed up and felt that she wasn't needed any more. But she said everyone feels like this from time to time. So it's been a bit of a revelation to me that people who are retired or elderly or people otherwise in a position where they are at home all day long, like carers, often feel like this. I think my mother initially held back from admitting this to me because she thought I'd be upset to realise that the rest of my family and I were partly to blame for her discomfort. I have to admit, I was gutted. And very apologetic too, I might add! My family and I actually live with my mum in her house and yet we never allowed her to help out around the home, even when she wanted to. "Just rest up," I'd say to her. "You've worked hard all your life." I mean for one thing she's in a wheelchair now and I guess we thought

7

that was reason enough to assume she'd just want peace and quiet at this time of her life. "Not so," she told me huffily. "I still need a reason to get up in a morning, whether I'm in a wheelchair or not," she said. So we sat down together, as a family, and realised that apart from activities for residents in local nursing homes, there's not an awful lot of meaningful activities for our ageing or housebound citizens to do on a regular basis, to prevent them from feeling lonely or bored at home. I mean, we're well served by the nursing and health community but there's nothing much that's *activity-based*. Would any of you agree with this statement? However, there has been talk and a bit of a national push about offering more stimulating activities to people who are not otherwise engaged in an ordinary working life and in some parts of the country localised organisations have already made a good start with this. Unfortunately, our area hasn't really jumped on that bandwagon yet. So we're starting to look at this now.'

The fidgeting had stopped. All faces had turned to study the two ladies in front of them. Was something actually being *asked* of them? One of the elderly gentlemen, seated at the back said: 'Hear, hear, ladies. Yes, it can be very quiet and lonely in the afternoons. I think this is a grand idea of your mother's. I, for one, would definitely come along again if you're going to be doing this on a more regular basis? Is that what you're saying?'

Eileen nodded.

'It certainly is. And this idea of my mother's is part of it. So, following on from the conversation with my mother, I suggested to my bosses at work that if we trialled something like this – an afternoon out with a cuppa or two – and if our community welcomed it, we could start to do more things like this on a regular basis. It's Taynor's and my long-term ideal, you see, to help our ageing or homebound community make the most of life. So the point of today's afternoon tea is to inspire you to mix with people you may not have met before with a view to possibly forming new friendships. You see, we believe that once you start making new connections with each other – once you realise that what you feel and think is still important to us all – you'll start to feel more *valued* within your own community. We're sure you'll agree that chatting and discussion creates camaraderie and a general feeling of wellbeing.'

'Yes, there's nothing like a cuppa and a good natter,' someone said, laughing.

'Exactly!' Eileen agreed. 'Being part of a social gathering generally makes people feel happier and accepted, doesn't it? So we think a concept like this would help lift your spirits and give you a new purpose in life. Plus by engaging in some new activities and experiences you would also play your own part by contributing to the wellbeing of your community.'

Murmurs of approval and slow head-nodding began to weave around the tables.

'So how else do we feel you could help your community?' said Taynor, taking over from Eileen with an encouraging smile. 'Well, following on from this initial idea, we'd then hope to get your feedback about new incentives to help enrich the lives of yourselves and those around you. This would be *your* chance to help us compile a document to present to our bosses about the needs of our elderly and housebound community. We'd need signatures from all your family and friends to give this project enough clout to resonate and make a real difference to all our lives. In other words, *your* opinion is being sought with a view to make positive changes within our community. How does that sound to you all?'

A ripple of surprise ran around the community centre. Marjorie wasn't the only one to realise that she and Gracie hadn't read the flyer correctly. Wasn't this meant to be a simple afternoon out, for afternoon tea, no strings attached? Taynor sounded like a political canvasser, touting for votes. But, golly, this was better than *that* kind of politics. Eileen and Taynor actually *wanted* them to join in and contribute to the society they lived in. Well, that was a first! The amount of times she'd have liked to have got on her soapbox and crow to anyone who'd listen about everything she thought was wrong with society today! And yet here she was now. Here they *all* were now, being *invited* to set the stage for the 'greater good'.

'Well, that's a marvellous idea,' said the elderly gent who had already spoken, intruding on the whispered confusion of the others. 'I'm all for it!'

'But would these afternoons stop then, after you got your, um, your data or whatever?' asked a canny younger lady, dressed in a pale grey trouser suit.

Eileen stepped forward to speak again.

'Not at all. As long as yourselves, as a community, want afternoons out, we hope to continue providing them. We'd also like suggestions as to what other activities you'd like to participate in. You know, things like a weekly art class or a drive out for the day. Activities like that. Of course, as you get to know each other you can start arranging your own afternoons out if you wish or you could start forming your own clubs and organisations. We're simply here to start the ball rolling, as it were, to help you help yourselves in order to improve your lives and give you your own voice within our community. We want to help you realise that, no matter what your age or circumstances, you do still count.'

Marjorie noticed the shift from complacency to murmurs of 'Oh right,' or 'Well, that would be rather nice for a change.' People were starting to put their hands up to ask further questions. *How often did anyone ask the elderly what they thought about anything?* As far as she was aware, there were plenty of activities for youngsters but Marjorie had never heard of any such events for anyone of her own age. Or perhaps there were things advertised in the daily newspapers? But she only read the Sunday papers and hadn't noticed anything like that in there and, as for things online, well, she couldn't even use a computer, despite Gracie saying she'd help her with that. Yet it actually felt *marvellous* to be permitted to stand up and be counted, for once! Oliver had never let her have her own opinions. She had never been allowed to voice her concerns nor her wishes in his presence. So being given consent to stand up and say something *meaningful* would be quite splendid.

'Can we tell our friends about this scheme? I think my friend Elsa would love to go for a drive somewhere. She's housebound at the moment,' said the girl in the yellow cardigan.

'Yes, of course,' said Taynor. 'We'd like to get the community involved as much as possible. We're here to hear what you have to say and then act upon it. All suggestions very welcome. Right, so we'd like you to have a think about what activities you'd like to do and if you decide to come back next week could you write out your ideas and put them in our suggestion box? We'll put the box at the side here, by the table, next week. Then we can discuss it all the following week, when we've read through what you've got to say. Oh yes – sorry – I forgot to tell you, we're going to be here next week as well, so do please come back and have afternoon tea with us again – same time, same place – and bring any friends along who might be lonely or a bit fed up or whatever. We'll also collate some name stickers next week for you to wear, which will make it a whole lot easier to remember each other's names. So now we just need to ask if you've enjoyed this afternoon? Oh and I need to let you know that we might have to change the venue in the future, depending what's in the bookings diary here, but if that's the case we'll let you know in advance. So now I *also* need to ask you, if you could and if you want to, please give us your contact details, before you leave, in case we need to cancel next week's tea or let you know anything else.'

'Right! So if none of you have any further questions, we'll just say, thank you for coming along today. We hope you've enjoyed it and we hope to see you next week,' said Eileen, with a slight bow.

Everybody started to clap. The tables of elderly women and the gents were quite animated by now, discussing the fact they were to be part of something – ahem – *meaningful*, and a social experiment, no less! Marjorie marvelled at the fact that Eileen and Taynor had managed to get an unrelated group of people, chatting freely together as if they'd known each other all their lives.

But best of all, Marjorie noticed, it had established the buzz of a sudden sense of, yes, *pride* in the room. Were the grey heads really starting to sit up and feel counted?

Marjorie liked that feeling, herself, too. So, yes, she might come back next week. She hadn't intended to at the outset; she'd just been doing it to appease Gracie. But now she might ask Lou if she wanted to come. Perhaps Gracie would even pick Lou up and drive them both here. Lou would love it here as she always had plenty to say about everything. Marjorie smiled at that thought.

Oh well, it took all sorts to make a good pie!

Chapter 2

The idea of afternoon tea with a group of total strangers had not, initially, sat well with Marjorie Sykes.

'When you reach a certain age,' she'd told her daughter, Gracie, 'you only really want close friends and family around you.'

But following her discussion with Gracie, when the flyer about afternoon tea at the community centre had landed on their doormat, and the subsequent afternoon tea meeting, she was now – surprisingly – warming to the idea.

She'd shared Gracie's flat with her for the last four years, and that had been lovely, of course, but forays out with her daughter or anyone else for that matter were sporadic. Her remaining friends were thin on the ground for one reason or another – mainly due to Oliver – or now lived elsewhere and Gracie was often shattered when she came back from work at night, after her train then bus journey from the out-of-town secondary school where she taught English. So Marjorie had very little interaction with anyone on a regular basis, apart from the man in the corner shop or the postman or occasional visits to see her doctor.

Her only child, Gracie, slim with a blonde bob, was the apple of her eye. She'd recently won an award from her pupils where she taught, who were encouraged to vote for the best teacher in their school each year. 'It's a new in-house award, following that incident last year when that boy attacked one of the tutors,' Gracie had explained to her mother. 'It's the Head's latest idea to help improve relationships between the staff and students. The children vote on three categories: respect, approachability and clarity of instruction. It's supposed to make the kids think about the role of a school tutor in their lives; and for us, it highlights any grey areas where we should be making improvements.' Gracie possessed a certain calm and poise and knew how to mete out the right degree of encouragement to her students, concentrating on their positive attributes rather than the negative, in order to encourage rather than discourage. Her approach had clearly earned the children's hearts.

Yet, her daughter's marvellous achievements aside, Marjorie was miffed to note that Gracie was being decidedly pushy, these days, about her mother needing to do something meaningful with her life instead of 'moping around all day'.

Admittedly, helping Gracie with the shopping, cleaning and washing took care of morning duties, but – apart from daytime TV – what was there to actually *do* during the long tedious hours until bedtime? She daren't admit to her daughter that most afternoons she simply sat on the sofa ploughing her way through books she'd acquired from the library because there really wasn't much else to occupy her time.

'Why don't you go do some voluntary work, Mum? Or help an elderly person with their cleaning or something?' Gracie encouraged, when her mother had moaned about the lack of activities during the afternoon.

But she was eighty-two, for God's sake! Not some idle teenager being encouraged that there was more to life than being 'poked' or snap-chatted by all her friends or whatever the latest devices-related craze was. Didn't the years of bringing up a family entitle her to a bit of peace, now she was old, craggy and tired? In the mirror, a grey-haired lady with a plethora of facial lines, born from far too much angst, stared back at her. Even with make-up, she looked tired.

That said, no one had told Marjorie about the inevitable boring bits she'd duly experience as she got older – especially the hardly-anything-to-do-all-day bit. And she didn't want to admit that sometimes she felt like screaming, trying to think up new things to do *every single day*. That was tiring enough in itself! Yet she realised having nothing meaningful to do on a daily basis *had* made her withdraw from life. Sometimes she paced the flat; sometimes she could only bring herself to stare out the window, arms folded, at the communal patio, watching the birds pecking at seed on the bird table she'd bought and set up, mainly to give herself something to look at when she had nothing better to do. Oh, she'd been thrilled when the other residents had congratulated her for that. But even though she was thoroughly fed up with things at the moment she certainly knew she didn't need another 'Life Goal' at her age.

'Besides, I still have a few friends, as you well know, daughter dear.'

However, it did irk Marjorie that the few friends she had left were all occupied by grandchildren or great-grandchildren and didn't see her very often. And being as Gracie was divorced with no little ones to occupy Marjorie's time, she couldn't even fulfil her own longed-for role as a grandmother. Marjorie often remarked that it was 'High time you got married again, Gracie dear, and gave me grandchildren! You're in your late forties now, sweetheart. No time to waste!'

And then their conversations would turn into a testy argument, with Marjorie wagging an index finger and Gracie insisting that since the collapse of her marriage – *not* due to them being childless, but because Harry had gone off with some 'young thing', as Marjorie put it – she'd wanted nothing more to do with men.

'I'm loving all this free time by myself, Mother. I can do what I want, when I want, which is great. Thought you – of all people – would understand that? I tried pandering to Harry's every need and where did that get me, huh? Still went off with someone else! What is it with you and I, picking the wrong men all the time?'

Marjorie had sighed.

So, no grandchildren for her, then. No rocking babies gently to sleep. No fun days out with tantrums in the park about whose turn it was on the swings. Nope! A life of solitary confinement, occasionally seeing friends whose lives *weren't* embossed with the embroilment of family life, was *her* luck of the draw.

Thus Marjorie's life, when she wasn't moping around the house, consisted of occasional visits to the library to borrow and return books, just to give her a reason to get out of the house; or occasional walks in the park with Gracie, *providing her daughter was free on a weekend*; or taking her oldest and best friend Lou to the chiropodist, to get her toenails cut; but no excursions to get a nice cup of tea somewhere afterwards. So it was far from an exciting existence and, yes, she conceded privately, Gracie was right; it was aimless at best, pointless at worst.

Living with her daughter hadn't turned out to be full of the promise she'd expected. But, tedium aside, Marjorie knew it was *infinitely* better than living by herself after Oliver died.

And thank the Lord he had!

Just as well he'd had his stroke because Marjorie couldn't think of any new ideas about how she could possibly get rid of him, without getting the blame!

Yes, that sounded bad. But Marjorie's husband Oliver had been a bully, both emotionally and physically, for most of their married life. Marjorie couldn't remember when it had first started. Possibly it had begun when he'd left the army 'under a cloud'. He'd been very morose around that time. But each subsequent job hadn't worked out for him, either. Not that Marjorie was making excuses for him, but she belonged to an era that truly believed in their 'for better or worse' vows.

Yet excuses aside, he'd hit her a lot. Oh, he'd been very apologetic at first, which had sucked her in, believing him to be remorseful. But it had continued. Thrice she'd been to hospital; once for concussion, once for a broken arm, once for her miscarriage due to his aggression. He'd become increasingly abusive after Gracie was born because he couldn't stand the fact that – suddenly – all Marjorie's attention was poured onto their new-born child.

'There are *three* of us in this relationship. Not just you and ruddy Gracie! Remember that, woman. Now go get me my dinner before I *really* lose it with you!'

Fortuitously he'd never laid a finger on Gracie. Marjorie knew she'd have had to leave if he'd done that. But when she'd turned to her mother for moral support and advice, her mother had shaken her head. Unfortunately, she was one of those women who considered it wrong to interfere in another person's relationship, whatever the circumstances.

'Yer makes yer bed, yer lies in it!' was her comment when Marjorie turned up, the first time it happened, to discuss Oliver's behaviour.

Another time, when she'd had her mother around for Sunday lunch – hoping for once that Oliver wouldn't let himself down in front of them – the meal had started off okay, until Oliver mentioned the fact that Marjorie had bought

19

him the wrong shaving gel that morning. As Oliver raged, Marjorie had overheard her mother calmly tell Gracie, 'Just leave them to it, lovey.'

Marjorie had no siblings and wasn't sure what response she'd get if she offloaded to her friends. She knew everyone had their own problems and where could she have gone for respite with a young child in those days? So she put up with their situation and suffered in silence.

However, Marjorie had been mortified when Gracie told her mother, on her eighteenth birthday, that she intended to leave home and go travelling for a year with friends.

'Oh but, Gracie, you can't just leave! You're my life!'

'Well, I know that, Mum. But I need some time out on my own – everyone's doing it before college or university! Besides, if I'm being really honest, I, um, I just can't stand being here any longer. I can't tolerate the awfulness of things any more. There's really no reason for you to continually suffer at the hand of Daddy. Why don't you leave him? Or ring the police? Or you could go and live somewhere else? Anyway, me and my mate, Rosa, will probably go and look for work in London, afterwards, because anywhere's better than being here!'

'But, Gracie, you can't leave. What about your education?'

'It can wait, Mum. Other students have time out and this is no different. Besides, I really think you should do something about Daddy.'

But Marjorie had always been frightened of Oliver and simply didn't know what to do. And even if she *had* told someone about her troubles with him, would they have wanted to get involved in all that? She suspected they'd have told her to leave him. But she was a housewife and funds were limited at best. She had no access to surplus money in order to move away, so she'd felt trapped.

Gracie had never understood the reasoning behind her father's venom. Weren't you supposed to have loving, caring parents around you as you grew up? She'd tried to intervene once, standing between her beloved mother and crazed father. But she'd got a furious verbal diatribe from him. He hadn't hit her but he'd sworn and yelled loudly enough to warn her off interfering again. And he'd also frightened their friends away over the years when they'd rung – often by brusquely telling them Marjorie or Gracie were out. So they'd stopped ringing. At school, Gracie had tried to explain to her friends what was going on at home.

'He's completely unreasonable, so never call me at home, okay? It's too risky. We'll make plans for the weekend here at school instead.'

Marjorie had been so wrapped up in avoiding Oliver's fury or trying to placate him that she'd forgotten what kind of impact it might have been having on their young daughter. The result of which was that her darling Gracie wanted to leave home. Yet why should Gracie suffer the consequences of her father's actions?

'Oh, darling, I'm so sorry it's come to this,' Marjorie had said, sobbing, as the reality of Gracie's words hit home. 'I know I should've sorted it all out, somehow, years ago. But I've never really known what to do about your father. Look, please stay. We'll work something out, Gracie. Please don't go, sweetheart. Oh, I couldn't bear it if you left!'

But Gracie had stood her ground.

'It's not your fault, Mother. He's unresponsive to reason. It's domestic violence, pure and simple. He's a wife-beater and it's a criminal offence. There's no other way to dress it up. So I can't stay. I can't stand seeing what he does to you every day and feeling helpless about what to do. It's not right. You should report him, even though I know you're scared. Anyway, my leaving will help – I know he didn't want me so that makes me part of the problem.'

'Gracie, none of this is about you!' Marjorie had pleaded. 'Are you listening to me? *None* of it. It's *his* doing. *He's* the problem. Good God, I should never have let it get this far. But I thought I was dealing with it in my own way. Darling, please! I'm so sorry it's come to this.'

'I know you're sorry, Mum, and I just wish I could make it all better for you but nothing I say makes any difference. It still goes on. Anyway, my friends have booked the trip now, so I'm sorry to disappoint you but I'm … I'm going.'

Marjorie knew she had to concede to her daughter's wishes. But she daren't tell Oliver. And so one morning, before Oliver was awake, she smuggled Gracie away to the bus stop. Time away from the family would probably be good for Gracie. She was young; she had prospects and her own life to lead.

Marjorie knew she couldn't hold her back indefinitely, even though she secretly wanted to hold on to her forever. And then, needing someone to tell, she'd gone round and offloaded to her best friend, Lou, sobbing remorsefully on her lap, whilst Lou had patted her friend's head.

'Oh, I thought summat was amiss with Oliver. I'd heard talk. And your poor girl. But you can't be standing for all that nonsense, love. Tell him I'll send my son Derek round if he comes for yer again!'

But Marjorie was convinced things would only get worse for her if she tried that suggestion. Instead, she found the courage to secretly buy a pay-as-you-go mobile phone, so she could ring Lou privately when things got too bad. Unfortunately, Oliver found it and smashed it to smithereens and then punished her.

'You'll not be going behind *my* back and gossiping with your friends about me!' he'd shouted at her, as Marjorie cowered in a corner, quietly sobbing.

He'd once, laughingly, justified his treatment of Marjorie to their friends, on an impromptu night out. They hadn't known what was going on until then. 'A good beating is all these women understand!' He'd smirked at their shocked faces.

Oliver's temper had continued to simmer under the surface until Gracie got married and moved to Dorset. Gracie's husband, Harry, was a police officer, but he'd told Gracie there was nothing anyone could *really* do unless her mother made a formal complaint or someone saw her bruises. So Gracie persuaded her mother to wear a light sleeveless summer top at their next summer barbecue and then, when Harry finally saw the bruises for himself that day, he stepped in to have a serious word.

'Fuck's going on, Oliver? What's this all about? If I ever see anything else like this again or if I bloody well even *hear* about it, I'm doin' you! So think on, mate!'

Outraged, Oliver had then been careful to hit Marjorie where the bruises weren't so easily spotted! But the frequency, Marjorie was relieved to note, dissipated.

After Gracie divorced Harry for his infidelities and rented a flat, back where Marjorie and Oliver lived in Hampshire, Gracie hoped she'd finally be able to help her mother, providing she could persuade her to be helped.

'You've got to leave him, Mum. Look, why don't you come and live with me, now I'm on my own? I've got the two bedrooms so we can have one each. It'd be nice to have some company for a change and we get on well enough, you and I, don't we? We could have days out and, well, I just think it would be lovely for us both,' Gracie had said.

It had sounded like a heavenly idea to Marjorie.

'Well, I'd like to leave, Gracie, but to be honest I'm frightened of him. What if he made life even more unbearable for us, in some way? Besides I don't want to involve you in all of that again. At least it's not as bad as it used to be. Anyway, darling, you deserve a happier life now you're free from Harry and you've got some lovely friends and a good job at the school. I know you mean well, sweetie, but I'll be okay. I've survived this long, haven't I?'

To herself, when she was alone, polishing and cleaning the house the way Oliver liked it or when he was down the pub, drinking heavily and playing snooker with his old army mates, Marjorie used to think, *Why are we still together if you don't love me?* Divorce might have been an option for some people but she knew Oliver would never grant her one and she wouldn't have wanted one anyway. So, mostly, she just wished he was dead.

And then he did die.

He died one Sunday morning sitting at the table, chewing his toast, waiting for his bacon and eggs, banging on the table with the handle of his knife, making dents in the table top.

'Where's my bloody breakfast?' he'd called from the dining room. 'And if you don't hurry up – aargh! Wha's happenin' to me? Marj! Marj!'

Hearing the change in his tone from anger to panic, Marjorie had rushed into the dining room and then stopped, realising exactly what was happening. Her father had died from a stroke too. They told you the signs to watch out for on the telly. She watched in disbelief as her husband slid from the table onto the floor; his right hand hooked like a claw, reaching out to her in his last gesture of anger.

'Do something, b-bitch!'

But something snapped in Marjorie at that moment. *How dare he!*

How absolutely *dare* he speak to her like that! She'd given him her *life* and he'd trodden all over it. His awfulness had even sent Gracie out of their door. And *this* was how he was treating her, even now? She'd been totally prepared to help him, until that point, despite the relentless abuse he'd inflicted on her.

Instead, she took a deep breath and folded her arms. She *would* help him – she'd be his wife to the bitter end, as per her wedding vows – but she had something to say to him first.

'It serves you right, you old bastard!' she said, exuberantly.

She saw one of Oliver's eyebrows flick up in surprise; she'd never dared answer him back before.

'Do you realise what you've done to us, over all these years? Did you enjoy inflicting all that pain? Did it make you feel more worthy as a man?'

He didn't answer. His eyebrow dropped; his eyes stared out in front of him.

She was aware of the tick, tick, ticking of the dining room clock, as she waited for an answer. She even thought at the very least he might say, 'I'm sorry, love.' How very different their lives might have been, if he hadn't been such a beast of a man! How very different their days might have been, if he'd been kind, instead of forcing his wife and daughter to walk on eggshells, fearful of what he might do or say to them next!

Why wouldn't he answer her? Clearly he wasn't remorseful in the slightest about the way he'd treated her over the years!

With a sigh, she turned to ring the doctor.

'Well, he's gone all red like he's choking or something. But I don't, um, I don't know how to dislodge anything if it's stuck, you see. Well no. We're old folks, love, and I wouldn't be able to do anything like that. The – the what did you call it? The something thrust? No, I don't know how to do it, love,' Marjorie replied to the doctor's receptionist. 'Yes, I think he was eating some toast. I tried banging on his back but nothing's come out. Oh, wait a minute. Oh, gosh! Oh, now it looks like he's not breathing. So shall I, um, shall I ring the ambulance instead?'

Chapter 3

Stacy was soaked from the hefty downpour by the time she got back to her flat, following afternoon tea at the community centre. She stood dripping on the doormat; her yellow cardigan now soaked with cold rain. She'd forgotten her umbrella and it had rained in heavy blobs, despite the heat. She hated her hair getting wet because it expanded, uncontrollably, into a frizzy mess if she let it. That's why she'd kept it long, a bit too long really, in the hope the weight would keep it down. It didn't make much difference though. Her clothes needed to go straight into a washing machine, but she didn't have one. She always did her washing at the laundrette next to the corner shop, so her clothes would have to wait in the washbag until she got around to doing that. The first thing she wanted to do, however, was have a shower, to wash away the stickiness from choosing the right colour but wrong fabric for her afternoon tea outfit. She didn't actually have any going-out outfits because she never normally went anywhere.

She felt quite relieved to be home, but as she turned the key in her door she was greeted with a cacophony of pitiful mews and yowling. It sounded a little different to usual. As she entered her flat a black and white cat slouched from behind the kitchen door and wound itself around her ankles, staring wistfully up at her with its lovely yellow eyes. Stacy bent down to stroke it.

'Oh, Pooch, my little pretty,' she murmured, picking it up and kissing its face. But the cat suddenly struck out a paw and clawed the side of her face.

'Ow! Naughty Pooch!' she exclaimed, dropping the cat, which ran off with a howl. 'Bad kitty!'

Stacy stomped along the corridor to the bathroom, holding her face. She glanced in the mirror. It was only a little nick but it had left a spotted trail of blood, sliding towards her chin. She dabbed at the blood with some toilet paper. Pooch probably hadn't meant it. He'd be skulking in the lounge now, fearful of another telling-off. But she had to get her wet clothes off first and get sorted.

However, turning from the sink, she could see some of her other cats – Ebony, Chater, Melanie and Dingle – leaping around in the bath playing with the shower extension. They were having fun. She didn't particularly want to disturb them. But then she breathed in smells she didn't really want to smell, either. One of them had probably weed and they were all in it now. Damn. The bath would need cleaning before she got in and used the shower attachment. But Chater was currently problematic and skittish following the incident with the toilet lid falling on him yesterday. Maybe shooing them out of the bathroom wouldn't go down too well with him at the moment, either. She certainly didn't want *him* hissing and clawing her again this afternoon.

Sighing, Stacy took her cardigan off and dropped it by the sink. She needed to see if Snowball looked any better. But the yowling was louder in the lounge when she opened the door. She sidestepped their climbing frames and empty tins of cat food, overflowing litter trays and unfortunate 'accidents' all over the lounge carpet. It really needed cleaning in here. John, her next-door neighbour often banged on her door to complain about the noise and smell. How, she wondered, could he possibly smell anything when they lived in separate flats? He was such a Moaning Minnie!

'Snowball, my little – oh! *Snowball!*'

Stacy gently picked up the tiny limp body from beside the radiator and held it like a baby in her arms. A tear slid down her cheek and plopped onto the little lifeless black kitten.

Casper tried to jump on her lap and sniff Snowball as she sat down on the sofa. She pushed him off. But he jumped back on again. So, *that's* why they're concerned, Stacy thought.

But what should she do now? She knew she had to get the kitten out of the flat. Maybe the odd-sounding mewing would stop then. She'd have to find a sealed plastic container to put him in, ready for burying somewhere. That would probably calm the others, too, she thought. Their mewing was constant. *If only she could switch that noise off, sometimes!* She needed her shower, yes, but her priority was to get Snowball away from the others because she could see the tiny kitten looked somewhat scraggy and when she turned him over – oh no – he'd been mauled!

She went into the kitchen, stepping over Rover the ginger tom – narrowly missing treading on Canterbury her pregnant cat. *How had Canterbury got out of the bedroom?* Had she left the door open, by mistake? And was Rover bothering Canterbury now?

'For God's sake, guys!'

She pushed Canterbury along the corridor with her foot, as gently as she could, and finally got her pregnant cat back inside the bedroom. But she'd had to put Snowball on the floor whilst she kept Canterbury just inside the bedroom door, with one hand, and then shut the bedroom door with her other. Unfortunately – quick as a whip – Rover spotted Snowball and went to paw him.

'Stop it, Rover! Was that you before? Get into the lounge! Now stay in there, naughty boy!'

Stacy was always stressed with the effort of trying to keep them all separated or stopping fights. She often got badly scratched for her efforts. It was partly the reason she always wore long-sleeved clothes, even in the summer; to cover her unsightly sores! She realised keeping all the cats in her one-bedroom flat had probably not been her best idea. And whilst she knew that cats tended to grieve a dead companion, both Rover and Chater had become unpredictable animals of late. Probably being cooped up in her small home meant their behaviours weren't as they should be. Yet her obsession with cats hadn't started off like this.

Stacy loved cats. They were her kind of animal. They weren't as needy as dogs, even though she knew dogs were loyal. As a child she'd lived on a farm with her parents and brother, so she was used to animals. However, the cats her father had kept were for ratting only. She'd never been encouraged to pet them, although she had done sometimes.

'Never know what germs they carry, so leave them be,' her father used to say.

So it was a complete joy to her when she was able to leave home and buy this flat with her half of her grandmother's inheritance. Having her own place meant living by her own rules and also meant she could have as many cats as she liked! So she'd started off by buying a couple of kittens from a pet shop. Then people had wanted her to take their cats when they moved house or if someone found a stray. She knew about the Cats Protection society but they always seemed to be terribly busy with their own intakes. So Stacy had thought she was helping everybody out by taking cats in herself.

Trouble was, working every day in the library meant she could only see them lunchtimes and evenings, and so she'd often come home to find chunks out of them when they'd been fighting and once one got stuck behind the back of the kitchen units, which had meant getting someone to remove the unit and rescue the cat. So vet bills were fairly high because she was at the vets quite a lot. Yet she still hadn't got round to sorting out a pet plan for them all yet.

Some days it felt like she was fighting a losing battle, trying to keep them all alive and happy and fed or separating them into the various rooms. And trying to find out who got on best with who was always a worry with new cats. Occasionally she found them new homes but not often. She'd had most of her current cats for nearly two years now – Snowball had been a new addition. Yet, despite their traits, despite being problematic, she loved them all dearly. It was wearing though. But she couldn't simply give them all away! Who would look after them like she did? Who else would spoil them with those little tins of sardines or smoked salmon, when she could afford it? Cat charities were probably overworked and no one else had the time to help her out.

Stacy didn't mingle with anyone from work and really only had the one friend, Elsa, from primary school days, although she hadn't seen her in ages. Elsa lived in the village Stacy was from and had been such a bright, happy girl, emerging from school with hordes of qualifications, destined for university and a life of amazing possibilities. But a skiing accident had taken all that away from her. Now she still lived at home, relying on her parents. Of course, they took her out in her wheelchair and looked after all her needs to the very best of their ability. But it was so sad. Elsa was the only friend Stacy had because all her time was taken up looking after her nine, no, eight cats and kittens. At least Elsa was usually in, when

Stacy found the time to Skype, even though she hadn't managed it in quite a while. In fact, Stacy hadn't been back to visit Elsa nor her own parents for a good few years. She hadn't learned how to drive, so it meant getting on and off the three buses it took, in order to visit them, which meant far too many hours away from the cats.

God, the place stank!

She knew she ought to get rid of the lounge carpet and buy laminate flooring. Much easier to clean, of course. Yet when did she have time to go shopping for new flooring? How could she make changes, in any respect, when she didn't have the time to do that? The afternoon tea experience had been a bit of an experiment for her. She'd seen the flyer in the corner shop window and because she'd known it was only for an hour or so and, fortunately, nearby, she'd risked going. She hadn't been anywhere in a long time, so it had been really nice talking to other people instead of trying to reason with her cats, for once. And the cake had been delicious! She couldn't remember the last time she'd had nice cake. Her weekly shopping jaunts meant only going to the corner shop or next door to the laundrette, and buying local was a much quicker option than getting the bus to the supermarket and leaving all her cats for hours on end. Yet she'd have *loved* to go shopping at a supermarket – any supermarket – with all the mouth-watering offerings they had on display, at far more reasonable prices.

'I need a shower,' she said out loud, above the mewing.

But to do that she needed to get Melanie, Ebony, Dingle and Chater out of the bath and wash the bath down. She chewed her lip, knowing she'd come out of that scenario with more than a couple of bites and scratches. Fortunately, she kept a lot of disinfectant to hand.

She'd considered getting separate cat carriers to leave the cats in, when she went out. That way she could maybe spend a bit more time doing things she wanted to do. But she knew that was a horrid idea because then they'd be stuck in them most of the day while she was at work and wouldn't be able to move around properly in them. So that's why she gave them free rein of the flat. Or rather, free rein of whatever part of the flat she'd allocated them to.

No, there was no other choice. She'd simply have to keep doing what she'd been doing these last few years. No time for boyfriends, shopping or living. Just time to look after her poor little kitties.

Question was, who was going to look after her?

Chapter 4

It had been a week of thunderstorms and drizzle, since the last afternoon tea meeting at Borough Community Centre, and the ladies and gents and the few younger people slurping tea and munching biscuits around the tables at this week's afternoon tea had been lamenting over that fact.

One lady had slipped in the doorway, due to the wet being traipsed in on people's feet. She'd been helped up by a woman who she was delighted to recognise as being her long-lost childhood school friend from a neighbouring town.

'Pauline? Pauline Rastock? Oh I don't believe it!'

'Goodness, is that you, Emily? Emily Blye? Well, what a coincidence!'

'Small world! Look, let me help you. Oh, your foot looks quite swollen. Can you stand on it?'

'No, not very well. It's quite painful! Now how are we going to get into the hall with me like this?'

'Right, well, just put your weight on me and we'll hobble. Yes, that's it. Let's get a table together. It'll be wonderful to catch up. Oh and I hear they've got *chocolate* cake this week.'

'*Chocolate* cake? Gosh, we are being spoilt, aren't we?'

Marjorie smiled as she passed the two enthusiastic ladies. People were making friends or rather reuniting with old friends. Unfortunately, Lou wasn't well enough to make it this week but promised she'd come next week if Gracie would bring her. But Marjorie's eyes lit up at the sound of chocolate cake being served this week. What a treat! She used to love baking but it tended to end up down a wall or trodden into her carpet when Oliver was alive. She shuddered at the thought of what she'd had to put up with throughout those awful years.

'Have you put your suggestions in the box yet?' said one of the elderly gents from last week. His question interrupted her thoughts, making her jump.

'What? Oh no. I'm perfectly happy just coming here for afternoon tea. Especially as we've got chocolate cake this week.'

'Ah yes.' The gent smiled. 'I can see everybody's thrilled about that. Although I must say I prefer Victoria sandwich, myself. My name's Raymond, by the way, like it says on my sticker. They wrote it out for me, which is helpful as I've got a bit of arthritis in my right hand, so I don't tend to write much nowadays. They're nice people, Eileen and Taynor, aren't they? It's marvellous what they're trying to do for us, don't you think? And I can't wait to see what suggestions everybody comes up with next week. So where's your sticker, then?'

'Er, I might get one later, if I remember. I don't think I'll necessarily be coming all that often. Maybe occasionally.'

'Ah,' Raymond said. 'Well, look. Do you mind if I join you at your table?'

Marjorie shook her head, although maybe a little too vigorously, and started to ramble.

'Um, no you can't join me. I don't know where I'm sitting just yet and I was just about to try and find the toilet. Do you know where they are?'

'Oh, I'm not sure. Maybe somewhere near reception?'

Marjorie sidled away. Oliver had always hated her talking to other men. Yet, despite him no longer being alive, she still couldn't seem to get out of the habit of making her excuses and leaving men when they approached her. Gracie got mad about it sometimes.

'I wish you'd see how rude it sounds to people when you're abrupt like that. They're *not* Daddy. So can't you learn how to let them down more gently instead of just saying "no" to everyone? My God, you're lucky to be approached at all. Some women never experience the charm of a man and there you are turning them away at eighty-two!'

Marjorie hated it when Gracie got angry with her but she could do nothing to change her behaviour. It was in-built from too many years of constant abuse. Even though Gracie had pulled her up about this unsavoury aspect of her personality and even though she'd tried to watch what she said to people, sometimes things just popped out unchecked. Unfortunately, it usually hit her that she was saying the wrong thing *after* she'd said it.

So she decided to stay in the toilets until she felt sure Raymond would have found a seat somewhere else. Then she went back and ordered tea and a piece of chocolate cake from the helpers.

'Oh and here's your name sticker. It's Marjorie, isn't it?' said Eileen coming up to her.

Marjorie turned in puzzled surprise. She'd told no one her name.

'The girl in the yellow cardigan, over there, overheard your daughter calling you Marjorie last week. Her name is Stacy,' Eileen said.

'Oh right. Thanks!' Marjorie said, relieved, but then nearly jumped out of her skin as Eileen positioned the sticker just below Marjorie's left shoulder and pressed lightly.

Marjorie already felt flustered by this week's experiences in the community centre. And she felt out of sorts at Eileen's easy manner as she stuck the name tag on her. Well, sure, Marjorie's hands were full, so it made sense, and it had been done with care, but it made her realise that the only person who ever really touched her, these days, was her daughter, when they hugged. Marjorie wasn't even one for hugging her own friends when she chanced to see them. It was behaviour she was not used to.

A tear pricked her eye. Everyone here was being really nice to her. It was a new experience for her and she was finding it difficult to accept.

'Hi, Marjorie!' called the girl in the yellow cardigan, loudly enough for Raymond to now know who she was, Marjorie realised. 'Come and sit over here with me.'

As Marjorie sat down with her tea and cake, she studied Stacy. In a way it was infuriating that she couldn't remember where she knew her from. But did the girl want to be her friend, like Eileen or Taynor had suggested they could if they wanted to, last week? Goodness, there was at least a sixty-year age gap between them! The thought made her chuckle as she placed her tea and cake on the table. She took a large mouthful of the cake to stifle her laugh and it was so delicious it made her sigh instead, which elicited a remark from Stacy.

'Good, isn't it? Everyone's saying they'll come every week if we get chocolate cake. It's a real treat isn't it? I don't get to eat cake much,' Stacy said with a sad smile. 'So did you make any suggestions? Did you put them in the box or just tell Eileen? I just told Eileen I'd like to go to the sea for the day. I'm a country girl you see. My parents have always worked the land. Mum said we stayed in a caravan in Mablethorpe when we were little. We went there to see our cousins, but I don't remember it. So I'd really like to go to the seaside proper. I work in a library near here. Don't mind it – it's a bit boring sometimes but it's near where I live and it means I can keep an eye on my cats. I've got eight cats, you know. They're a bit rowdy and I got scratched recently but I do love them. So what do you usually do with your time or do you—'

'Good grief! Please *stop*!' hissed Marjorie, covering her ears.

The other women around the table gasped, their mouths

opening ever so slightly in shock at Marjorie's response. Marjorie glanced about herself nervously. *Oh no, I'm doing it again!* she thought in dismay, judging by the way the other women were scowling at her. Stacy's eyes dropped to the table. The poor thing suddenly looked as if she was about to cry.

One of the women with the name Doreen on her chest took hold of Stacy's hand.

'It's okay, love. I think this woman probably has a headache or something. I'm sure she wouldn't have meant to be rude to you otherwise, would you, Marjorie!' the woman said, glaring at Marjorie.

Marjorie felt flustered. Well, that had all come out wrong! She *had* wanted the silly young woman to shut up, of course, but she shouldn't have said anything. She should have simply moved tables when she'd started annoying her – that much was clear. So she mouthed a 'Sorry' to everyone on the table and then gathered her tea and cake and moved to a different table – a table where there was just one other little old lady sitting there, eating her cake with a fork, and who seemed much more civilised.

However, whilst Marjorie munched her cake, she suddenly felt tearful. She was sure she didn't really belong here, amongst these people, despite the delicious chocolate cake. No, this experiment wasn't working for her. Perhaps she'd persuade Gracie to take her out for *proper* afternoon tea in an upmarket hotel somewhere instead of having to deal with these unbearable people, here, with their funny ways.

Then to top it all off, Stacy approached her table with two paracetamols in her hand.

'I'm sorry you've got a headache, Marjorie. Here! Take these with a glass of water. You'll soon feel better!'

Chapter 5

Gracie stood, with her hands on her hips – just like she used to do when she was a little girl, trying to stop her mother and father fighting, Marjorie thought wryly.

'So when this girl approached you, you got up and left. Is that what you're telling me, Mother? After what you said, which was totally rude and nasty, and then the sweet little thing gave you tablets because she thought you were ill? How can you ever face her again, after that?'

Marjorie didn't want to row with Gracie today. And it irked her that Gracie used the kind of language that only someone who looked after schoolchildren would use when the students needed reprimanding. Not that Gracie reprimanded anyone at school. She only scolded her mother, which made Marjorie *feel* like a naughty schoolchild.

'But she was so annoying; so needy. All her words were tumbling out and running into each other. There was no "off" button. It was like she hadn't spoken to anyone in years and it was all just dribbling out of her!'

'So *that* was enough to make you tell her off? This poor

young woman's manner? I thought the organisers said they wanted you all to make friends with each other?'

Marjorie buried her face in the tea towel she was using to dry their dinner plates.

'But I don't want to make friends with all those people down there. They're a funny bunch of characters. And some of them don't seem right in the head.'

'Well, now I've heard everything! Have you heard yourself? You're starting to sound like my father!'

'Well now *you're* talking rubbish. I'm nothing like Oliver,' Marjorie snapped.

'But we all know that the abused often become the abusers, Mother,' Gracie said quietly. 'You've let yourself down at that place and I must say I'm disappointed by your behaviour.'

Marjorie bit back the tears that threatened to overflow. Saddened by her daughter's comments and unable to justify herself, she stomped out of the kitchen and snatched her coat off the banister, intending to go for a walk to calm herself.

A light drizzle accompanied her down the street. She found a wet bench in the little park nearby, and sat down. A man threw a stick for his dog. The dog kept retrieving it delightedly and running back for the man to throw it again and then they left. Marjorie let her tears stream down her face unchecked whilst no one was around. She sat there deep in thought until the rain matted her hair and she didn't even flinch when a slow trickle wound its way down her neck.

She didn't understand herself but, more importantly, she

didn't understand others. Their behaviour was different to hers. Sure, she knew they all had challenging lives; they'd seen and done numerous things and that made them speak and act differently to her. Horses for courses! She'd had a horrid life with Oliver apart from their wondrous gift of her dear Gracie and maybe some of those people at the community centre had lived through horrid lives too. That said, Marjorie could see there was something wrong with Stacy in a way that there was also something wrong with herself; loneliness being at the heart of it. But she couldn't deal with other people's problems – didn't *want* to deal with other people's complications – when she didn't know how to deal with her own problem of coming to terms with what she'd suffered. The isolation, loneliness and fear she'd lived in because of Oliver had been debilitating. She was aware that the way he had treated her was probably the main reason she dealt with other people the way she did.

Because that's all she had known for so many years.

She didn't intend to go around hurting people but she expected them to understand when she felt annoyed about things or when she felt justified in pointing things out that needed saying. Problem was, people seemed to easily take offence at her words.

She'd often wondered if she'd spoken to someone in a professional capacity about how Oliver's terrible behaviour had affected and hurt her over the years, would she have been able to put the past behind her and move forward in a more positive light? She knew that abused people didn't *always* become abusers themselves, as Gracie had said.

Part of the problem was that she'd never managed to fathom why Oliver had been so angry towards her. His own mother had never understood it or been able to explain it, when she'd witnessed it first-hand and she'd refused to discuss it with Marjorie – just like Marjorie's own mother. Perhaps the older generation preferred to sweep things, like that, under the mat.

When she'd sat and conferred with Gracie, years later, they'd realised Oliver's problems couldn't have simply stemmed from his stint in the army. Maybe his problems had started before that. Maybe there were things she'd never known about him, before they'd met? She'd known he'd never been a particularly warm and caring soul and even though she'd found out he'd been in prison for grievous bodily harm she just thought that was part and parcel of his 'macho' image – something she'd probably been attracted to in the first place, if she was honest. When she'd met him in her late teens he'd seemed exciting in a way that the other boys in her village never were. Of course, Marjorie also realised that preferring men with a 'bad boy' image had been many a woman's downfall.

Or had his problems been the reason he'd left the army in a dubious way?

Marjorie sniffed miserably and tightened her coat around her. The drizzle was starting to make her feel cold. And now that she was thinking about things, she realised she hadn't been happy for a while.

She felt as though she lived on the outskirts of other people's lives. Sure, Oliver's behaviour had initially alienated her from her friends and family. She'd felt so alone back then and she knew her 'people skills' were somewhat lacking. And, yes, his manner and the way he'd dealt with everything in his destructive, derogatory way had rubbed off on her, even to the point of her being rude to people, the way she had in the community centre with Raymond and Stacy today. But Marjorie also knew that if she didn't come to terms with this unsavoury element about herself and do something about her behaviour, she might end up completely alone. Even her darling daughter might withdraw from her.

She shivered, partly because of the weather, partly because of that dreadful thought.

'Oh, Gracie!'

She couldn't bear to be without Gracie, now her life was entwined with her daughter's. But what if Gracie asked her to move out or find somewhere else to live? She might do that for lots of reasons, one being her mother's inability to be kind to others. Or, even more worrying, what if Gracie acted on her mother's advice and found someone else to love and they got married? Her new husband might not want Marjorie living in their midst.

Wake up, Marjorie! *Of course they wouldn't want you living in their midst, if Gracie married someone new.* Besides, who, these days, invited their mother to live with them?

That was a terrifying new thought to Marjorie. But,

whether she liked that thought or not, it was a possibility. It was a possibility that could very easily turn into reality, especially if Marjorie gave it reason to. Falling out with her daughter about this unpleasant aspect of her personality wasn't an option. Her outbursts had wrecked other possible friendships in the past, so she knew she couldn't go on being destructive. It had to stop.

But how could she stop the things she said, when her words often popped out, unchecked?

She knew it had a lot to do with her indignation at all things unfair, unjust and unpleasant, zipping straight up to the surface and barrelling out of her. Life with Oliver had been all of those things. Oliver had never let her voice her thoughts, good, bad or indifferent. He liked women to be quiet and respectful of him, even though he'd certainly never been that way with them.

Marjorie's insecurities probably stemmed from her not knowing how to deal with Oliver's behaviour. Oh, she'd have liked to have fought back, just once. It would have made her feel a whole lot better about things; she might have even been able to move on, more successfully, if she'd ever had the guts to do that.

Gracie had wanted Marjorie to see someone about her problems with Oliver.

'Maybe it'll help you move on,' she'd suggested.

Yet Marjorie conceded that she hadn't wanted to speak to anyone about her problems with Oliver because she didn't want to go over all that hurtful old ground again – especially spilling her guts to someone she didn't know. And she also didn't want to keep going back to see a counsellor week after week, forcing her to live through the whole sorry mess over and over again. That period of her life, Marjorie insisted to Gracie, was well and truly over. She didn't want to keep thinking about it. On the other hand, she'd realised that there was no way she could change her behaviour by herself. She'd tried and failed miserably.

However, the incident at the community centre had brought it home to Marjorie that things *had* to change and not just because she wanted to be accepted by the wider community.

Primarily she had to change for her daughter. Gracie was young and vibrant in a way that Marjorie had never been allowed to be. And despite Gracie saying she hated men, she didn't hate them in the same way nor for the same reason that Marjorie hated and mistrusted them. And despite her fear of being asked to move out if Gracie *did* meet someone new, Marjorie had no intention of standing in Gracie's way when her daughter found someone to love her again. Gracie *deserved* to be loved again! The gift of love had never touched – would never touch – Marjorie and she was completely accepting about that. But she wanted Gracie to find that special someone.

Marjorie let out a long sigh. *Why is life so darned hard sometimes?*

She knew she no longer wanted to continue living as a

bitter woman, marred by her past with an abusive husband. Marjorie wanted the chance to live as a woman other people would *like* to get to know because she was kind and considerate. She certainly realised she would never be classed as a sweet little old lady. But she could start by trying to be better; by trying to unlearn the wrongful message Oliver had taught her with his offensive actions.

She thought back to the situation with Stacy a few hours ago. Marjorie already knew that, deep down, her behaviour towards the nervous young woman had been wrong. Oliver had told their friends he felt justified to treat his wife howsoever he chose and Marjorie realised she'd done the exact same thing to Stacy that afternoon.

But it had made her miserable; it had made her daughter hate her a little and, worst of all, it had made Eileen take her to one side and suggest she go home, to have a think about how she treated people because they didn't want any bullies in their midst. She hadn't confessed *that* bit to Gracie. It was too shameful.

She'd been branded a *bully*! How totally devastating! Luckily, Eileen had been discreet enough to make sure no one overheard what she'd been saying to Marjorie. But even so, Marjorie had been so shocked at Eileen's words, she'd wanted to shout out: 'I'm not a bully! *Oliver* was the bully!'

Pricking tears filled Marjorie's eyes.

She looked up into the large thunderous clouds that seemed to have made their way over to her side of the park. The day had started by being bright and hot. Yet the sky was now stubbornly dark and ominous and as Marjorie searched the sky for answers, the darkness suddenly broke and emptied its hefty thunderstorm mercilessly down on her heavy heart.

Chapter 6

Raymond's son Simon was stirring their teas in the kitchen, whilst staring out of the window at his parents' beautifully kept garden. The lawn was trimmed and weed free, blue-tinged lacecap hydrangeas graced the far hedge, pale pink clematis climbed the garage and brightly coloured perennials sat in a small circular raised bed, towards the bottom of the garden, surrounding the base of the elaborate bird bath.

Raymond had lied about his arthritis to Marjorie. It was getting into all his joints now. He'd argued with his doctor as to whether it was partly hereditary or not.

'It's unclear,' Dr Hien told him. 'But we think familial concurrence has some bearing, yes.'

Why did professionals always talk in riddles? But when Raymond told his doctor about symptoms he'd found online, pertaining to something *he thought* he might have, she'd told him she would check him over and assess for herself what may or may not be wrong with him, based on *clear medical evidence* – not Google say-so!

Raymond knew Dr Hien would argue blue was black if he let her. But the point was, on his recent visit to her she'd told him that his increasing pains were probably his arthritis getting worse. She'd given him some medication, a list of exercises and a squashy ball for his hands that he quite enjoyed using now.

'You know, Dad,' Simon said suddenly, snapping Raymond out of his reverie, 'I think we should do something about these steps by the back door. Makes it awkward going down to the garden, when you've got something in your hand. You'll be tripping over them next.'

'Well, son, you're right, of course. I've no idea why someone would build a bungalow and then have steps of any sort coming off it. It certainly makes carrying tea or a meal out into the garden most precarious.'

Raymond had made Dianne's mug of tea exactly how his wife liked it – quite strong, with only a little milk and just half a teaspoon of sugar. And then he picked it up and carried it outside to where she was in their sunny garden. Simon followed behind with the other two mugs of tea, setting Raymond's down beside him before retreating to the shade by the house, to read his sporting newspaper.

Raymond sipped his tea, enjoying the comforting feeling of the hot sun on his face.

It was stickily hot today after the thunderstorms yesterday. Should've cleared the air a bit but it hadn't. There'd be no working in the garden today. Not that anything really needed doing. But Raymond did like to potter, liked to keep on top of things. Before Simon had rung and said he was coming round to see them today Raymond had thought it best to put his feet up and chat to Dianne in their favourite spot. Isn't that what long hot summers were for? Relaxing? Yet he could have easily fallen asleep in the sun if it wasn't for Simon calling round.

When Raymond gave up his carpentry business and Dianne retired from nursing, they'd decided to sell the family home and retire to this little one-bedroomed bungalow. They'd also given Simon and his wife, Jo, a cheque for £10,000 from the proceeds of the sale of their house, 'to help with anything you need help with!' and then they'd gone on the journey of a lifetime, visiting the famous blossoms in Japan, sightseeing in New York and finally staying with Dianne's sister in California for three weeks, before hanging up their travelling hats to spend the rest of their days, enjoying being near to their family and grandchildren.

Dianne had loved their little garden when they first moved in. It wasn't so big that they'd be constantly working on it. Neither of them had wanted that. It was just right. It was one of the reasons they'd bought the bungalow, six years ago.

'We need to get something manageable now we're retired,' Raymond had told her in the garden centre, when they'd first moved in. 'Slugs like all the little colourful perennials and annuals you like! And you know I don't like killing slugs.'

She was the one for flowers but she'd relented.

'Okay, but we'll still have a little patch of *my* favourites as well as your shrubs,' she'd laughed. 'Or I can put them in a raised bed.'

'Ah, but slugs can climb, my love!'

Yes, he was a shrub man, through and through, he'd told his son, which had made Simon laugh.

'Sounds like you've got a beastly ailment when you say it like that, Dad; doesn't it, Mum? Or you sound like a super-hero! Not Superman but Shrub Man!' Simon had grinned.

Simon was a postman and had married his childhood sweetheart, Jo, a hairdresser and they'd had twin girls.

'You see? I get to have girls in the family, after all!' Dianne had informed Raymond proudly, all those years ago, when Jo had let her hold them at the hospital, a few days after their birth. Their skin tone was a soft caramel, much like hers; their hair in dark wisps, too. She'd always wanted to present Raymond with a daughter but it hadn't happened. Yet now she had *two* girls to mollycoddle. Oh, it had been joyous babysitting them, whilst the twins were growing up and then keeping up with their exploits when they went off to college, unsurprisingly, both wanting to be hairdressers and opening their own salon.

'Confusing to your customers though,' Dianne had said when the girls had told her what they wanted to do.

'But we have to be together, Gran,' Maya told her. 'It's what we're about. We'll make it work. I've told Esha I'm happy to dye my hair if there's a problem.'

And she had, too. Aubergine purple! Dianne couldn't imagine a worse colour but it actually suited her. Luckily her sister Esha never had to dye her wonderful dark curly locks, although in the course of their work she had experimented with lots of different 'looks'. But Dianne and Raymond had been completely proud that their granddaughters' business had been a roaring success. Both girls were married now, with tiny babies of their own.

Raymond loved to reminisce in the garden with his wife, especially on beautiful summer days like this. It was their thing. They always took their tea together, at the bottom of the garden where the hedge shaded them from their neighbours, near Raymond's crimson azaleas, until they fell or his lacecap hydrangeas for which – they were both surprised – he'd won prizes several years ago!

'We do have to make the most of life, though, don't we, love.' Raymond smiled but the air around him was warm and still, apart from a couple of sparrows squabbling in the bird bath.

'Well, I went to the second afternoon tea party at the community centre yesterday as you know,' Raymond told her. 'And I took my suggestions, as Simon recommended I should. It's so nice to have your say and be heard, sometimes, isn't it, dear? Did I enjoy it, you ask. Well ...' He looked down at the grass between his toes. He liked the feel of his bare feet on the cool lawn, even though Simon had mentioned earlier that his father ought to have been wearing sandals, in case he trod on something unpleasant. 'There was some trouble there, unfortunately. One of the ladies was very rude to a young girl who I can tell has problems of her own.'

Raymond finished his tea; his wife's had gone cold when he picked up her mug.

'I think I might just try it again next week, too, love. I'm starting to make some new friends there and I know you said you wanted me to do that sort of thing when you got ill. Wouldn't have dreamt about going anywhere without you at first, though, would I? But I'm improving now because they're an easy crowd to get on with, in general.'

He stood up with a bit of a wheeze as the deckchairs were quite low; perhaps he should buy some new ones, more upright, easier to get in and out of. But he and Dianne had had those deckchairs forever. So it was quite hard for him to think about giving them up. Just like it was hard to give up his darling wife to the dreadful accident she'd had last year.

'We'll leave you alone now, love; Simon's taking me to go watch the footy again with him. That's nice isn't it? He looks after me now his Jo's left him. That was a shock though, wasn't it? Never saw that coming, did we? The girls are good about taking turns visiting them both, though. So he's not too lonely. Truth be told, I'm still a bit lonely, love. But on the whole, life's not too bad. Anyway, we'll speak later.'

He kissed the top of the urn, sitting proudly in centre stage of the bird bath, at the bottom of the garden by the hedge, shaded from their neighbours, surrounded at its base with all the pansies, peonies and marigolds that Dianne used to love and enjoy when she was alive.

Chapter 7

'For God's sake, Dora! You're like a flibbertigibbet. Go find something useful to do instead of moping around like some gangly teenager. It's a shame your father treated you like a ruddy princess when he was alive because, as I constantly need to remind you, real life comes with hairy armpits. And will you leave your ruddy face alone? It's how God intended,' her mother, Yvonne, bellowed.

At forty-nine, Dora was fed up of life.

It hadn't turned out the way she'd hoped because she'd never really known what she'd wanted to do in life. At school, the careers advisor had tried to encourage her with things like hairdressing, floristry or nursing. But none of those professions had appealed to her. And whereas her friend Jodie always knew she wanted to be a beautician, Dora never had aspirations in any particular direction. And because she knew her father would always be there for her, picking up the tab, no matter what happened, she'd drifted through life, cherry-picking, knowing she never really *needed* to have any career aspirations.

'If I choose wisely, I can always be looked after by a wealthy husband,' was her comeback, whenever her mother had asked what she intended to do in life.

'Better get a move on then, love, because there's a ruddy great long queue in front of you, all looking for the exact same thing!'

Her mother, ever sceptical, had never stood for what she used to call Dora's 'nonsense' back then. Even now, at the ripe old age of eighty-nine, she was a still force to be reckoned with. When Dora had been a young girl she'd been spirited, too, and not quite as respectful of her mother as she had been of her father, when he'd been alive. She'd never questioned anything *he'd* said or done. Didn't need to. His word had been king. Not that there was ever anything to judge him by or criticise him of. He'd been one of those exemplary people whom everyone looked up to: staff, customers, his children and wife. And he'd done very well for his family.

Her father, Martin, as her mother liked to tell everyone, came out of his mother's womb, 'knowing what was what from the get-go!' A shrewd businessman, all his business deals turned to gold, which meant his family would never want for anything in life.

Even as a boy, he'd been at his happiest selling things like his brother's old bike or an old chest of drawers from their garage while his parents were out shopping. And when he'd left school with few qualifications, Martin had worked in an auctioneer's, doing what he'd always liked doing best – buying and selling. He'd beavered away, saving up all his commission and wages, with his heart set on buying cheap decrepit old buildings in the right location, and turning them into profitable themed accommodation, one by one.

By being in the industry he found out where all the best places, for the best prices, were. So by the time he'd got married to Yvonne and long before they'd started their family, he'd procured four properties and turned them into Hen & Stag Hotels, sited just outside London. They became incredibly popular and did a humongous trade because of Martin's relaxed attitude to the clientele's private enjoyment of the Jacuzzis and other raucous entertainment, setting the scene for riotous but very profitable behaviour.

And once they'd settled into their enviable lifestyle with a big house overlooking the sea, they'd had their kids. Stuart first, followed by Dora, possibly a little late in life. Then with Yvonne's insistence Martin did an about-turn and purchased another property which, between them, they turned into their Arts & Crafts Hotel in the Cotswolds. They aimed for a different clientele, offering mid-week inclusive breaks for Painting and Drawing or Photography for Beginners, as well as weekend courses of Basket Weaving or Jewellery Making: Beads, Bracelets and Clasps.

It seemed Martin's magic touch could do no wrong within the industry of themed entertainment. All his properties were highly profitable and constantly packed to the rafters. Martin's dynamism had set his family up for life.

'And the "B" plan – if it doesn't work out, guys – is that we'll become property developers and turn the ruddy lot into flats or houses and make our fortunes that way!'

But it had never come to that. Updating his properties whenever necessary meant they hadn't fallen victim to changes of trend. So they all had jobs for life. Dora's brother, Stuart, married but with no children, was the manager of the themed hotels; her father was overall sales and marketing director and her mother, even up until very recently, had headed up the bookkeeping and bookings team.

As a teenager, Dora had reluctantly done stints as a waitress and chambermaid in the hotels during the school holidays, at her mother's insistence to gain a bit of what she called 'real-life experience' rather than swanning around spending the family's fortune, as her father would've had her doing. Dora had certainly been a daddy's girl, and her father had doted on his precious daughter. He certainly wouldn't have had her paling at the sight of vomit in the Hen & Stag Hotel bathrooms that she'd had to clear up, her mother standing over her with a bucket of hot soapy water, when Dora first started working there. But he wouldn't have sided with his daughter against his wife, either.

'We have to teach her *some* responsibility and life skills, Martin. She has to learn that life isn't always about spa days and holidays in Florida,' her mother had pointed out, as Martin slipped his daughter a couple of crisp £20 notes for her troubles.

At odds with her mother, Dora finally left the family home; left a hated secretarial job and dumped her two-timing fiancé at age twenty-six, to travel Europe and America, refinancing her travels with bar work or nannying whenever she felt like it. She never settled anywhere or with anyone for too long; slumming it on Californian beaches with sun-bleached surfers or bedding down with arty types around the theatre scene in Paris and generally having the time of her life, whilst she tried to decide what she *should* be doing. It was a far cry from the constraints of family life in Hampshire, even though she didn't have to want for much in her family's luxurious surroundings.

Back then, however, even though Dora still didn't know what she wanted out of life she realised she wanted to live her life on her own terms. Not her parents' terms.

'Secretarial and hotel work is simply not for me,' she'd told her best friend Jodie, who'd repeatedly asked what Dora was going to do next in life, each time her current foreign boyfriend dumped her.

'But don't you *want* to come back and settle down at some point, hon? We could have so much fun again!' Jodie pleaded.

'But they want me to work in our hotels and it's just not what I want. My mother won't let up about it. She says it's where I belong.'

So Dora continued to kick back at what her parents wanted for her by staying away and living as freely as she pleased. However, her father's first stroke – which, fortunately, didn't kill him – had seen her running back to the family fold. Dora had missed her father. She hugged him while their tears mingled as he held her tightly, forgiving everything, pleased she was finally home.

'I've missed you so much,' they both spluttered.

His health scare had, however, made him reassess his life and he'd called a family meeting to discuss the pressures of running their family businesses and the toll it was taking on everybody, not just himself.

'I mean, aren't we doing this so we can have a good life? We don't want to be killed off too early because of it,' said her father, convalescing, afterwards. 'And I think I need to change my tune about you now, Dora. You're what? Bloody hell! You're thirty-two and still single? Your mother is right, princess, it's high time you took on a bit more responsibility. You've enjoyed a carefree life for years. But we need some help, here. Your mum's seventy-one, even though she doesn't look it and even though she's still got plenty of get up and go in her. But she should've retired by now. Heck! We both should've retired by now. I'm seventy-four.'

'But, Dad!' Dora had started to pout and then got a 'quit whining' look from her brother, Stuart.

'Leave it out, sis,' said Stuart. 'You've had a cracker of a life so far. But back to reality. This is what's real!'

'Your brother's right, Dora,' her mother snapped. 'So we're getting the staff together and putting some new priorities in place. You're not tied to anyone and you don't have kids or a husband anywhere we should know about, do you? Don't pull that face. You never tell us anything. That's why I'm asking. No? Right, so therefore you've got no particular reason to go running back to wherever it is you hang out these days – Spain, did you say?'

Dora had stared sullenly at the patterned carpet and took hold of her father's hand.

'I don't want you to die, Daddy.'

Stuart had scowled at her but her father had drawn her into a long hug.

'I'm not dying today, sweetheart. But it's going to happen some other day. And before that day comes we do need to sort some things out. So can I count on you to help towards that or at least help us make some decisions about things? Your mother will need all the help she can get whilst I start taking things a bit easier. That stroke has put my left hand out of kilter. And that's my phone and writing hand, so things are going to be a bit difficult for us at the moment. I've already spoken to Stuart and he's going to take over my role whilst I'm off sick with a view to taking it over permanently, even when I start to get better. He's recruiting that Damian chap as the manager. He's a reliable sort I believe. Been with us three years already, as bar manager, so he should do a good job. And your mother needs a certain someone to step up and help out, too. So do you think you can do that for us, Dora darling?'

Dora didn't want to be stepping up anywhere. She was still searching for her life, the last time she looked.

'I guess, Dad. But it's not where my heart lies. I still don't know where that is but I'm pretty sure it's not in cleaning up after people or making their beds. I mean, there's no way I could be a nurse, that's for sure!'

'Of course, darling.' Her father had nodded soothingly. 'But I think your mum could do with some help behind the scenes in the office, just until we sort things out on a more permanent basis.'

She'd pulled a narky face, despite her mother shaking her head. Inwardly, she'd have liked nothing more than to run away from *that* responsibility. She'd never liked the hotel life she'd been made to endure when she was younger. She'd have enjoyed working on the front desk as a receptionist in those days, but her mother had insisted she start at the muddy bottom and work her way up, which had put her off working in hotels for life!

'Look, Dora, surely you realise you'll be able to offer a better service to your customers as well as understanding the problems the staff face on a regular basis by doing this. And then, of course, the hope is that it'll make you a better boss at the end of the day, when you and Stuart inherit the businesses,' her father had said.

Inherit the businesses? So *that's* what all this had been about? Dora had never wanted to inherit the sodding businesses. She'd always intended that to be Stuart's baby when the time came for her mother and father to check out, as it were.

That type of commitment, whereby she'd have to cultivate and tout for business and then maintain that business, was too much for her. She wouldn't be able to live a carefree life, that's for sure. And though she'd never really known what she wanted to do in life, she'd certainly never envisaged taking on the family businesses.

All she'd ever loved doing was romping around interesting countries with equally interesting men in tow, even though she'd blown the last one, Pepe, out after she'd caught him stealing her money for his roll-ups and vodka. He wasn't the love of her life, even though the sex had been terrific. So, at the time, her foray home because of her father's ill health had coincided with her limited choices of what to do next. Their tiny airless studio flat in Alicante was still there awaiting her return if she decided that was her plan, though she'd told Pepe it was not.

On the other hand, it was marvellous to be back amongst the lavish trappings of her family's home environment. She could sleep in her beautifully furnished bedroom when she wanted and eat what she wanted, when she wanted. She didn't have to do things like go out with Pepe on his boat to catch flapping, gasping fish for their supper or spend hours scouring the markets for all the items she needed to make everything from scratch. Dora simply did not expect to have to do things like killing, skinning and gutting things in order to eat. That's what supermarkets were for, to take the stress out of finding food on a daily basis. She found life so much more *civil* at home in the UK. She knew she would starve if she ever found herself stranded on a desert island.

So looking down on her father, on his sick bed that day, Dora had sighed deeply, just to let everyone know she wasn't happy with the suggestion that she 'pull her weight'. Yet whilst she didn't like to admit it, she could see that it *did* made sense for her to stay and help her folks get things sorted and settled for a little while because she really had nowhere else to go. Plus a stint in the office would be infinitely better than cleaning up after their mainly boozy guests. So it just *might* be do-able.

Yeah, but then I'll be gone, she'd told herself.

In fact, not only had Dora stayed to help out for a few months, but she'd stayed working in the family business for a good few years longer than she intended. And she did everything from bar work to, yes, cleaning toilets when the situation arose, as well as running the accounts team and sitting in on the monthly meetings and putting her points across in a professional manner. Remarkably, she found she quite enjoyed managing people and, surprise, surprise, her parents had been right – working from the bottom up *had* put her in a good place for dealing with problems the staff faced. Thus business and life in general, for Dora, was trotting along at a good pace and they'd just secured another small hotel in London with a view to turn it into a boutique spa hotel when her father suffered his second, fatal stroke.

And then – almost overnight – everything suddenly changed.

After the funeral, one of Martin's business associates asked if he could buy the four Hen & Stag Hotels and Dora's mother said 'Yes,' without flinching. Those hotels might have given them an enviable lifestyle but they'd never been places Yvonne had felt comfortable in, even though that's where she made Dora do her first few years' work experience.

Stuart had just gotten divorced and decided to take a year out and tour Australia. And there, on a train between Sydney and Brisbane, he met Hazel, the woman he was now married to. They'd moved to Devon and ran a hotel there, complete with her young daughter, Stephanie, and a rescue dog they'd called Ozzy. The Wallabies, Dora called them all. A property developer bought the boutique spa hotel in London and Dora's mother sold the family home and flat but kept the Cotswolds hotel she now lived in and ran with Dora. And even though Dora would later admit that it wasn't such a bad thing, no longer running around the world with the likes of Pepe, she still had her off days when she wished she could just do that.

Hence why her mother's recent outburst had Dora lamenting to her friend Jodie that life was becoming 'predictable'.

'I'm still living at home with my ox of a mother, for God's sake! And she thinks I should be settled and married like The Wallabies by now.'

'Aw, honey,' Jodie had crooned. 'But you're not the marrying kind.'

Admittedly, Dora had certainly evaded that institution! But she'd soon be fifty, a fact that concerned her greatly because, *where had all that time gone?!* She was certainly at an age where she no longer felt happy in her own skin and had not been on a date or hooked up with anyone delectable in years. She felt as though she was drifting again, with no particular direction in mind. She seldom went out, unless Jodie rang out of the blue and they spent a rare weekend together at Jodie's home, back down in Southampton, getting rat-arsed down the pub, whilst her bloke was working night shifts for his security company. Yet it somehow felt wrong that she was still living with her mother. In fact, everything felt wrong with her life.

'It's all slipping away from me, especially since my looks have faded,' she'd whine to anyone who'd listen.

So, fed up of her friend's whinging, Jodie had rung one day with a suggestion.

'Look, why don't you have a shot at Botox or whatever. Works wonders for me.'

'No chance! I don't like pain and what if it all went wrong?' Dora had blared, robustly.

'Look, just have a think about it. I can send you a whole bunch of literature on it.'

Just a little nipping and tucking could work miracles, the brochures had said. The glittering photos of the before and afters had certainly looked inspiring. And there were all sorts of procedures to choose from – invasive and non-invasive. And so, reassured by Jodie, Dora had asked her friend to drive to their hotel and then dragged her along to her appointment to try out a bit of Botox.

When they got back to the hotel Yvonne had squinted at the results, and then pulled a face. 'Is that a botch job or what?'

Disillusioned, Dora went back to try and get it sorted out the next day.

'Oh I'm sorry, love,' the receptionist had told her. 'You have to wait till it wears off. Round about three to four months after your first injection, sometimes less. And then we can have another go at it.'

'What? So I'm supposed to look like a frog in the meantime, am I?'

'You must've moved while they were doing it,' Jodie had said, supressing a giggle. 'It should've been fine. Oh, don't worry about it. Just put a bit of lippy on and smile more instead of frowning. Anyway, I thought the intention was to get your forehead done? Not your mouth.'

'I know but I hate my saggy face! And anyway, you should've persuaded me to use your chap.'

'But you rarely get leave of absence from your hotel. Plus, like I said, he's on holiday. Anyway, it doesn't look that bad.'

Despite her friend's encouragement, she didn't feel any better and her smile was definitely wonkier than it had been. She wasn't sure that a bit of lippy would help but clearly there was nothing she could do about it all now.

'Oh, how I hate getting old and decrepit,' she'd groaned to her mother.

'You behave like a small child!' her mother had snapped.

'Just grow up and find yourself a man and settle that roving spirit of yours.'

'Well, that might happen if I looked prettier than I do. But just look at my crow's feet, my lined forehead, my crappy skin.'

'What do you expect after sitting on a beach for nearly ten years?' her mother had shot back. 'And do you hear me whinging about my looks?'

Dora snapped. 'No. But you're allowed to be wrinkly at eighty-nine. It's expected of you.'

Their sparring had become amiable over the years. True, she had been a daddy's girl and absolved of all failings and errors because of that. But now she was much closer to her mother. She was even closer to The Wallabies and popped over to see them sometimes, when being in one place for too long took its toll.

Yet it was on a rare couple of days' visit to see her mother's sister, Aunt Philippa, in Southampton, after nagging her mother to leave the staff in charge of the hotel and come with her because she was fed up of doing things by herself, that Dora spied a flyer in a shop window offering free afternoon tea at a nearby community centre, the following day. And it transpired that the building was on a road parallel to where Philippa lived.

So because Dora was feeling out of sorts and generally fed up with her life she decided to act on that flyer and find out what afternoon tea at the Borough Community Centre was all about. And as her bloody mother had complained about her moping about, she intended to leave her mother and aunt to catch up whilst she went off on a little adventure for the day.

Who knows, Dora thought, *it might just cheer me up a bit*. Plus it said she was going to get a free cup of tea and a piece of cake.

Chapter 8

Stacy was lounging on the reception desk with her head in her hands, daydreaming.

She loved her work in the library and had been there so long she knew her duties back to front. She loved all of it, the cataloguing, the classifying and developing of library resources; dealing with reader's queries on reception and showing people where the magazines or non-fiction or the microfiche machines were – yes, people were surprised they still used those. But today was exceptionally quiet for some reason and her supervisor had already mentioned her lacka-daisical manner. Yet it was so easy to get side-tracked, ruminating about other things, when nothing much was happening. She did have a list of literature searches to do and needed the books ready for when the gentleman in ques-tion came in to collect them at 3 p.m. today. But that was a good few hours away yet.

Abstractedly, she was remembering the woman who'd upset her at the community centre. There were a couple of tetchy women who frequented the community centre, she'd noticed. Stacy couldn't understand why some people had to take their annoyance out on others. Didn't they throw plates and smash things in the anger rooms in China to vent their frustrations? She'd read about that. What a good idea that was!

One of the women had, at first glance, basically looked all right. She reminded Stacy of her kindly Sunday school teacher when she and her brother arrived late, slouching and poking about around the graves, trying to find the oldest gravestone or the one with the youngest occupant, because they didn't actually want to go inside the church and do yet *more* colouring in of the three wise men or make paper angels.

But the woman had screwed her face up and pouted when Stacy had sat down next to her.

'Good grief! Please *stop*,' she'd said, making Stacy feel uncomfortable, until someone had suggested she might not be feeling well.

Then after the tea party, Stacy remembered hurrying back to her flat because of her cats. But she'd called into the corner shop, en route, to get them a little treat. In front of her in the queue was a tiny, frail-looking old lady with a faded flowery summer dress on that looked six sizes too big for her. She was stooped so that her head nearly touched the counter where her purchases – three tins of cat food, a tin of peas and the cheapest packet of dried mashed potatoes – sat on the conveyor belt.

Stacy had wondered if the peas and mashed potato were to pad out the cat food? She often spiced up her own cats' meals with other ingredients. Just for variety. Who wants to eat the same things all the time? And why should pets be subjected to the same old tins of food just because they were animals?

'Hello! I see you have cats, judging by your purchases. Do they eat peas then? Mine won't eat anything like that,' she'd told the old lady, bending down so she would hear her.

The old lady had jumped a little, as Stacy's face came into her periphery, then she smiled.

'Oh hello! No, the potatoes and peas are mine, deary. Don't eat much these days. You don't when you get to my age.'

Stacy had heard this sort of thing before, especially with elderly people who had pets. She'd sincerely hoped she wouldn't only be able to afford peas and powdered potatoes when she turned eighty or so. As the little old lady paid for her purchases, Stacy put hers on the conveyor belt.

The old lady was ambling along, leaning heavily on her walking stick when Stacy caught up with her and 'bumped' into her.

'Oh sorry,' Stacy had said. 'Not watching where I'm going. Silly me.'

She'd smiled as the little old lady trundled off into the distance, hoping that she would be tempted to eat the sardines and smoked salmon she found in her coat pocket later.

I wonder if anyone else is just as lonely as me? Stacy thought, with a sigh, and then sat bolt upright as the first customer of the day walked into the library and she was brought back to the present.

Simon dropped his father off at the community centre for his third visit to the afternoon tea party and waved goodbye. Raymond watched him drive away.

Raymond was very proud of his son and felt blessed that Simon cared about him the way he did. He was always ringing and making sure he had enough shopping for the week and that his washing was done. Simon said he wanted to make sure that the ordinary things that kept life ticking over got done. Yet Raymond knew Simon's attitude was mainly down to Dianne's unswerving love and devotion towards all things familial when she'd been alive. He knew he had a lot to be thankful for.

'They're going to read out our suggestions this week, so I can't wait to hear what everyone else thinks,' Raymond had told his son in the car, earlier, en route to the community centre.

'So the old dear who caused an uproar hasn't put you off going then?'

'Well, like I said, it wasn't nice. But I'll give it another shot this week and see where I go from there. I did enjoy that first week and I didn't expect to. You don't mind dropping me off again do you, son?'

'Good heavens no, Dad. I'll drop you wherever you want to go and at any time. You only have to ask. So go enjoy it and see what else they have to offer by way of outings. Have some fun!'

'Do you mind if I sit here?' the middle-aged woman with faded blonde hair curled up into an untidy bun, huge dangly gold earrings and bright pink lipstick covering slightly wonky lips had asked Marjorie.

'How she looked! And why nobody said a thing about the way she looked is mind-boggling, dear. That cheap lipstick just didn't do her any justice at all. In fact, it drew attention to her crooked lips. Why she didn't go for a nude colour, instead, I don't know,' Marjorie had said dourly, recounting that week's afternoon tea over dinner with Gracie later that evening.

Gracie had given her a stern look and then shaken her head, despairingly.

'I can't believe you're telling me this, after what we spoke about the other day, Mother. You tell me you want to change but all I hear from you is how you simply can't stop putting other people down or criticising some aspect of their looks or behaviour. But it's *got* to stop, Mum. It drives me mad. You've got to realise that nobody is perfect and they shouldn't be berated for their imperfections! Now, I've got quite a lot of marking to do tonight, and I'm going to do it at the desk in my bedroom so I'm not disturbed,' Gracie had said with a frown.

Marjorie knew Gracie meant that she didn't want to be

disturbed by her mother. That thought made her want to curl up and hide at her daughter's harsh words. Yet hadn't she given herself a strict talking-to in the park that wet afternoon? Hadn't she already convinced herself she was going to change for the better? But when would she be able to implement that change in herself? It was so easy to simply mock or scorn the afflicted. It tripped from her lips or flew into her thoughts the minute she spotted someone acting or looking *different*. Yet Marjorie knew it was wrong. She knew it was unfair of her. It was Oliver's bloody fault but she simply *couldn't* shake his awful behaviour. It had somehow disgustingly rubbed off on her after all the years she'd been subjected to his foul mouth and nasty ways.

She had to make it up to Gracie. 'Well, look, darling,' she began uncertainly. 'By way of talking about something, um, happier. I did apologise today about that incident before and I think that helped.'

Gracie stared. 'You *apologised* today? My God. The woman has a heart, after all!'

But it was true. Marjorie had taken her first step towards being more positive and civil to others. And it had started with an apology, at the community centre earlier that day, because she did not want to be excluded from the possibility of making new friends. Lou had gone with her and Gracie had dropped them both off.

Marjorie had been pleased that Lou had been able to come to the community centre with her because they hadn't seen each other in ages, due to the fact Lou had been ill, with flu. She realised they needed to start doing more things together now she was better, even though they did live a good few miles apart.

'S'lovely this is, here!' Lou had grinned, looking around at everybody as she started on her second piece of lemon drizzle cake.

Lou didn't drive and being overweight meant it was difficult for her to get out and about easily, even for something as simple as a walk, although she did have a walking frame. Gracie occasionally dropped Marjorie off to see Lou at the weekend or would pick Lou up and take them both to a café, for a cuppa. But they hadn't done that in a while. Yet, although Lou was happy enough eating her afternoon tea, Marjorie had already noticed that her old friend was not her usual jovial self. She'd been very quiet and seemed depressed in Gracie's car on the way over. And when she'd come to get out of the car, Lou's movements had been very laboured. Both Gracie and Marjorie had struggled to get her out. She had no family to speak of, well apart from her son Derek, who she rarely saw and who rarely visited her in her tiny ground-floor flat. And because a carer only came in once a week to bathe her, to help with the shopping and clean the flat, Marjorie wondered if it was time to start having a talk with her friend about an alternative arrangement. Crikey, she knew Lou would balk at the idea of going into a home but it might simply mean that since she was finding things more difficult she'd probably only need more regular help. Either way, Marjorie decided to ask Gracie if she'd drop her off at her friend's next weekend so she could talk things over with her.

With Lou by her side, Marjorie had stood up, when everyone had eaten their fill and asked Eileen and Taynor if she could speak before they got down to the business of reading out what excursions had been suggested for the new community project. The young girl she'd spoken sharply to wasn't there but Marjorie was hoping that, by apologising to everyone, it would put her firmly on the road to *behaving* like a well-adjusted member of the community, at least. It was a start, for her, at any rate.

Both the organisers had looked surprised when Marjorie came forward and stood next to them and then turned to the audience.

'Um, sorry, folks. Can I just have a minute? Um, I'd just like to say that I'm very sorry for my outburst last week. I know it upset some of you. But I've, er, I've been having some difficulties in my life. Things I'd, um, rather not discuss here. But I just want to apologise and let you know it won't happen again. That's all really. I've ... I've come here to make friends. Not to alienate anyone. So that's all. Thank you.'

There was a surprised silence at first. Then people started to react.

'Apology accepted!' shouted someone who started clapping. Eileen smiled at her and said in a low voice, 'We all make mistakes and we're sorry you have troubles in your life, Marjorie.'

'It was nice of you to apologise, Marjorie. Thanks for putting things right,' said Taynor, as Marjorie returned to her seat.

'Takes guts to apologise,' said someone else, also clapping.

Marjorie suddenly felt better about things as she approached her table and sat down, amid the whole room clapping her.

''Ere? What was all that about then, Marj?' said Lou, in wonder.

But Marjorie just smiled and tapped the side of her nose. 'Oh, don't worry about all that. Question is, are you enjoying yourself?'

Lou nodded vigorously. 'It's been wonderful, thanks. I don't get out much any more, you know. And they all seem like really nice people 'ere.'

'Yes they are, Lou. So you'll have to come again!'

And then Marjorie even forced herself to smile at the woman with the brightly coloured wonky lips.

'Right! So to finish up, now,' Eileen said, shuffling the sheets of paper in front of her. 'The activity suggestions are as follows. That's most of you wanting regular afternoon tea but not always in the community centre. Well, like we said before, it won't always be here. It depends what other events they've got on here. Sometimes you'd like to go out on a country drive, finishing up somewhere pretty for afternoon tea. Most of you also want an afternoon where you go to learn something new. So the top three topics suggested are, learning how to use a computer and the internet; painting and drawing; and an occasional day trip out to the seaside. You'd also like us to arrange a mini trip away somewhere for three days or less, once a year, and you say you're happy to pay for it, as long as it's not too expensive or problematic. Okay. The two top spots for that outing are overnight in London to see a show and probably Bournemouth – to frolic in the sea, as Raymond puts it, which did make us laugh. So would you say that is a fair representation of what you'd all like? Would anyone prefer anything different, apart from Margo at the front, here, who would also like swimming lessons? There's a pool nearby, so that can be easily arranged.'

'I never learned to swim, you see,' Margo said to the woman next to her. 'And my family said I'm too old to go learning about that now. They say I should be at home resting and just watching telly. But I'm bored with all that.'

'Okay, good people,' said Taynor. 'Now Eileen and I will type up our findings and get you to all sign a sheet that we'll eventually submit to our bosses. Please bring anyone along with you, next time, who might also like to sign our sheets. And, of course, they can have afternoon tea, as well. Obviously the more people who wish to make this happen, the more weight this will have when we finally have our meeting in two weeks' time. At that meeting we will try to firm up all other possible trips or courses we'd like to secure on your behalf. And if this means that a small charge is levied for, say, the services of a coach driver, would you be happy to pay for this? Unfortunately, at this stage, we don't know how much will be allocated for these community activities.'

Murmurs went around the hall. People were fidgeting from sitting in one place for too long. A couple of people moved off to use the toilet. Some people said they needed their families to take them shopping before the shops closed. Marjorie was watching the proceedings with interest. They seemed to be balking at the mention of charges being necessary. Yet did councils store excess funds for the elderly or homebound, to have a lovely time out once or twice a month? Probably not!

'Actually, let me clarify a thing or two, first.' Taynor began to explain, 'You see, whatever else we can agree with our bosses regarding ongoing activities for the community, Eileen and I have been told we can get funding to at least be able to offer you afternoon tea on a monthly or possibly twice monthly basis, somewhere else, once we find a suitable full-time venue. So that's a given. However, what Eileen and I want for you are more engaging activities as well. Yet this is an unknown. We don't know what else they'll agree to, over and above your afternoon tea. Do you understand?'

Everyone stopped fidgeting. Marjorie saw Raymond on the other side of the hall put his hand up.

'Well, as long as it's not too expensive, love. We're pensioners, most of us. Every penny is accounted for. That's the trouble. But I think I could spare six or seven pounds a month for an occasional trip out somewhere. You'd have to let us know how much you're thinking about.'

'Yes that's a fair comment, Raymond,' Eileen said. 'Right, well, I can see you all need to be going home or elsewhere, so we'll leave that thought with you and see what our bosses come up with. Just on another note, though, I would like to call our regular get-togethers the Afternoon Tea Club just so when you mention it to your friends they have a sense of what we're all about. Does anybody think that's a good idea?'

Everybody cheered and clapped at that. Well, yes! It sounded as if they really belonged to something now. Plus it would be something positive and enjoyable for them to look forward to every month. Hopefully, though, the council would advocate other activities when they saw how popular the Afternoon Tea Club was.

'That's a good idea!' said Lou.

'Yep, I like it, too,' said someone else.

'Feels like we're part of something with that name. Yeah, it's good!' said another.

'Right, well, have a good couple of weeks and we'll see you all, the week after next, if any of you can make it. That's the week after next because I'm on holiday next week. Yes, love, here again in two weeks, same time. Okay, well cheerio then for now folks. Cheerio,' said Eileen.

Marjorie found herself thinking that she'd definitely come back. She felt she'd overcome something today and they weren't such a bad lot here after all.

Chapter 9

Stacy had decided against afternoon tea this week.

She'd had too much going on at home with her cats – three of which had been fighting – and then there was the inevitable trip to the vet with the three of them; putting them in their carriers and carting them down the two flights of stairs because she didn't like using lifts. The lift that serviced the flats she lived in was rarely working anyway. But with the three of them it was heavy going, leaving one at the top of the stairs, taking the other two down and then going back and getting the one at the top. And then she'd had to lie to work by saying she was off with food poisoning. *Yet again.* Caring for her cats sapped all her energy whether she was taking them to the vets or just looking after them in general. Oh, she knew that trying to maintain eight cats was far too much work for her, even though she loved them all dearly.

'Can't go on. Cannot go on!' she was muttering on the way home from the vets in a taxi. All her earnings seemed to evaporate buying food and tending to her cats or paying for their vet fees. She knew she should've got a pet plan sorted out for her bills but had simply never got around to it and because there were so many cats her vet bills were getting out of hand. Granted, she did have a little more money at her disposal than the little old lady she kept seeing in the corner shop – Mrs Michaels – who had tried to give Stacy her smoked salmon and sardines back. Stacy's overly feigned refusal that those items were simply not hers did not sway the old lady from trying to return them, each time they saw one another.

But there was certainly nothing left over for things like holidays or nice clothes. Plus, how could she even *think* about having a holiday with the worry of what to do with her cats while she was away?

Stacy felt stressed and anxious about the fact that she did not seem to be coping with anything in life at that moment, never mind the spiralling situation with her cats.

'What to do? What to do?' she muttered.

The taxi driver glanced at her periodically and she wondered what he saw. She was young with dark rather bushy long hair, no make-up. She wore a long featureless pale green dress with capped sleeves, ankle socks and pumps. Probably a bit old-fashioned in his opinion.

Stacy was out of breath by the time she hauled the last of her cats in their carriers up the second flight of stairs to her flat. It was too hot for all that. It would've been so much easier to just stick them in the lift. But she'd got stuck in one once. The call button was broken and no one had heard her cries for hours. *Never again!*

Coming back through her door to the regular cacophony

of meowing and the awful stench, Stacy placed the three cats in their carriers outside the door in the corridor, whilst she sorted herself out. It was much cooler, out there, for them anyway. She'd decided she wasn't going to work the next day either. She was going to start to get some *real* sorting out done in her flat. She just couldn't stand it any more. She no longer wanted to endure the stench of faeces and the chaos of unhappy, noisy cats clamouring for attention, every day of her life. All she wanted to do was put her feet up, have a cup of tea and watch some daytime television. *Things ordinary people did.* She paid for the TV licence every year but never got the time to watch anything properly or in peace.

She sighed despondently; her life had become unbearable.

For the umpteenth time she considered ringing her mother. She hadn't spoken to either of her parents in years because she knew they'd be full of 'I told you so's'. They hadn't wanted her to leave home but their rules and antiquated ideas were so suffocating. No friends had ever been allowed over for tea, no pets, no boyfriends, bed at 7.30 p.m. prompt, no this, no that and so many rules, rules, rules that she'd left pretty soon after turning eighteen and went to live with the boyfriend her parents didn't know existed. Unfortunately it hadn't worked out with him. But luckily she'd just started an apprenticeship with the library – where she still worked – and one of the girls there said she could share with her, splitting the bills, until she found her own place. So it had all turned out okay for her until she started getting the cats.

'It all went wrong then, didn't it, my lovelies?' she said out loud, into the chorus of cats vying for her attention.

She'd also not rung or Skyped Elsa in months – maybe longer. She'd often wondered if their conversations ever got back to her mum and dad, being as they all lived in the same village. Her father would explode if he found out she had *lots* of cats; she was sure of that. Anyway, they'd had plenty of time to ring *her* in the past, if they'd chosen. She'd rung and given them her telephone number and address years ago. Her father was always a stickler for all sorts of odd rules and regulations so he probably wouldn't have rung. But she was surprised she hadn't heard from her mother, apart from cards on her birthdays: 'Happy Birthday love from Mum and Dad xx'. No letter included. No gifts or a tenner shoved in the card. Yet her mother could've easily opted to ring or leave a message for her. Or perhaps she had tried to ring and not got through for some reason?

Ah, but you still haven't sorted the answer phone out have you? she reproached herself.

She sighed, wondering what to do next. *Cup of tea first*, she thought as she moved towards the kitchen to put the kettle on, stepping over cats trying to curl around her feet and dodging faeces and tins, empty of cat food, along the hall. It was then she heard a strange noise – partly a meow and partly a muffling, scratching noise – coming from the kitchen.

'Oh no,' she wailed as she kicked off her pumps to climb

up on the worktop. She knew that noise! One of her cats was either on top of the kitchen wall units, stuck behind the heavy pans or had slid down behind the back again. She'd asked the carpenter to make sure there were no more gaps on top of the units, when he put them back the last time a cat got stuck. But she had no idea if he'd done that.

Ah, she could see a black tail. Was it Pooch? Well, at least he hadn't slipped behind the units then. But was he otherwise trapped? She reached up to carefully start pulling the pans aside, one by one, when suddenly Pooch's black and white paw shot out and viciously scratched her hand. Stacy snatched her hand back in shock.

'Ow!'

Why was Pooch becoming more and more unpredictable these days?

'Naughty puss. Bad puss!'

She knew the scratch had drawn blood but she still had to either free him or get him down. She was nervous about moving the pans now. She cautiously shifted another pan when suddenly his mouth clamped down like a vice around her fingers!

The pain was like tiny searing hot blades stabbing into her hand, all at the same time. She cried out, trying to yank her hand away but overbalanced and slipped in her socks on the shiny work surface, pulling Pooch down with her as she fell in a heap, clipping her head on the sharp corner of the work surface.

She remembered thinking, *Why do my cats hate me so much? I give them everything*, before she blacked out.

So peaceful …

And white. White? Yes, peacefully white. And nice dreams of pink candy ice creams tasting divine. I want to be a ballerina but Mummy won't let me. They want me to be another boy, so I can help with the farm. But not even Peter wants to do that.

Who are those people with big faces, like out-of-focus gargoyles? Ugh! And the bloke? A bit rough-looking. Familiar. All around me. Staring. No, frowning. An angel in the background. The angel is going away now. No, don't go! Stay and protect me from all these ugly creatures.

'She's coming round, now Jerry!'

A familiar voice. Can't place it, though. And a grunt.

'About time! Wasting public resources because of her silliness—'

'That's enough, Jerry. She's our daughter and she's in trouble.'

Another grunt.

Oh no! Stacy's eyelids flickered open but she wanted to shut them, immediately, after she spied her mother and father peering over her. But where was she? She wasn't at their place. The farm was a cold, dark, repressive place to bring up children. There was no love to speak of there. Just rules and practicality at every turn. Stacy snuggled into the bed she was

90

lying in. Her scratched and bitten hand ached but it was bandaged professionally.

'Come on, Stacy love. Wake up, now. We're here for you,' pleaded her mother's voice.

Stacy opened an eye and looked into her mother's tired, lined face. Her once light auburn hair was greying and she looked downbeat. Farming was heavy going. It was a daily chore; a calling. It had taken its toll on her mother. And Stacy knew she would never want that for herself. Her father sat back on a chair at the end of the bed. His face was dry, leathery and wrinkled from years in the sun working the fields. He was frowning at her – a look she remembered from way back. She had never seen her father smile.

'This man, here, found you. He's your neighbour, John. Nice of him to call us,' began her mother.

'Though how he found our number in amongst that pigsty you call home I'll never know!' barked her father before her mother could stop him.

'Now that's enough, Jerry!' her mother hissed. 'I told you she needs our help and we're going to give it to her, whatever you might think. So hold your tongue! I'm not putting up with your nonsense any more. It's sent our children away from us, never to return. That farm is my father's, don't forget! And we're going to be doing things *my* way for once. I want my children back around me at my time of life. And that's my final word on the subject.'

Stacy gasped at her mother's uncharacteristic tirade. Wow,

she'd actually stuck up for her for once. And, double wow, the farm didn't even belong to them! It belonged to their only remaining grandparent, who lived in a care home. Her mother's family had been reasonably wealthy through farming, she realised.

Stacy slowly sat up in bed, leaning on her good hand, noting the hospital monitoring equipment, flowers on her bedside table, a pale green gown on the back of the door.

Her next-door neighbour John was standing nervously beside the bed, looking as though he no longer wanted to be there. But why was he here? Ah, didn't somebody say he'd rescued her?

He bent down so suddenly Stacy thought he was going to kiss her. Then he whispered, 'No wonder you're the way you are with this lot looking out for you. Anyway, I've got to go. Bye.'

Suddenly Stacy remembered her cats. 'Oh no. What about all my little kitties?'

'That bloody mad lot have gone to Cats Protection!' roared her father, now John had left. 'And we've had to get the place fumigated and the carpets ripped out! The whole ruddy place needs completely sorting out. It's a disgusting mess! So like it or not, you're coming home with us!'

Chapter 10

Stacy awoke in her old bedroom, her hand still aching from the cat bite and scratches. She knew it could have been a whole lot worse but at least the hospital had managed to wash it out and give her a tetanus injection. Thankfully, there was no cellulitis, nor septicaemia – both potentially life-threatening; a cat bite could be pretty serious. She still had a lump on her head though.

She sat up in her childhood bed and studied the dulled flowery wallpaper and the single bulb hanging from the ceiling in its faded pink shade. The room had always smelled damp and it still did now. Glancing around, she saw the small single wardrobe still sitting in the corner with two school desks next to it where her mother had started to school her and her brother before the authorities had forced her parents to send them to the primary school in the village. Stacy was shocked to note that her bedroom hadn't changed since the day she'd left her sombre family home, dragging an old heavy suitcase of her mother's down the drive and struggling to push it into her boyfriend's car, whilst her mother was out collecting apples and her father was out in the barn working on one of his tractors.

93

The whole place was stuck in time but those memories, from the day she left, suddenly whooshed back, like it happened yesterday.

She remembered she'd walked a fine line that day. She'd known about the problem with the tractor but her mother had flitted in and out all morning, preventing an easy escape at the pre-arranged time of 11 a.m. with Mike.

Yet how she'd ever fortuned to meet Mike was one of the biggest wonders of her life, at the time.

Mike had drifted into the village, in a clapped-out old mini, looking for farm work. Someone had given him her father's name and he'd turned up unannounced looking for any part-time work her father could offer. Her parents ran their small family arable farm of 300 acres with a couple of farm hands, apart from harvesting time, when her father joined forces with a neighbouring smallholding to help with the harvesting and drying process of their grain. But their recent employees had left and so her father was able to give him some work in the role of odd-job and maintenance man and said he could stay in the tiny room at the side of the barn with its outside privy and chipped sink, no bath or shower. Mike had stayed and helped her parents with all manner of niggly tasks around the farm for a good few months before his wandering spirit got the better of him.

But in that time Stacy experienced the first heady stirrings of love with twenty-nine-year-old Mike.

She'd met Mike on the day of her eighteenth birthday. She'd been having an argument with her mother, as usual, about the lack of freedom afforded her and her brother throughout their lives, hence the reason for her brother Peter's early departure. She'd been having a lot of rows with her family of late.

'Growing pains, Jean. Ignore her!' her father had scoffed. 'When she behaves like a young lady, she'll be treated like one!'

It wasn't a happy household to live in and hadn't been for years, with all the rules and regulations, even down to how long they had to spend sitting at the dining table for meals, chewing their food slowly so it would digest properly. And no speaking, no conversation, at all, was permitted whilst they were sat at the table. No friends were allowed over for tea. Bedtime was always at 7.30 p.m., after homework and chores. They weren't allowed mobile phones and Stacy had to do the washing up, after tea, every day apart from the weekend when she did other housework for her mother.

Peter had to chop wood for the fire, every day in the winter months, and help his father around the farm. The TV was rarely switched on and when it was it was because there was a football match their father wanted to watch or something to do with the royal family. Every weekend, from when she and Peter were around seven or eight years old, was spent helping their parents run the farm, instead of running free with their friends in the village while they were youngsters or having fun with their friends in town when they were older. And their tasks became more demanding the older they got.

One year, their father took ill due to the stress of trying to cope with the farm by himself after two farm hands left. Peter was fifteen at the time and had to run the farm for months, missing out on school, until their father recovered and was able to hire more staff. Stacy had always washed and cleaned for her mother without the assistance of any mod cons. Her mother only bought a washing machine the year before Stacy left home.

Peter got out as soon as he turned eighteen, a year before his sister. As Stacy's eighteenth was fast approaching she remembered praying she'd be able to leave then, too; hoping there was nothing her family could do to stop her leaving, whilst simultaneously worrying whether she'd be able to make it by herself in the outside world, even though she had inheritance money from her grandmother.

On the morning of her eighteenth birthday she'd been given a card with a country scene on it – no mention of the fact she'd turned eighteen at all – from her mother's shabby card box. Inside, with a crumpled ten-pound note, all it said was 'Happy Birthday love Mum and Dad xx'. There was no explosion of bright encouraging emotions for her future. It was dowdy and not even something she'd have longed to cherish as a special childhood memento. Her mother had also told her they couldn't afford a party for her. But there'd *never* been parties for Stacy and Peter – they'd never been allowed to go to school friends' parties, either.

She'd heard about parties and seen how *wonderful* parties were, on school friends' social media. Her friends, at least, knew how she and Peter were treated at home and commiserated with her about her parents and so she often went to town with them, during lunchtime at secondary school, so she could try out things like alcohol, curry, chicken tikka or a Big Mac. Stuff she never had at home. Her friends had opened up the world for her – also helping her experiment with make-up and trying clothes on in shops – before she left school. Her parents had never taken her out for meals or shopping in town. Weekends were always wrapped up helping her parents on the farm.

So her parents' apathetical response to the milestone that was supposed to be her wonderful eighteenth birthday had resulted in her throwing the birthday card on the floor, to stop herself from bursting into tears.

'I was hoping for a mobile phone, at the very least. You've never, ever given us anything nice, Mum!' she'd whimpered.

'How dare you speak to me like that, Stacy! You should be thankful we've looked after you the way we have over the years. There's plenty in Africa who don't even get anything decent to eat!'

Grrr. That old line!

It made Stacy furious with her mother. She always wheeled out the flagrancies of Africa whenever she felt like using them.

Stacy felt trapped by the injustices her parents meted out. What a crap eighteenth! No cake. No brightly wrapped special gift. No love. No joy. And not even a birthday party for once in her lonely and miserable life.

At that moment Stacy had hated her mother.

So she'd bolted out of the house, bolted away from her mother's holier-than-thou speeches. Luckily she had her little bolthole at the top of the hayloft where she'd fashioned a little hidey-hole for herself. There were a couple of books up there so she wouldn't get bored. Her mother would never find her up there although Peter had known about it.

Yet, as Stacy ran from her mother in tears, she'd run slap bang into Mike, coming out of the barn. He'd been shown around the farm by her father, the day before and was about to start work that very morning.

'Whoa there! What's the rush? Stacy isn't it?' Mike grinned, holding her away from him to look her up and down. It was the first time he'd seen her. And then something weird had happened to her. She'd suddenly felt hot and peculiar and quite out of sorts.

'Um, yes. And you – you're here to help my, um, dad, aren't you?' she stumbled, blushing madly, trying to wipe her tears away.

'Yep. I'm Mike. That's me,' he said with a grin, noting her discomfort.

He took a creased tissue from his pocket and offered it to her. She shook her head.

'Oh, it's okay. I'm, er, I'm fine!' she said, shrugging.

'No, Stacy. You're upset about something. Here. Let me help.'

Then he'd softly wiped away her tears with his tissue. His touch had made her jump. She wasn't used to being touched by anybody, let alone a stranger, so she excused herself and backed away towards the barn and had gone up into her hidey-hole, opening one of the books. But she'd not been able to read at all. She couldn't stop thinking about Mike's unshaven but sexy face.

When she eventually went back into the farmhouse, her mother was busy making lunch and would not meet her eye. Her birthday card, however, had been propped up on the mantelpiece. The farm hands always ate with the family in the evenings but her father brought Mike into the farmhouse, explaining about the repairs he needed help with, and sat him down and told him he'd be sharing lunch with them that day, too.

The four of them ate silently, with Stacy shooting sly glances at Mike every now and then, whilst he shot equally sly glances at her, when her parents weren't watching.

A few days later, Mike crept up behind her, whilst she was pinning washing on the washing line.

'Well, hello there. Fancy walking with me to show me the countryside around here, when you've finished your chores? Your dad's gone into town for something so I think I deserve a little break.'

Stacy had been hoping for an excuse to see Mike by herself.

So she finished up and took the washing basket back into the house. They set off at a brisk pace down the drive, together, then sauntered into the village whilst she pointed out her friends' houses, the church, the school. On the way back, he took her hand and guided her into a field, beside a hedge. He sat down and patted the earth beside him.

'Come. Let's sit and talk a while and maybe even make daisy chains!'

Stacy beamed at him. She hadn't made daisy chains since she was a child. But as she sat nervously beside him, he reached out and stroked her cheek. She felt herself shudder uncontrollably. But it was a nice tingly kind of shudder.

'Or maybe not,' he murmured, pulling her towards him.

They sat, seemingly millimetres apart, as he cupped her face and with a hungry moan he'd pressed his lips against hers. She'd nearly fainted. A murmur escaped her lips. She'd never been kissed by anyone before. *Was that even a kiss?* It felt as though she'd been infused with an electric current.

In between gasping, fevered kisses, she'd willingly succumbed to Mike's frenzied examination of her, but she stopped him going too far.

To Stacy, it felt as though she'd finally been *freed* from something!

She'd never met anyone like Mike before. He was so knowledgeable and easy-going. She knew she was smitten by him; enthralled by him, bedazzled by him. He'd opened up a very different aspect of life to her. His actions made her feel *valued* for once in her life, because here was someone who was prepared to give her some much-needed attention for once. When they finally made love she experienced pure joy and lust and feelings surged within her she never knew she was capable of. She felt alive and worthy. She was no longer so anxious to leave the farm, because *he* was there.

But they could only get together when her father was in the top fields, mending a fence or patching holes to stop kids or stray dogs running all over his crops. Stacy's mother wasn't a problem because she was usually busy making fruit pies or jam to sell at local markets or craft fayres. And if she wasn't making anything she'd be collecting or freezing fruit or preparing meals for everyone twice a day. And when it seemed to be getting too dangerous, they had an arrangement whereby Mike would meet her down the lane and Stacy would slip into his clapped-out Mini on the lower road and they'd drive away for exploratory time by themselves, elsewhere. Her excuses to her mother as to why she'd gone missing, each time, were that she was mooching around the village or had gone for a walk down the back lanes.

However, when Stacy finally plucked up courage to leave her parents' home for the last time and with Mike, to boot, what Stacy had never guessed was that he was one of those men who didn't understand the word 'exclusivity'.

Living with him in the bedsit, which he'd promised would be their first home together, where he encouraged them to share their lives *and their bodies* with other people drifting in and out, as well as plying her with booze and drugs, brought home a certain reality to Stacy and was not her idea of happily-ever-after.

So one Saturday night, whilst Mike and the others were getting stoned on the stained mattresses, Stacy had dragged her heavy suitcase outside to her colleague's waiting car, and they'd driven away without a backwards glance.

'Come and get some breakfast, Stacy! Are you up yet?' her mother called up to her, interrupting her daydreams.

Stacy tutted at feeling forced to jump to her parents' commands once again. Yet she went downstairs having found her old fusty dressing gown and tatty slippers, which still fit. The kitchen still looked the same but the smell of bacon dazzled her nostrils from the Aga in the corner. She couldn't remember the last time she'd had a fry-up. Or perhaps it had been here, when she'd last lived at home?

As she was sitting down to eat, her father came in the door with a grunt, removed his cap and went to the sink to wash his hands.

Stacy wasn't really sure what to say to her parents.

She'd been away such a long time, dreading the wrath she expected to receive if she ever showed her face at their door. Maybe she wouldn't mind her mother so much now she'd stood up to her father for once. So that might be something positive. But she could see her father had permanent frown lines down the middle of his forehead. His features were dark and glum. They were what – in their late fifties or sixties? She had no idea. It was something she'd never been interested to find out. They were just her parents. She didn't think about them in terms of how old they were or who they were as people. Nor did she care. They'd never cared properly about her and Peter when they were children; never allowed them their childhood or freedom or a special treat occasionally. The injustice of it all had chewed away at her, when she'd had time to mull over the hardships her parents forced them to endure, back then. But she also knew she couldn't just sit down to breakfast with them, without saying something.

'Hi, Dad.'

Stacy's father glanced in her direction as he sat down and her mother placed a huge plate of bacon, potatoes, fried eggs and toast in front of him and then sat down herself with scrambled eggs on toast, something she'd always eaten for breakfast back when Stacy and Peter still lived at home. So some things hadn't changed.

He started eating his breakfast but didn't speak to Stacy. Stacy paled a little. Was he going to blow his top because of everything that had happened? She was sure he must've been highly annoyed about her sudden departure years ago, even though she'd left a note saying she was leaving home and would let them know when she got settled somewhere. But she'd not said why she was leaving, nor where she was going or with whom, although she was almost sure he'd never found out about Mike. Her mother had never asked her about boyfriends. And since she was once again trapped – as she saw it – in her family's midst, he might think it was his right to mete out some harsh words or punishment about the way she was conducting her life. She tried to think of something else to say, to break the ice and gauge what his thoughts were. But it made the eating of her otherwise delicious breakfast, uncomfortable.

'So do you, um, see Peter, at all?'

'No, but he's doing all right, love,' her mother answered, quickly, her eyes fixed on her breakfast. 'He bought a flat out Kent way with his part of your gran's inheritance. He's into computers. And he, he lives with, um—'

'Yes, well we don't want to bring all that up again, do we? Can't we just sit and eat, woman, without going on about all that?' shouted her father, thumping the table, making everyone jump.

Her mother dropped her fork but got to her feet, angrily.

'How dare you, Jerry!' she said pointing at him. 'He's doing very well for himself, as you well know. He lives with a man, Stacy, and they're in love and thinking about getting married, which is what your father *refuses* to accept!' she shot back.

'It's not right, all this new gender stuff!' her father said, glancing nervously at his wife. 'It was never like this in our day. So, no, I don't accept it.'

Stacy raised her eyebrows as she shovelled a forkful of fried eggs into her mouth. Wow, she hadn't known that about her brother. Yet Peter had always been a very good-looking boy with his blue eyes and blonde hair and gentle ways, despite her father always saying he wanted to 'make a man out of him' with all the work around the farm he gave Peter to do.

'Gosh,' she said, covering her mouth and chewing as fast as she could, so she could answer her father. 'But that's how things are, nowadays, Dad. He's still our Peter, though, isn't he?' Stacy risked saying, keeping her eyes low.

Her mother nodded. 'That's very true, Stacy. So you've got no choice but to accept it, Jerry. And that's final. You'll give yourself heart failure if you keep going on about all this stuff all the time. Now eat your breakfast. And no more talking until we've finished or we'll be getting indigestion next.'

It was a hot sunny day, again, with a light breeze slicing through the heat, keeping the temperature around twenty-two degrees and bearable. After breakfast, Stacy and her mother did something they'd never done before; they walked around the farm, arm in arm whilst her mother explained what they'd been doing since Stacy and Peter had left, and told her about the plans they'd been discussing for their future.

'And it's been nothing but hard work, every day here, just as usual. And, well, you know what it's like. I've told your father I'd like to persuade your grandfather to sell it and then we can retire and get a little cottage somewhere by the sea. We've got some savings put aside, you see. So it'd be nice to do that.'

'I didn't know it belonged to Gramps. But Dad'll never let

it go, will he? He's got nothing else in his life and he's just too stubborn.'

'Well, he's not always such an ogre – your father,' her mother said carefully. 'Just old-fashioned. Unfortunately, he'll never change, love.'

Stacy had forgotten how serene it was here in the top fields, with only the swishing of the wind and leaves rustling on the hedges for company. But now they were alone there were some things Stacy needed to discuss with her mother; some things she needed to get off her chest. She folded her arms, bracing herself.

'Well, I think you should move, Mum. I hated living here, I'm sorry to say. Peter hated it too. So many hard-edged rules and Dad's word was final. But also we felt you could've stuck up for us or at least been on our side sometimes. That's one of the reasons we left. The other reason we left is because you didn't allow us a childhood or any nice treats occasionally. You made us work as if we were your staff or something. All our lives. Please tell me why you did that, because I've never understood it. No one else I know has ever been treated like that. It hurt us both, considerably, you know.'

Stacy watched whilst her mother's eyebrows rose and fell, as though she was searching for the right words. An apology and explanation would have been nice; some outpouring of remorse and love would have been wonderful. Or were her parents incapable of giving or showing love, as she suspected they were?

'Oh, Stacy. It was just our way, you see. We've always had to work hard throughout our lives, with little reward and—'

'Oh,' Stacy exclaimed, her indignation rising to the surface. 'So because *you* didn't get anything nice out of life meant that *we* shouldn't have expected anything nice? Is that it?'

'Well, no, but it builds *character* to struggle, my father told me. And look at you both! You and Peter have made something of yourselves, haven't you? You, in the library and Peter with his IT?'

'Right! So your reasoning is that you *both* made us suffer – you were unkind to us, you showed us *no* love – so we'd get good jobs?' Stacy said resentfully.

'No, I don't think we were unkind, exactly, love. And childhood doesn't last, does it? So, well, I suppose we thought it would prepare you to be strong and independent. But I will admit that I've realised since then that our, um, behaviour, let's say, drove you away. You were both out the door so quick after you turned eighteen. And I am very sorry about that. But I don't want to go over old ground and start worrying about all that now. We've made our beds, all of us, and it's done now. So, anyway, tell me, do you have a nice boyfriend now?'

A tear teased her eyelid as Stacy sighed.

Her mother clearly didn't understand how unloved and lonely she'd felt throughout her childhood. So it wasn't just their father who had odd ways about him. Stacy could see that her mother had her own very fixed ideas about life, too.

She realised they'd never understand that it was their lack of love and care that *really* drove her and Peter away. It was as she thought: her parents were simply unloving people.

'Nope,' Stacy said finally. 'I never have any kind of life because of my cats.'

'Well, they're gone now so maybe you can have some kind of life. At least your father's sorting out your flat for you. Got someone in to freshen it up with a lick of paint, too, apparently. He likes things to be done in a certain way, as you know. So it'll be nice when you go back in. What you had before wasn't really working was it, love? We spoke to that John. He says you yelled at them all the time. But it wasn't the cats' fault, love. They were cooped up and that's not right for animals like that. You'd become a cat hoarder and that's not healthy living either. So you just need to find a nice boy and settle down before it's too late. I'd love some grandchildren and we won't be getting them from Peter, unless him and his partner decide to adopt some kiddies, you know?'

'I know. But I feel sad about my cats. I tried my best with them. But it all just got to be too much, which is a shame, really. Mum, tell me, do you ever see my friend Elsa who had that skiing accident?' she asked, determined to change the direction of the conversation because thinking about her lost cats was too painful. 'You know Elsa? She lives at the bottom of the hill. You know, that girl I used to go to school with? Or do you see her parents at all? I wouldn't mind going to see her while I'm here.'

'Bottom of the – oh, yes! They moved last year. They got a bungalow somewhere near Bognor. Nicer for their girl, you know. No stairs or hills to bother about. And she's got one of those electric chairs now. So she can manoeuvre herself about, instead of her parents pushing her everywhere. Much better arrangement for them all. No forwarding number but I suppose they might be in a phone book.'

As they turned and headed back towards the farm Stacy realised something. *So there's nothing left for me here, now. Nothing left for me anywhere, really, now my cats are gone and Elsa's moved.*

Chapter 11

Stacy relented to staying with her parents for a couple of weeks, taking the time in paid leave from the library. However, her supervisor had told Stacy that she needed to have a serious think about things, before she came back, because she'd been taking far too much time off work lately.

'Do we bore you, Stacy? Are you thinking of leaving us or something? You really don't seem to have the same motivation you used to have. Or are there difficulties we need to be advised about?'

'Well, I have had some, er, personal problems recently but I'm just about on top of all that now. So when I get back everything will be different, I promise.'

She couldn't go back just yet though because her flat wasn't ready, for one thing. Her father was still busy trying to sort it out during the evenings after his farm work, doing the long drive to her flat and back twice a day. Stacy did feel a bit guilty about that. He always worked very hard, her father; she'd give him that. But she surprised herself by acknowledging that she *did* want to stay with her parents and try to patch up some of the holes in their relationship. She'd been away eight long years and not seen them in all that time. She'd only spoken to her mother once on the phone, when she first moved into her flat. Yet her mother hadn't responded with much enthusiasm when she'd asked how they were.

'Oh, you know,' she'd said. 'Everything's pretty much the same, as usual. Nothing much changes around here.'

Her mother's complacency had left Stacy feeling empty. Why hadn't her mother said she'd missed her? And even though her parents had never expressed loving feelings of any kind – even to the point of them never having kissed either of their children goodnight when they went to bed – Stacy would secretly have liked her mother to have told her, just once in her life, that she was *loved and missed*. But no one had ever told her she was loved. Not even Mike, although she had loved him. So that was the reason Stacy had stopped calling her parents all those years ago. There was no point looking for love where it did not exist. She knew she had to try and find it elsewhere.

So whilst she stayed with them, she helped her mother, like she used to do, washing and cleaning and even collecting the apples. Their house looked tired and dated and Stacy mentioned this to her mother who said, 'Decorating is your dad's department, love. But he's always busy with other things. Anyway, he's busy with your flat at the moment, isn't he?'

Her mother even persuaded Stacy to let her cut her hair, sitting on the old three-legged stool with her knees nearly up to her chin, in the middle of the kitchen, while she snipped away like she used to. It completely irked Stacy that she'd acquiesced to allow her mother to do that on this occasion, like she was still a little girl, even though her hair *had* needed sorting out. Yet it was just another thing, Stacy realised, she hadn't been able to do because of the cats. The amount of time it took looking after her cats had meant they'd prevented her from organising essential life events like dental appointments, having a haircut or doing the weekly shop. Perhaps it was best, all around, that they'd gone to other homes. But she knew she'd miss seeing them once she stepped back into her newly decorated flat.

'Seems funny that I used to cut both yours and Peter's hair with these old scissors. But there now. Your hair looks much better shoulder length and I've given you that fringe so you won't need those awful hairbands. Right, now keep still a while longer and I'll plait it, like I used to. You can keep this old scrunchie. You could easily plait your hair yourself, you know. Plaits keep that wild hair of yours tame. Plus, you'll see how pretty it looks. Much more feminine. Unfortunately, you got that frizz from your dad's side of the family. But plaiting it will help with that. There you are. What do you think? You look so much better now!'

Every afternoon Stacy would wander down the potholed drive, which her parents had done nothing about fixing since she was little. That took her onto the lower road and then down the hill to the village. Her mum was right in one respect, that everything pretty much was the same. A few people had

112

added extensions to their homes, though. She was especially keen to see the old village school because it had been one of her favourite escapes from her oppressive childhood. When she saw it nostalgia swamped her. The climbing frame was still in place. But no sand pit. Of course, it looked smaller than she remembered, as she leaned on the outside railings, looking in. Then she went round the corner and found the brook and sat on the bank a while, playing games on her phone. It was good to feel the fresh air on her face and relive old memories. It was even good to be doing something other than working and looking after her cats for a change.

The run-down pigsty where Mike had stayed had been knocked down and turned into a proper studio flat for Bob, who had worked for her father, since Mike left. He ate with them each night, as usual. He was a lot older than Mike and nowhere near as fanciable! Her father came and went each day grumbling about this and that, or with news that Stacy's flat was nearly ready. She wondered if her mother would be sad to see her go but didn't really care either way what her father thought.

When the time came for them to say goodbye, Stacy could see that her mother was fighting to keep her tears at bay. Ah! So maybe her mother did care a little about her then, in her own way? But she wasn't going in the car with them. Stacy relented and gave her mother an awkward hug. It felt so strange hugging her mother. It was something she'd never done before. She was surprised to note that her mother's clothes smelt of mothballs and she felt very thin. She couldn't remember the last time she'd touched her mother.

'Bye, Mum. Look, when I'm settled I'll ring you and you'll both have to come for a proper visit or maybe I can cook lunch or something for you.'

Her mother had nodded, a handkerchief in front of her face, probably masking her real feelings about everything, Stacy hoped.

Her father had driven his daughter home without a word passing his lips. Stacy had spent the entire journey just looking out of the window. There was no way she could make conversation with him for the whole journey. But when he dropped her off outside her block of flats she did assent to thank him for his trouble.

'Thanks for everything, Dad. Um, I'm sorry I've caused you some grief. I'll see you soon.'

'See you later then,' was all he could manage, looking out of the car window as Stacy got out of the car.

Stacy kept walking without looking back. She could tell he'd paused for a moment because his engine was still idling. But whether it was to check on something or whether he was thinking about how different their lives could have been if only he'd been a more loving father, she could only wonder. At least she'd finally broken the ice with her parents again. So maybe there was a tiny ray of hope about striking up a better relationship with them in the future. She also wanted to phone Peter and catch up with his news.

'But first,' she said firmly – and she slid the thank you card, from her mother's old box of cards, under John's door and then inserted the key in the door of her own flat.

The change was dazzling!

As she walked from room to room in wonder, she could see all the walls had been repainted in an off-white colour, which brightened everything considerably. The bathroom had been scrubbed and was gleaming and there were no piles of dirty washing lying about. Even her washing had been done and put away!

'Oh, wow!'

It was as though Mary Poppins had come in and swished a magic wand and everything had sorted itself out. Everything was clean and tidy and the piles of paperwork and books that had been stacked on the lounge table had been whisked away into a new low-level cupboard, which had been added to the room. Oh, that would be useful as she'd never had enough storage for everything before. Her sofa had been replaced by another infinitely better one. It was not new but that didn't matter. Her old one had been stinky with cat pee. The disgusting lounge carpet had been replaced with laminate flooring. Her torn cat-pee-stained duvet had also been replaced. And there was food and fresh milk in the fridge.

What a difference!

And it was a very pleasing difference, she was happy to note. A tear escaped down her cheek, as the enormity of all the changes finally hit her and as she realised she had even more reason to be thankful to her father.

However, it was completely silent and that was an experience she was not used to! No little Pooch or Chater was there to come and welcome her or wind around her legs, expecting their dinner. Stacy sighed despondently. No longer having her little kitties would take some getting used to; she knew that for a fact.

Chapter 12

Eileen wiped the back of her hand across her tired face. She felt she was starting to look a lot older than her fifty-three years. She really needed to get her mother to help her colour her hair again. She rarely had time for hairdressers but her roots were starting to look like a runway at Gatwick. Yet there was always so much washing and ironing and feeding of everyone in her household. No time for herself what with work and her two boys. Marcus and Troy were in their early twenties yet told her regularly they had no intention of leaving home until they found their Mrs Rights. Sure, they both had jobs, down the local supermarket and training up for management, no less, and she'd loved having them around since her husband Graham walked out of their lives, saying he was going down the pub one evening, never to return. But sometimes some help from them – offered, not cajoled – would have been nice.

She'd long given up hope of ever finding Graham. The police had done their best, they'd told her. There had been sightings of course and CCTV had showed grainy images of someone who *might* have been Graham. But nothing had come of it. Eileen knew that if his intention had been to disappear then that's precisely what he would have done. He'd been gone for over three years at any rate.

Not that Eileen had really minded. He'd been a drinker, had Graham, and not a very nice man when he was on one of his benders. He'd also never really managed to hold a job down for very long, so Eileen had always been the main breadwinner. Anyway, since she'd always had so much to do there wasn't much time left for lamenting over her loss in that respect. So she and her boys had got on with things without him.

At her mother's request, though, she'd moved out of the rented flat she'd been living in with Graham, and she and the boys had moved in with her mother, Veronica.

'It's a bit of company for me, rattling round this big old house. And I won't charge you rent just as long as you do all the shopping. Plus it'll be easier on your purse strings now you're the only earner.'

Eileen had never known her father. 'A quickie behind the coal shed, with an old boyfriend,' was how Veronica laughingly explained her daughter's parentage.

But Eileen knew life was full of glitches, grievances, problems. 'You have to make do and mend,' her mother was fond of telling her. Eileen agreed with her mother that having plenty of problems herself made it so much easier dealing with other people's problems.

Anyway, she was busy putting the washing into piles, setting up the ironing board and checking the temperature on the iron and then while the iron was hissing away, climbing to the correct heat, she got a saucepan out. She filled it half full with cold water, added a bag of frozen peas and then began filling up the sink to wash the potatoes.

'Chicken and leek pie tonight, Mum. That do you?'

'Of course. You know I'm happy with anything, love.'

Eileen took the pie out of its carton, placed it on the side by the oven and switched the oven on.

'Hi, Mum,' said Troy, coming in from work. 'Marcus is gonna be late. Problems with cashing up. So he's got to stay and sort things out with that new cashier. She's not very good. She'll be getting the boot if things don't improve with her.'

'Uh-huh. Well dinner's going to be a bit late. I'm just catching up with the ironing.'

'Whatever. I'll be in my room. Just yell when it's ready.'

Veronica tutted. 'You know, you ought to teach those boys how to look after themselves, love. What if they decide to leave home? Neither of them can cook. Neither of them knows what a washing machine's for. They're pretty useless!'

'Uh-huh. Well maybe one day when I've got time and a whole load of patience! Oh, can you pass me those jeans, Mother? No, not those. Those there. Thanks.'

'You're running yourself ragged, love. And then you've got work on top of that. Don't know where you get all your energy from.'

Eileen put the iron down and sighed. 'You're right, Mother,

as usual. It's funny. I love my work. I love helping people help themselves. But you're totally right. I get stuck when it comes to sorting out my own family, don't I? I'm good at giving advice but not so grand at taking it. Anyway, we've got another Afternoon Tea Club meeting on Saturday. Why don't you come with me? You started all this lot off in the first place and I've got the results back from that meeting we had. I think it'd be really nice for you to meet everybody. What do you think?'

'Dora? Is that you?' Yvonne called from her office.

She rubbed her face and stared bleakly out of the window, even though the view of the hotel garden with its colourful herbaceous borders, two willow trees and pond that attracted squirrels and hedgerow birds was a delight to behold. She tutted, trying to solve a problem on the supplier's invoice in front of her. Yvonne was getting behind with her paperwork these days. She'd have liked nothing more than to take a breather outside in their garden, with a glass of white wine, for half an hour or so. She couldn't remember the last time she'd actually had time to do that and, come to think of it, it had been ages since she'd read a good book, let alone gone for a walk in the lanes with Dora, like they used to do.

Everything seemed to take so much effort these days. But it didn't help that their last bookkeeper had left and they'd not found anyone to replace her yet. Was it her imagination or were the staff starting to take liberties with her now she didn't have the same verve she used to have in her seventies?

A door slammed and she heard rustling in the kitchen.

'It's okay, Mum. I'm back. I've got the lot. Right, so that's one thing done. We'll get dinner sorted out and get them fed first. Now I know Richmond is usually here to give them a talk after dinner. But we can do that between us, can't we? We've listened in on the way he does things often enough. They'll have the usual mix of cameras, iPads and phones so we can have a chat about what they want to get out of the course, make some notes and that will buy us even more time!'

Yvonne closed her laptop and started filing her invoices away. Even her desk seemed to be unusually cluttered. She removed two empty coffee mugs and brought the overflowing paper bin into the kitchen to empty, as Dora was putting the shopping away.

'God. Another day's work almost over. But you know, Dora, I really think I'm getting too old for all this now. This is the fourth time Richmond's let us down. I mean we simply can't keep digging photographers out of a pot for a last-minute reprieve, can we. It's too stressful!'

Dora poured two large glasses of icy sauvignon blanc and gave one to her mother. She then continued putting the shopping away.

'You're right, Mother. It's bloody mental. The art classes are great. The jewellery and basket weaving courses are great. But it is all a bit of a faff, as far as the photography classes are concerned. And you're right. You should definitely be taking things easier now you're nearly ninety. I don't know how you've done it all these years. Not that I want to run the place, I hasten to add. But I think we need to put our heads together and work something out regarding our retirement or retirement of sorts. So what do you suggest about tomorrow?'

Yvonne eased herself onto one of the barstools and took a long swig of her wine. 'Oh, this wine is rather delish. Hmm. Right, well, we don't want to lose their business, darling, so I suggest we take them all out tomorrow morning in the minibus, as usual and they can take whatever photos they like. Then we'll get them back in time for lunch. And then. Um. Well, unless we can grab someone else at short notice, I think we might have to say he's just rung and says he's ill, can't make it, was hoping he'd be okay, et cetera. Unless you have any better ideas?'

Dora shrugged with a frown. 'I think that's by far the best idea, Mother. Right, well. I'll get the dinner on then and after that I'll try ringing and texting him again tonight and if there's still no response, I guess we'll have to go with that!'

'Right, folks, so this is the lady who started the ball rolling! May I introduce you to my mum, Veronica!' Eileen explained, standing back as Taynor wheeled Eileen's mum to the front of the room in her wheelchair and up a slight ramp they'd fashioned, so everyone could see her.

'Oops, brakes! Don't want you rolling back down the other

side, do we, love.' Taynor grinned, manoeuvring Veronica into place.

'Well done, Veronica,' someone yelled and everyone started clapping.

'You've made a big difference to my life, you have!' shouted someone else. 'I'm loving all this. Never used to get out before.'

As the clapping faded, the members of the Afternoon Tea Club could see how flushed with pride Veronica was. She was beaming and thanking everyone for their kindness.

'Thank you. Thank you all,' Veronica said. 'It was only a tiny suggestion. I never thought it would go as far as it has. But I must say it's wonderful to finally meet all of you. It seems to be going great guns, doesn't it!'

'You've got me and my friend out of the house to meet all of these people here. It woke us up, in a way, it did,' said one lady.

'Never thought anything interesting would happen at my time of life now I've reached eighty-six. But you've made that possible for me,' said someone else.

'You see, Mother? I told you they'd welcome you with open arms!' said Eileen, grinning. 'Right, well thanks for that, everybody, and now let's get down to business.'

Taynor gave Eileen a clipboard with lots of paperwork attached.

'Okay,' Eileen began. 'Well, the good news is that most of what we've asked for has been approved at the meeting. So what we've got is this. We've got afternoon tea twice a month.

123

And we've got it on the first Saturday of the month here at the community centre and the last Saturday of the month at one of two garden centres. And we'll alternate those. Now, don't worry about keeping up with me on this because we'll be giving you all a sheet to keep, at the end of today's session, with extra sheets for any of your friends. And we've also secured two Friday afternoon sessions a month, to help anyone who's having difficulties with their smart phones and iPads et cetera or wants to learn about computers and the internet. Now, these computer courses are limited because there's only a certain number of computers available in the classroom. It will be at the local college but you'll have to ring and book that yourselves, direct with the college. All the telephone numbers you'll need are on the sheets. Right, on to swimming lessons! We've managed to fix the second Saturday of the month for a two-hour session if any of you want to learn how to swim. I've got four names down for that, already. Yes, Margo, your name is at the top of the list, love. And last but not least, art. We can do two Friday afternoon sessions a month at another community centre for those of you who want to either learn how to draw or paint. All the venues we've decided on have parking and disabled or wheelchair access, of course. Now refreshments will be available but they're from a machine. So you'll need to bring fifty pence with you for that. All other information is on your sheets. So just to be clear, the computer and art classes will be on different Friday afternoons.'

Eileen paused and looked around at the group of people

in front of her, allowing the information to sink in. People were commenting in surprise at what Eileen had managed to secure for them.

'Didn't think she'd be able to get half of what she's got!' said someone.

'Well!' commented another. 'Isn't it lovely being able to have a choice about what we get to do? I think I fancy learning to swim but I'll have to get our Sandie to help me buy a new swimming costume.'

'And finally,' Eileen continued, 'as far as trips go, we can arrange *either* a trip to London each year to see a show, with an overnight stay, or it will be a day out to a seaside resort of your choosing, including lunch in a hotel. There will of course be a charge for the trips but this charge will be agreed later on. Now we're looking into whether there might be additional charges for any of the courses or afternoon tea at the garden centre. But my bosses have assured me that nothing will be prohibitive. And we haven't got prices for the London trip yet. Right now, regarding the trips, you need to be aware that each of the trips will probably be early morning starts from a set location. So you will need to be dropped off at these locations at the exact times stated because, unfortunately, the coach companies say they won't be able to wait for stragglers. So please make sure you're on time for those. We haven't been able to secure any mini-breaks due to the fact they might be problematic as one of you suggested. But either way we hope you'll be very happy with all the things we have managed to sort out for you. Right, now in a minute Taynor will come around and hand out the sheets to you all. Now another thing I need to tell you is that we're going to initially run these courses up to Christmas to see how they go. We might need to change or alter them depending on turnout. If no one takes up the art or computer classes they'll either be cancelled or replaced by something else. So please let us know by the date on the sheet which courses you or your friends would be interested in. And we'll need those sheets back by next week so we can start putting things together and getting hold of tutors and the like. Yes, love, that's a week from today!'

Eileen stopped to take a couple of gulps from a glass of water. Taynor took over.

'Okay, so just to let you also know, we've already arranged a trip to Bournemouth on the fourth of September, which will be our trip out for this year, just to start that ball rolling. The date is on the sheet. And we can do this particular trip for £15.00 including a three-course lunch. The reason we're arranging this now is to see what sort of response we get. And it'll be a cracking day out. You'll be dropped off at the gardens for a meander down to see the sea and paddle if you wish and then lunch in one of the hotels nearby, with a bit of shopping if you're up to it after all that paddling! And also, once we've sorted out tutors and firmed up definite venues et cetera, everything will start running straight away. So I envisage the art classes being the first courses to start up on the third and fourth Fridays of the month. So have a good think about what you want to sign up for and we'll let you know prices, if any, next week. Then we'll start. So how do you feel about what we've managed to secure for you?'

'Fantastic!'

The room erupted with people shouting joyously, clapping, banging on the tables and even a couple of sun hats being thrown into the air!

Chapter 13

Dora was drinking a cup of English breakfast tea with her mother and her brother in the residents' breakfast lounge, at their Arts & Crafts Hotel, as Handel's 'Water Music' was playing its jovial tune on the iPlayer. Richmond, the photography tutor, was neither Dora's nor her mother's favourite person, but he'd seemingly, of late, got his act together and was driving the photography class to Bourton-on-the-Water in the minibus that Wednesday morning, for a lesson on how to capture reflections over the River Windrush.

'If this music is supposed to wake me up gently, Mother, it's not working. It's just bloody annoying after the session I had with Jodie last night!' Dora snapped, holding her head.

'Well, whose fault it that, I wonder? Anyway this music is supposed to be inspiring for our photography guests. Nothing to do with you, you silly child! Is Jodie still asleep?'

'She wants to sleep in until at least midday, she told me, because it's so blissfully quiet here. So after we've had our meeting, me and Jodie are going out for lunch somewhere. So can we crack on with things!'

'God! Do you two ever come up for air?' Stuart griped, shaking his head slowly. 'Look, are we going to talk about things now or what? I was up bloody early this morning to drive up here for this meeting. And even though I love you both dearly and would like to stay a bit longer I really do need to get back to my own hotel. I'm not blessed with time to slouch around like you two.'

'There's no slouching here, son! We're your father's family. It's not our way,' Yvonne stated, indignantly.

'Look, Stuart, it's not just the hotel; my fiftieth is coming up in a few months' time and I think that alone warrants some thought. But on the other hand, Mum's a bit of an old croc now and doesn't want to be doing this forever more, do you, Mother dear?'

'There's nothing like being disrespected by one's children!'

'There certainly isn't, Mother, and that's why I'm so pleased you enjoy it! Anyway, what do you want to do about things?'

Yvonne poured herself another cup of tea, offering the teapot to her children. They shook their heads. She glanced around the dining room and sighed. The breakfast things still needed clearing off the tables and Debbie was late in again today. What was it with her ruddy staff these days? Weren't they motivated enough with better than average wages, six weeks' holiday pay with additional time off for their birthdays, Christmas and emergencies, no questions asked? Or was it something else? It was certainly getting her down. It never used to.

'Right, well, I don't want to be a useless old stick at any age. I'm still fit at eighty-nine. I'm not on tablets. If I take up residence in an old people's home, I'll be fit for the scrap heap. I had thought about getting a little cottage or a little flat somewhere. But I'm not so sure where. And I think that with your fiftieth birthday fast approaching it's a good time for *you* to start thinking about things too, Dora. You've been a wandering minstrel for *far* too long. But I'm not sure it would work out if you and I moved in together somewhere. I think we need to find our own new lives now. However, I will say you've been a great help to me and great company these past few years. Yet nor would I want to put on you, Stuart, and demand you leave Devon and come up here to take over things. Other than that, I really don't know, dear children. What are your thoughts?'

Stuart shifted uncomfortably and looked down at his hands.

'Okay well, I think it's probably time you sold. The reason being, I have a life – no – I have a *great* life in Devon with Hazel and Steph. We've already discussed things and none of us wants to move up here to take over this place. You have far too many problems with people like Richmond for starters. He should be ousted as the photography guy and you should either change the course or get a more reliable tutor. It's as simple as that, Mother. But I think you have to decide what *you* want out of life, before you start questioning everything and everyone else. And what about Aunt Philippa? Couldn't you move down there or move in with her? She's got that lovely big house and that annex and you get on okay.

'Southampton's still a great city with London a stone's throw away. That's what I'd really want for you because then you'd have some permanent company and lots to do in your spare time. Of course, you're not short of a bob or two, so in all honesty you could live anywhere you wanted, at home or abroad. But I think you need familial company at your time of life and I think Philippa is the best person to give you that. What say you, sis?'

'Well, to be honest, I agree with everything you say, Stuart. You should definitely sell, Mother. And I also think you should move back down south to be near Philippa. You're both healthy women with similar interests. Dad's brother is still in the area; it's where we're all from originally and I wouldn't mind going back there myself. Hey, it's been fun being here. And, sure, I'd miss stuff like sitting out in our lovely garden and the friends we've made around here. But the older I've got the more I crave family and old friends around me. So, yeah, it's time for another life change now.'

'You and your changes, child! But this time I actually agree with you,' Yvonne said, and sipped her tea. 'Hmmm. Well, okay, I'll admit I've been doing a bit of thinking myself and what I think is this: I will sell. I've been speaking to my sister and she says she'd love me to move in because – like you say, Dora, we like similar things. Plus she's been feeling lonely and we're of a certain age, of course. So we'll probably try that. But you, Dora, you need your own space, a place to call home. So both your immediate inheritances from me, apart from when I finally croak, of course, will be a straight half cut from the sale proceeds of the hotel. And you'll only get yours, Dora, as long as you buy yourself a little place somewhere with it. In other words, I expect you to finally put down some roots, darling. Okay? I will also give you both these inheritances on the proviso that you come visit your poor old mum on a regular basis, as I don't *only* want to speak to Philippa for the rest of my life. And you need to stop messing around with that bloody Botox or whatever it is you're doing, Dora, because it's ruining your looks!'

Rat-a-tat went Stacy's door.

Who the hell is that? she thought. No one ever banged on her door. She took a final swig of her morning coffee, tightened the towel around her wet hair and secured her dressing gown belt because she was naked underneath after her shower. Then she cautiously opened the door.

The corridor beyond her door was dark because the lighting had failed again, something she'd mentioned to her mother the previous evening, during their first telephone conversation since she'd stayed with them to recuperate. Her mother had rung to see how she liked her newly redecorated flat and to find out how she was doing. Ordinary family stuff that Stacy had never experienced before. At least her mother's phone conversation proved she was actually interested in her daughter's wellbeing, now, for some reason. Or had she finally awoken to the importance of family? Her mother told her she would ring every week if she'd like.

'Well, I'll ring you sometimes,' Stacy had said, with what she hoped had been a smile in her voice because she actually thought it was going to be nice reconnecting with her mother again after such a long time apart.

Her next-door neighbour, John, was standing on the mat in front of her.

'Oh, hi, Stace. Sorry. You just up? Sorry!'

'Um, yes I'm just up. So what did you want? I've got lots to do today.'

Stacy felt highly uncomfortable standing in front of a stranger when she wasn't ready to receive guests or otherwise. Besides, what did he want now? All he'd ever done in the past was moan about her cats and complain. She had no time for Moaning Minnies, even though he had contacted her parents about her fall.

'Um, well I just wanted to say thanks for the card you gave me. Didn't spot it till this morning. It went under the mat, you see. Not that I'm saying I don't clean up much. But I rarely move that mat unless I'm having a real good clean throughout. You didn't need to give me a card, though. I only did what anyone would've done. But thanks anyway. Er, and you're okay now, are you?'

Stacy didn't like the fact that he was dressed but smelt as

though he hadn't showered recently. She tried not to turn her nose up in disgust. But it happened anyway.

'Yeah, I'm fine,' she managed. 'Thanks for saving me. But I've, um, got stuff to do now. So I'll see you later. Right, bye then!'

She didn't wait for his reply but turned and closed the door. At least she hadn't slammed it.

Her breakfast eggs were boiling away in the pan on the hob, with two minutes to go. Stacy had never even been able to have her favourite brekkie of six-minute boiled eggs and toast soldiers because there were always so many other things to do first thing in the mornings, when she had the cats. Things like having to get up really early to sort out all the cat food and change their cat litter plus giving them all a little pat or cuddle *every single day*. Melanie, especially, had loved lots of little cuddles. Breakfast, for herself, used to be a snatched banana or yoghurt because it was easiest. She didn't know herself now, sitting down to what her mother would call a proper breakfast of cereal followed by eggs of some sort, toast and tea or coffee. It felt luxurious to actually have the time to do that, for once.

That said, she was missing her little kitties. She wondered how Pooch, Rover and Chater were faring now. They had socialisation problems and how would anyone know about all that unless they took the time to find out? She wanted to ring Cats Protection to see if they'd housed them yet. But, like her mother said, they would only probably reassure her they were okay, no matter what was going on with them, whether they'd managed to secure new homes for them, or not.

She had to stop thinking about all these unpleasant things. But what else was there to do, now, either side of work? She'd lied to John when she'd told him she had lots to do. It was Saturday and she had *nothing* to do now her kitties were elsewhere. Maybe she should get the bus and go to one of the supermarkets instead of the corner shop? Yes. She could do that. She'd always wanted to have the freedom to do that. Oh well, that was worth drying off for and getting dressed, instead of mooching around the flat or watching morning TV. But she promised herself that morning TV was going to be a special treat for later in the week.

Goodness, she wouldn't know herself!

'Okay, Mum, sit down. I've, er, I've got something to tell you,' Gracie began after they'd put the breakfast things in the dishwasher and before they went to do their weekly shop at Waitrose, as they usually did every Saturday morning.

Marjorie always felt worried when anyone said they had something to tell her. It was especially worrying if they also added that they wanted her to *sit down*, as if preparing her for something awful. But Marjorie already had an inkling what was coming; she'd been waiting for this particular conversation for a while now, despite Gracie always telling her she was happy they were living together.

135

'You've met someone!' Marjorie said, folding her arms, leaning against the sink.

Her daughter looked surprised. 'Well, um, yes! I have actually.'

Marjorie's tut slipped out before she could restrain it.

She hadn't meant to tut. Well, maybe deep down she had. But she hadn't thought it would escape quite so successfully. What she'd really wanted to say was, 'Oh, that's great news!' She wouldn't have meant that, either, but it's what she *should* have said.

Trouble was, it meant things were moving at a speedier pace than she'd hoped they would. She still hadn't managed to pick up the phone and speak to someone about the devastating impact Oliver had had on her life and she certainly *needed* to speak to someone about that. Otherwise how could she move forward? She also wanted to make friends at the Afternoon Tea Club because it was the most likely of places for that to happen. But things like that rarely happened quickly; they happened at their own pace. And even though Marjorie had sort of wanted these things to happen, for both their sakes, she hadn't wanted them to happen until she was ready.

So even though she thought she'd mentally prepared herself for it, Gracie's news had still taken Marjorie by surprise. Plus Gracie had recently pooh-poohed the idea of finding love again. At least if Gracie had informed her she was ready to look for love, rather than saying she'd already met someone, it would've given Marjorie the time she needed to fully adjust to that idea.

She shook her head by way of an apology. 'I didn't mean that.'

'Didn't you?' said Gracie, crossing her own arms defensively.

Marjorie then took her daughter's face in her hands and stared deeply into her eyes.

'That tut was for me. Don't you understand, darling? Look, I wanted you to find someone else way before you and Harry started divorce proceedings, once you told me what he'd done. But since moving in with you – since being with my precious, wonderful, funny daughter on a day-to-day basis – well ...' Marjorie felt tears pricking. 'Since then I've known no other life. I've wanted no other life. Yet despite all that, I've always known that one day you'd fly the nest, for a second time. And me? Well, I've realised two things. One, I need to get over Oliver. I need to talk to someone about that time and move on. And two, I want *you* to find some happiness with someone who is wonderful and completely right for you. And so that tut was me realising that everything has to happen a lot faster than it has been. So I'm going to ring my doctor this very minute and go talk to her. Not before time, I know. I might also see if she can prescribe me something for my anxiety.'

'Oh, Mum, I'm so sorry,' Gracie whispered, stepping forward and hugging her mother, as their tears started to flow.

They were both lamenting the passage of time, Marjorie thought, despite realising the future would very probably bring a hopeful new and exciting beginning for them both.

Chapter 14

Marjorie was looking at the timetable she'd got Gracie to type out for her before she went along to the art class that afternoon. She was quite excited about the prospect of possibly meeting some new and interesting people at a learning event like this. She'd always liked to dabble at drawing as a girl and she'd liked doing trees. So she was hoping she might excel at something like that today.

The Afternoon Tea Club
Monthly Activities

Day Of Month	Activities – mainly afternoons				
	Afternoon Tea CC1	Afternoon Tea GC	Computers CL	Swimming (local pool) (**Mornings**)	Painting (P) & Drawing (D) CC2
1st Sat	√				
2nd Sat				√	
4th Sat		√	√		
1st Fri			√		
2nd Fri					

3rd Fri					√ (D)
4th Fri					√ (P)

CC1 – Usual Community Centre; CC2 – Art Classes, Community Centre 2
GC – Garden Centre; CL – Local College

'Right, class!'

Class? Marjorie wondered. There were only four of them! Stacy had come and she looked completely different. Well, her hair was a lot better, she smelt a lot nicer and she was wearing jeans instead of the fuddy skirt she'd worn on previous occasions. Raymond was here. Was art even his thing? And there was also the woman with the wonky lips, who she'd seen at the community centre before. But hadn't someone told her that Dora lived miles away? So what was she doing here? She did look a bit stern, though. Or maybe she was worried about her choice of art class – drawing.

Marjorie was happy to be trying something new but she was very disappointed that there were no new people in the class. She had rather hoped an art class might attract a certain type of person – people she could start making friends with or someone of a similar age, who liked similar things to herself. She never for one moment thought people like Raymond, Stacy and Dora would join!

'Right, so my name is Eva,' the girl at the front was saying. She had very short blonde hair, brown eyes and she was small, stick-thin and waif-like. She certainly didn't look old enough to be knowledgeably teaching anything to anybody in Marjorie's eyes. 'And I'm going to be here on the third Friday of each month for those of you who wish to try your hand at drawing like the mighty greats. People like Leonardo da Vinci or Michelangelo or even artists like George Stubbs who was a famous painter, known best for his paintings of horses. Right, so you've all tackled drawing or sketching before, I presume?'

Eva, Marjorie thought, was one of those people who clearly knew her stuff. *Probably fresh out of college or university with all sorts of highfalutin' ideas.* Yet she would probably have no notion what it felt like to be confronted with the bravado and confidence she was spouting to the four uncertain people in her class, that Friday afternoon.

Raymond and Stacy shook their heads. Dora looked thoughtfully at Eva.

'We're here to learn, love, so we're not gonna be a clever clogs like you just yet. Obviously.'

'A-ha! Well, you don't know what you can do until you put your mind to it. And this is certainly not going to be any kind of class where you hold yourselves back. It's *not* "Drawing for the Terrified" because I don't do anything terrifying. Now, you might all have lived with terror and fears and worries in your past. But please leave that kind of thing at the door before you come in. We don't want anything to cramp your abilities here. So art – any form of art – is about self-expression. And there's no particular right or wrong way with art because

140

whatever you choose to create, be it a sculpture or a painting, for example, is something that comes solely from yourselves. So no two people can create the exact same art, unless they're very skilled forgers. But we're not doing forgery in this class today; we're doing copying,' she said, grinning.

Her students exchanged anxious glances.

'Right, so I want you to step up and self-express, people. I don't want you to be maudlin about all your worries, whilst we try to work! And, after you've all written your names on the pieces of card in front of you, so I don't forget you, and after we've run through the fire drill, which is a necessity, the way we're going to do this is to start by taking up your pencils. Yep, that's the way. They're all nicely sharpened and ready to go. So pop your names on the card right now please. Lovely, that's the way. Right, well, we won't worry about whether you're using the correct pencil for the type of drawing you're going to be doing, at this stage. You may know that pencils are classed as graphite and commercially they *mainly* range in hardness from 9H to 9B, although you can occasionally pick up others, like a 10. H means Hard and B means Black and softer. So an HB pencil is sort of the middle of the range and that's the pencil you've got in front of you today. There's a fine art to knowing what each one's suitable for – in fact, it's almost a subject that can be studied by itself. But for this class, we're simply going to use these HB pencils and put something down on the paper in front of you. But we're going to do it *together* because it's easier than everyone doing their

141

own thing and then getting lost in the process or thinking that someone is better than you and going home early because you feel like failures. Got it?'

She stared eagle-eyed at the four of them as they nodded vigorously, surprised by her ferocity. *Bit like a madwoman*, Marjorie would tell Gracie later. But after Eva had showed them the fire exits and ran through the fire drill they returned to the art room.

'Right! Now I'm going to draw something on the blackboard in chalk and I want to you to copy exactly what I've done on your piece of paper and in the exact same spot. Got it?'

Everybody nodded obediently and Dora had started to smile. Marjorie thought she heard her say the word 'nuts' under her breath but she couldn't be sure.

Eva drew a circle at the top of the blackboard in the middle and she had to stretch up to do that. She checked her four students did the same. Then she drew a line from the bottom edge of the circle straight down. Everybody did the same. Next came the stick arms and stick legs.

'Right, so what have you got, guys?'

'Stick people!' said Stacy happily. 'I can do stick people, though.'

'Correct! Now *everybody* can do stick people. So what does that very simple fact convey?'

Dora sniggered. 'It means everybody can draw stick people, love. Heh, heh!'

That made Marjorie smile.

'No, wrong!' Eva cried.

She glared at the students, willing them to answer. She was obviously very passionate about her subject, Marjorie thought.

'What it means, people, is that everyone CAN DRAW!' she said, triumphantly.

'Oh, rubbish!' snorted Dora. 'Well, I can't ruddy well draw! That's why I thought I'd come here today, to give it a go!'

'Me too,' said Marjorie.

Eva clapped her hands.

'Okay, well look at it this way then. Everything in life – *everything* on the planet – is made up of either straight lines or curves. Correct? Don't shake your head, Dora! Okay, let me explain. So there's architecture or buildings. They're made of straight lines and curves; a cup – straight lines and curves; the moon, obvious; a donkey – wonky lines but even its mane is made up of straight bits and curved bits. And the sea is connected by its undulating waves or rather its *curves*. Think about a forest of trees. But it's *not* a forest of complicated trees – it's merely shapes with some dark detail and lighter bits. Simplistically, it's just a matter of getting the curls and squiggles and straight bits into a certain likeness with the subject you're drawing. So to recap, even the most complicated of structures has either curves or straight lines connecting them, making them what they are. And art is one of those things in life that you can see the results of straight away. That's one of the reasons it's so satisfying. So therefore, guys, *what* have you just done on that piece of paper?'

Raymond was nodding slowly and answered her with a smile.

'We've just drawn a picture!'

'Correct! Now, who said they couldn't draw?'

Eva had gone outside to use her phone in the refreshment break.

'So what do you think about our first drawing lesson?' Stacy said to Marjorie.

Marjorie grinned. 'Well, the tutor is completely nuts for starters, of course. But I like her. She knows her stuff and she's not worried about our concerns about not being able to draw, which is probably helpful. I've always liked drawing but I really fancy being able to draw properly and now I'm older I certainly need something to do in my spare time. So, yes, I fancy learning to draw the Eva way as a hobby. What about you?'

'Well, I've changed a bit since I was last at the Afternoon Tea Club. I've had a few issues to deal with. But yeah, I think this is my way of giving myself a bit of time out if you see what I mean.'

'Yes I do, dear. And isn't this nice being able to have a chat in between lessons, too?'

'Yes, it is. And, so I was wondering, Marjorie, could we be friends? I don't have many friends and I'd like to mingle and, um, maybe make some new friends through the Afternoon Tea Club, like they said. I mean, don't worry if not. You might be thinking I'm too young or we're too different or whatever.

But I would really like to start to get to know people, you see. If that's okay?'

Instant derogatory thoughts flew into Marjorie's brain. *Make friends with Stacy?* Well, no, she certainly didn't think so! She wanted to meet people of her own age. But, but, but! She took a deep breath. What had Dr Baxley said?

She'd recently booked a double appointment and been to see her doctor to finally start discussing the far-reaching implications of her life with Oliver. The doctor had wanted her to see a psychiatrist but Marjorie had refused point blank. However, Dr Baxley spoke to her at length and gave her medication for her anxiety. But the one thing Marjorie had tried to take from this first meeting and fix inside her head was that if someone riled her, *say nothing.*

'It's about changing the way you've been thinking about Oliver. So the technique is this: you think of a happy thought or word and you replace all negative or stressful thoughts with said happy thought or word. So, if your husband pops into your mind, for example, you'd replace him with a happy memory about your daughter, say. Or you'd just say the word "Gracie". You just need to replace Oliver's image or whatever stressful situation you're in with something more powerful. But you need to have this happy thought in your mind *before* you go out to mix with friends or acquaintances, because it might need to be used instantly,' Dr Baxley had told her.

Marjorie's hands had immediately got sticky as she wondered whether she'd be able to do that or not.

'Think of it as a get-out-of-jail-free card. So the minute someone says something you don't want to hear or don't like, you take yourself away from them with your special word or thought. Just try it, anyway, and then come and see me next week to let me know how you've coped. Oliver was a bully. Don't play into his hands by replicating his behaviour. You're so much better than all of that!'

Marjorie could have hugged her doctor when she said that. She'd made it sound so easy.

So that one piece of advice she'd been given – change your thought pattern by replacing it with something positive – had meant that today when Stacy had asked Marjorie her rather irksome question, the happy joyful word that sprang into Marjorie's mind was, of course, 'Gracie', because Gracie certainly conjured up everything that was beautiful within her life. Gracie was the *only* thing that was beautiful in Marjorie's life.

In fact, Marjorie was so fixated on the word 'Gracie' that she forgot who had said what to upset her. But that wasn't a particular good thing because *now* Marjorie was starting to worry about whether Gracie would ask her to move out so she could move her new boyfriend into their flat.

Snapped out of her reverie by Eva blustering into the canteen and shooing everyone back to class, Marjorie was pleased to discover she'd got herself out of a potentially awkward moment with Stacy by saying they'd *talk later*. More importantly, the doctor's advice had worked on this occasion.

146

She hoped it would continue to work when she came across other instances she felt stressed by.

'Right, class, so what we're going to do until the end of this lesson and each subsequent lesson, I might add, is to draw something you'll be amazed you can actually do. Something, in fact, you'll be proud to take home to your adoring family. So for today's lesson we're going to draw a building from memory – something you're familiar with or really care about. Like your home or a favourite school or church. Anything, really, and I'll be coming round helping you all out. Small classes are the best because I get to give everyone premium learning time. Okay, Stacy, let's start with you, shall we?'

At the end of the lesson, however, Marjorie didn't think Dora would be proud to show her mother the picture of their hotel with the chimney, looking like a giraffe poking its head out.

'Not quite a chimney pot, is it, Dora!' Eva had said.

Nor Stacy who, in a fit of annoyance with herself, had torn her paper into a zillion pieces because Eva had said, for the second time, 'No, it's not quite right. Start again and just draw from the heart.'

Stacy said she hadn't been in touch with her heart recently. Plus they only had fifteen minutes to go and she certainly didn't have the *heart* to start over.

As they all left the premises, looking somewhat glum, Marjorie wondered if anyone would be attending the drawing class, again, next month.

Chapter 15

Marjorie was fidgeting with her sleeve. She'd wanted to look fresh and relaxed but it was another of those clammily hot July days and whilst her pale blue jacket, edged in silver, looked the epitome of summer, the synthetic fabric made it feel a tad damp around her shoulders. She was also sure she'd put on weight because it didn't seem to hang the way it used to, over her matching dress, which – in turn – made her feel uncomfortable with her choice of outfit.

She'd asked for a glass of water to take her mind off things. Things being that she'd arranged for Gracie and her new boyfriend Steven to meet her for lunch in one of the light and airy restaurants near the waterfront because she felt it was the right thing to do. She knew she had to meet Steven before things progressed further between him and Gracie, as she suspected they might, but she didn't want to meet him in their home. That would've been a step too far. To Marjorie it would have felt as though he was intruding on their life, and she wasn't ready for that kind of intrusion between herself and her daughter in their own environment. She'd deemed it far better to meet up 'off site', as it were, in a more controlled environment and sincerely hoped it wasn't going to turn into an ordeal for her, rather than a pleasant afternoon out.

Marjorie glanced at her watch. They were late. What was Gracie thinking? Surely she'd realise her mother would be highly anxious about the whole situation and its implications? Gracie was never normally late, unless they couldn't find anywhere to park? She checked her mobile phone to see if Gracie had sent a text. Nothing. Or maybe the lateness was down to this new boyfriend? Maybe he wasn't the punctual sort. Maybe he wasn't even the right sort of person for her lovely daughter. Marjorie's mouth felt dry. She took a large gulp of water and then realised she had hiccups.

Oh no!

Marjorie didn't normally drink alcohol but this wasn't a normal situation. It was fast deteriorating and she hadn't even met the chap yet! 'I need a drink,' she said to herself but it came out rather loud. Oh boy, did she need a drink. Maybe just a little one, like a sherry, to calm her nerves. It's what she'd used to drink when Oliver was alive. *Oh, please stop thinking about him, Marj.* That's what her doctor told her to do when thoughts of him popped up from the depths. (Push them back down again.) Oh no! Now she couldn't *stop* thinking about him. Right, that's it. She needed alcohol to calm her frayed nerves.

She was about to call for a waiter, when she felt a hand on her shoulder and she turned.

'Hello, Mother,' Gracie began, with a wide smile. 'This is Steven!'

Marjorie, nervously, glanced up at the tall young man by her side, wearing a light-coloured suit; his dark hair was short, his face freshly shaved. He, too, was smiling, genially. It was also a smile that reached his dark grey eyes, Marjorie noticed, as he extended his right hand and gave a slight bow.

'Very pleased to meet you, Mrs Sykes. Or may I call you Marjorie? Gracie has told me so much about you ...'

Stacy had always wanted to be loved, she realised. But the relationships she'd had so far hadn't yielded the feeling she associated with the word 'love'. Love was what she'd felt for her cats; a cuddly, peaceful feeling. Well, apart from Pooch and Chater. And there was that chap on the telly she used to fancy on one of the TV programmes, although she couldn't remember the programme nor his name.

She stared absentmindedly out of the window as she chopped the cucumber and the peppers and prepared the salad. Her mother had told both her and Peter to never expect too much of anything from life because life wasn't usually kind. She had felt badly let down by Mike. They could've taken the world by storm the way she'd felt about him all those years ago. And she'd never met anyone else since, mainly because of her cats. She'd let the cats rule her life. That way, she hadn't needed to feel pressured about meeting anyone new or having a fabulous social life because the cats always served as an excuse as to why she never had time for all that.

Her work colleagues asked if she'd come to their Christmas staff party, every year, but she'd always refused. Elsa had once asked if she wanted to go on holiday with her and her family because she said it would've been great to have Stacy with her instead of just her mum and dad. But she'd turned the offer down because she said there was no one to look after her cats for the week. Perhaps that's why Elsa had started pulling back from their relationship and had never been at home when Stacy had rung? Perhaps that was why people had stopped asking her out? Was she even worthy of being asked out?

She'd been so pleased – and also relieved – that Peter had been thrilled to hear from her.

'Wow, sis! Is that really you? Oh wow! Hey, Marvin, my sister Stacy's on the phone. I can't believe it!'

They hadn't communicated in over nine years, but they'd never been close as siblings. Maybe it was different when you got older; maybe you just felt differently about things, she'd thought. His boyfriend, Marvin, even spoke to her on the phone that day. They'd already moved in together and couldn't speak highly enough of each other, putting the phone onto speaker, so they could all have a proper conversation together.

'Thanks, princess,' Marvin said hoarsely when Stacy invited them over. 'We'd simply lurve to come over for the afternoon to have a meal so I can meet you. Wouldn't we, Pete?'

It had seemed like a great idea at the time. Or was she being naïve? But Stacy couldn't wait to see either of them. Would Peter's good looks have changed? Perhaps he might have filled out more. And what would Marvin look like? Oh well, she'd soon know. She'd invited them both for a late lunch that Saturday, being as there was nothing on in her Afternoon Tea Club diary for that weekend.

She'd already decided it was going to be a lovely weekend. She was going to watch as much TV as possible and she was going to go into the city centre to have a stroll around the park tomorrow. People did things like that at weekends, she knew. And she'd even booked one of her holiday days off, from the library, on Tuesday because a) it was usually very quiet on a Tuesday and b) because she was going to spend some money on revamping her wardrobe for once. She hadn't done anything like that in years. Yes, life was certainly starting to look a lot better for her now; even though she did feel guilty about the cats not having the benefit of her care. But her mother was right. It had to be done because it had all got out of hand.

She'd had another conversation with her mother only last night and she'd invited her parents over for Saturday lunch too. She knew things could be quieter on the farm on Saturdays and from what her mother had told her when she was last there, they rarely did anything with their Saturdays. In fact, her mother had jumped at the chance to visit her.

'Oh, Stacy, I've been waiting for you to ask us over. I can't wait to see what the flat looks like now. I came with your dad when that John rang us about your fall, you see. I saw how awful it was. So it'd be lovely to come and see you tomorrow. Wouldn't it, Jerry?'

Stacy couldn't hear her father's response in the background.

'Okay then, Mum, I'll see you around 1.30 p.m. tomorrow. Bye then.'

It was almost that time now, Stacy noted as she put the salad bowl on the table. But they might all be late. Lots of things could hold them up, she knew. She'd rarely been bang on time for work when she'd had the cats.

There! All done. The table looked nice, anyway.

She didn't have enough chairs but someone could sit on the sofa if they wanted. She'd put slices of ham and cheese and chicken pieces on serving platters and there was the salad and cold potatoes and some olives and some bread and butter – all things she'd got from the supermarket that morning. She'd taken ages in the supermarket just picking things up and marvelling at how much choice there was. She'd even managed to pick out a bottle of red wine. She hoped they liked red wine. Well, the assistant in the supermarket had said most people liked red wine best. But they could have lemonade if they didn't like red wine or if they were driving. She didn't want to get anyone into trouble with drink-driving. And for afters there was lemon mousse or chocolate cake, which was her favourite. Plus she had some whipped cream if they fancied that as well.

So that should be it.

The tring-tring of the doorbell made her jump and as she opened it, Peter bounded in followed by his boyfriend Marvin. Peter was much taller than she'd remembered him. Yes, he'd filled out more but he was still good-looking. He lifted her up in the air and hugged her. And when he put her down again, Marvin gave her a kiss on the cheek.

'How are you, sister-in-law-to-be? And, oh wow! Just look at that spread, Pete! Tickles my taste buds, it does. And here. Do you like flowers?'

Stacy liked Marvin immediately. He was full of energy and the perfect opposite of her lean, blonde brother, with his dark hair, beefier build and his zany personality.

'Nice flat too!' he said after he took himself off for a quick look-around whilst Stacy was looking for something to put the yellow roses in. 'Oh, Pete, honey. Who's driving? I fancy a swig or two of that wine over there.'

'Just help yourselves, guys,' Stacy called as she went to answer the door again.

And there stood her mother with a gleeful smile on her face as she spotted Peter down the hall, chatting to Marvin. Her father was ambling along the dark corridor. The lights still hadn't been fixed, despite the landlord being notified.

'Oh, Peter, my darling boy!' her mother cried, racing down the hall to him. 'Oh how wonderful to see you. I didn't know you were invited. Oh, how you've grown. Oh, isn't this wonderful, Jerry? The whole family's together again. We should've done this, Jerry. We should've been the ones to have done this.'

'Mum! Hi!' Peter yelled, happily opening his arms to her and lifting her off her feet.

She hugged Peter, tears in her eyes, as he hugged her back, burying his face in her hair.

'Well hi there, mother-in-law-to-be. I'm Marvin!'

Stacy's mother broke away from her son long enough to shake hands with the person he intended to marry.

'Oh my goodness, Marvin. I'm so pleased to meet you finally!'

But as Stacy's father reached the front doormat, he visibly recoiled as he spotted Marvin and then his face turned thunderous as he saw Marvin put his arm round Peter's waist.

'Well,' he barked. 'I didn't realise you'd got us here under false pretences for a bloody charade!'

Raymond looked at his watch again. She'd been gone almost twenty minutes. Why would any woman need to be in the toilet that long unless she had an upset tummy? He'd have to give it a little longer, though. Or should he ask someone to go and check she was all right?

They'd had a very nice starter of poached eggs on what they called smashed avocado; a rather aggressive description for something that merely looked like avocado paste, he'd thought. And for their main course they'd both opted for the same choice, again, entrecote steak with roast veggies and

155

chips, although he'd liked his well done and Coralia had liked hers rare. Too rare, he'd thought; put him off his own meal, it had, all red and runny like that. So if it was an upset tummy that sent her running to the ladies, maybe it was because her steak hadn't been cooked well enough? Or maybe she'd got a bug? Or maybe she'd eaten something dodgy the night before?

Coralia was a lady his son had introduced him to. She was one of the counter staff at his place of work – someone his son felt his father might gel with.

'You know how I worry about you, Dad. Plus I've just met a new lady myself so I'll be spending more and more time with her. You and I will still be close, of course. But life has to move on.'

So Raymond had taken the phone number his son had given him and rung Coralia, and they'd chatted by phone, a couple of times, until Raymond felt confident they would get on really well. Then he'd asked her out. He'd decided on dinner at a nice restaurant Simon had recommended.

Coralia was a buxom Jamaican lady with a big personality, much to Raymond's delight. But as the evening had worn on she'd become less engaged and less chatty. Then she'd excused herself and gone to the ladies.

Raymond looked at his watch again. Hmmm. Twenty-six minutes since she'd left.

They'd been on their dessert course, so Raymond finished his Black Forest Gateau and asked to speak to his waiter.

'I'm sorry to ask but could you get someone to see if my

date is all right? She went to the ladies half an hour ago and I haven't seen her since. She might have a poorly tummy or something but I didn't think it right to go in there myself. Thanks.'

'Ah,' the waiter began sheepishly, 'I'm sorry. I should've told you. But I've been busy serving, you see. She, er, asked me to tell you she was going home because she didn't feel so well. She, um, passed me this note, which I should have given you earlier. Sorry, sir. Here you are.'

Raymond took the little scrap of lined paper, torn from a larger sheet of paper – probably from the restaurant – and read the hastily scribbled note, as the waiter hovered nervously nearby. '*Not feeling too great, Ray. Decided to go home. Thanks for the meal. Coralia.*' A tear escaped down his cheek and he quickly wiped it away, embarrassed.

'Um, excuse me?' he said to the waiter. 'Right well, could I have the bill now please? I-I don't much feel like coffee now.'

The waiter hesitated. 'Yes, of course. I'm so sorry, sir!' he whispered.

'Erm, thank you for your concern. I guess some things don't work out, do they.'

The waiter shook his head, vehemently.

'They do not. But then true love, so they say, does not run smoothly either.'

Raymond thought about that.

Oh, but he'd experienced true love once; Dianne had been the love of his life. These other women were not a patch on

157

his poor wife. How could he ever have expected to replace her? But perhaps he wasn't trying to *replace* her. Maybe he'd just been trying to find some kind of reprieve at a time of his life when any kind of affection would have been greatly appreciated. Yet it wasn't what he'd really wanted to do, despite Simon's best efforts on his behalf. The other dates, if he could call them that, had also been hit-and-miss affairs.

As he rose to go, with a heavy heart, he vowed he would bow out gracefully from any further attempts on Simon's behalf to secure meetings with women who probably wanted a bit of company for the night, instead of cherished companionship in the long term.

Besides, he thought sadly to himself, how could he entertain going out with anyone else when he was still very much in love with his beloved Dianne?

Chapter 16

'Okay let's try it again, boys! Don't pull that face, Marcus. It will all be worth it in the end because your mum will love you even more and probably spoil you even more if this goes according to plan!' Veronica informed them from her wheelchair, her arms waving as if she were conducting an orchestra. 'Right, so it'll be you first, Marcus, because of that attitude of yours. Tell me what you're going to do and then I'd like to see you do it.'

Marcus scowled and tutted like a child. He looked at his notes.

'I put the clothes in the washing machine.'

'Is that the first thing you do?'

'Oh, for heaven's sake, Gran! I go get them from wherever we've put them and stick them in – no, I don't! I go get them. *Then* I open the door by first releasing the catch to *open* said door and stuff 'em in! Then I get the powder or the tabs or um—'

'Or?'

'Or the liquid. We have powder, Gran.'

'I think liquid is best, actually, but anyway, go on.'

'Then I turn the dial to Intensive 60 if it's all our jeans and things, or Quick 30 if it's stuff that's not so dirty. And you tell me that the LG we've got is easier to use than some of the other washing machines out there. Thank God for that!'

His grandmother nodded, trying to suppress a smile.

'Very good, my boy. Right, now go find me some of your dirty washing. Troy, do you think there's a better way of keeping your dirty laundry together or do you think dropping it all over the house is acceptable?' she said, turning her attention to Troy.

'Ha, ha, Gran. You and your trick questions.'

Marcus slouched off upstairs looking for dirty washing and finding some in every room; he came downstairs, his arms full. He stared at Troy, now positioned behind his grandmother, pulling a face at Marcus.

'Piss off, Troy. Can't wait to see how you fare, cooking breakfast next. God help us; that should be a *real* laugh!'

'Yeah, well. If it wasn't for the fact Gran's giving us fifty quid each for getting this right I wouldn't be doing it. But I s'pose it'd be useful knowing how to cook breakfast for some bird on a sleepover?'

'Oi,' Veronica said. 'Language. I don't like you disrespecting the female of the species. That's the way your father carried on. But it won't be the way you two carry on under my roof. Do you hear? Right, now, Marcus. Is all that washing going in together or do you think you should separate the whites from the colours first?'

'What do you mean?'

'I'm sure you've seen your mother separating the clothes, so the dye from strong or dark colours doesn't run or seep into the white or lighter clothes? No?'

'Oh, you're such a dorkbrain, Marcus. Even *I* know that!'

Veronica smiled to herself. So now they were even competing for bragging rights as to who could do better than the other.

Now we're getting somewhere, she thought to herself.

Dora slammed the phone into its cradle, then jumped up to get a tumbler out of the cupboard. She liked the sound of alcohol glugging into her glass. She took a long swig. Ah, yes that felt much better, but boy, was she mad.

Nine phone calls in two days, just to get one simple answer. Someone was certainly giving her the runaround.

She returned to her list with a sigh and then crossed a few more names off the sheet. Frustration and aggravation etched her face. Nothing would shift that, she knew. Not even Botox. When would she get her answers? No wonder she needed quick fixes via alcohol, she thought, as she looked at the whisky in her hand. It wasn't everyone's tipple. She'd grown accustomed to it, after finding nothing else in the drinks cabinet one time. But it was a hard drink, scorching her throat every time she took a mouthful.

She was getting nowhere fast, doing this. But who the hell else could she call to help her? Or was there someone she could pull in a favour from? Unless— Ah, yes! Tony Gallagher.

Well, why not? That might work. Her father used to trust him implicitly and it was one phone call she might just get a positive answer from.

But at least one other nagging problem had been solved at the Arts & Crafts Hotel. Richmond had finally been dismissed. He'd taken one sabbatical too many for her mother's liking. Dora rang her brother to tell him their good news. Then Stuart had rung his mother to say he was pleased she'd finally done something about him. Dora had overheard them on the phone, as she downed her whisky.

'Thanks, son,' Yvonne had replied, sounding relieved at her own decision. 'But I don't find it easy firing people, as you well know. Your dad was best at that when he was alive. Anyway, our other news is that I think I might've found a buyer for the hotel. Yes, it's all happening. Well, I rang Roger – oh, you know, *Roger* – who bought the Hen & Stags? No, he's not buying it. Well, I knew he wouldn't be interested, Stuart. It's not his sort of thing at all. But he's given me the number of a lady who I hope is. So that's uplifting news. Oh and Philippa and I are going to try living together. I might just start packing some stuff off to her because I've already decided – Dora knows, before you ask – but I've already decided if the hotel doesn't sell for some reason I'll move out and put a manager in and sign it over to you. I'm too old for all the shenanigans now. And Dora wants out too. Yes, I think she's going to look for a flat in the city centre and get a little part-time job somewhere. Could be the making of her.

162

Anyway, I want to start putting my feet up and enjoying life. That's what your dad always used to say, wasn't it, and he was right. It's time for that now. In fact, I think Philippa and I might go visit your dad's sister Emily in Melbourne for a month. She's always asking us to come and stay with her and we've never had the time nor the inclination before. So things are looking up, son. We'll speak again soon. Love to the family. Bye for now, darling!'

Chapter 17

'Well, how nice to see you all again! I really didn't think any of you would be coming on the painting course after your experiences with the drawing course last week,' said Eva, with a wicked smile, as she handed out empty jam jars, small paintbrushes and tubes of acrylic paint.

'If we'd have known it was going to be you on this course, I doubt we'd have come!' Dora grinned, nodding at the others.

Although it was quite a hike for Dora to keep coming down to Southampton for the occasional afternoon tea and various classes that Eileen offered the community, she was pleased she'd made the effort. It wasn't a long drive over, at any rate – a couple of hours, tops. But each time she came, she'd bring yet more of her mother's belongings down to Philippa and then stay over at her aunt's after the classes; going back to their hotel the following day.

Marjorie chuckled at Dora. She was hilarious sometimes. But she was right. She'd have expected there to be a different tutor for each course. But then art was art, she suspected, in all its forms. So why shouldn't Eva be the one to do both?

Anyway, she didn't particularly mind. Eva was a lively, uplifting character; a bit of a rogue, too, despite her youth. But, primarily, she was clever and genial too. Marjorie could see that Dora wasn't particularly enamoured. But then Dora hadn't mastered any of the courses yet and Marjorie could see she was feeling out of sorts.

'Okay, people. Well, sitting next to you here, today, is Michael. Say hello Michael.'

'Hello, Michael!' he sniggered.

'Now, I can see from your expressions that you're wondering why Michael is here, aren't you? Well just because Michael's in a wheelchair and almost totally blind doesn't mean he can't draw or paint, does it, Michael?'

'No, miss,' he said, grinning. 'Probably better than the ruddy lot of you, actually.'

Marjorie sucked in her breath with a wheeze. Stacy gasped and Dora just tutted, saying, 'Well this I gotta see!'

Eva chuckled to herself.

'Okay, folks. Well, following on from our class last week, I'm going to test exactly who can do what here before we progress onto colour and paint. So I'm going to level the playing field. And the scarves in front of you will certainly do just that!'

Everyone looked at each other. Michael sniggered again.

'Right, people. We're all going to be doing some drawing again first and I'd like you to draw what I ask you to draw. The only difference, this time, is that you'll all be singing from the same hymn sheet, as everyone bar Michael puts a scarf over their eyes!'

'Eh?' spluttered Raymond. 'Is this some kind of joke, Miss Eva? I just came here to do some painting. Thought it might relax me after the awful week I've had.'

'Ah, well, remember what I said about leaving all your worries at the door before you come in? Can you do that please, Raymond. We don't want to be hindered by the chaos of your mind. We're just here for enjoyable artistic sessions, as you know!'

Raymond scowled. Marjorie raised her eyebrows. She certainly didn't stand for any nonsense, the young Eva.

'Now as you're all part of the community programme I wanted to see how you fared if I forced you to walk in the shoes of a different person for a change. So I'm giving you the opportunity for a couple of hours to understand just how tricky it is to paint and draw if you can no longer see. I want to see if your other senses kick in and guide you through this very difficult task. To help you out, I'm giving you a piece of paper with a balsa wood border, so you don't drift off the edge of the page. You can actually buy this sort of thing but I find it quite restrictive because you have to follow the makers' guidelines and I prefer free artistic licence. Michael tells me he does too.'

'Yeah I do because this way I can create a more sizeable painting and paint anything I want.'

'Right, folks. Now keeping all things equal Michael will

have the same edged sheet. So you'll all be able to feel where the edge of the paper is and you'll know the subject I give you to draw. You simply have to do your best by keeping within the frame and working out, to a certain extent, how you'll be able to complete the drawing. Are you all up for it? I know Michael will be. It stops him feeling the odd one out for a change. That okay?'

There was an initial silence, followed by an uncomfortable shuffling of feet and further anxious stares at each other.

'Sure, I'll give it a go,' said Dora.

'Yes why not. It's a bit of fun,' said Stacy.

'It's not fun for me. I've got Type 2 diabetes,' said Michael. 'Welcome to my world.'

Stacy reddened. 'I, er, I didn't mean it like that. I'm sorry, Michael. I'm not being flippant.'

'Sure don't worry about it. It's cool,' said Michael. 'We live in the worlds we inhabit, that's all.'

Marjorie and Raymond exchanged wary glances.

'Okay, I'm up for it,' said Raymond with a resigned sigh.

Everyone slowly put the scarf around their eyes as Eva handed out the boards and asked if everyone was ready.

'Okay so I want you all to draw a house. Keep it simple. You know, four windows, a door, possibly a couple of trees if you're feeling adventurous. A chimney maybe. Not if you don't want to though, Dora. You could just stick to whatever you feel comfortable with. I'm only going to give you a couple of minutes to do it, otherwise you'll start to panic and think you can't do it. Okay, got pencils? Oh, here, Dora. Yours was on the floor. Right three, two, one – go!'

Before Marjorie started to draw she felt for the four edges of the balsa wood. Right. That was just about fixed in her mind. Now, where would she start – the first wall? Hmmm. She realised she'd need to keep her left hand on the frame to direct her right hand when she'd put the walls in and then she might just remember where she could try to put the windows. She wasn't going to make this hard for herself. It was simply going to be a box with four windows, a door – if she could squeeze it in somewhere – and a roof. Anything else might just fuzzle her brain and prevent her from accomplishing her task. Blimey even a simple drawing was going to be difficult.

Michael had finished his drawing long before anybody else's pencil had even touched their paper. 'Right I'm done. What's next, miss?'

'Well, that was one of the most difficult things I've ever done,' Marjorie said, breaking the ice when they were all sat around a table in the canteen, during the tea break. Eva was outside again on her phone.

'Yep, it certainly took more than a few minutes by the time we'd sorted it all out,' Raymond admitted.

'It's logical when you think about it, though,' said Michael. 'Like anything, whether you're blind or not, once you work out how to do something, logically, it's easy enough.'

'So, um, how long have you been blind?' Stacy asked, and took a sip of her coffee.

'Well, I'm not completely blind, but it's as near as, dammit. It was an ongoing thing. Didn't know what was happening at first. Used to be a carpenter, ate whatever I liked, then going out for pints of ale at the end of the day, before I met my Janice and never doing any exercise. General unhealthy living I suppose. Guess if I'd stumbled across what I'd got long before I started to deteriorate summat might've been done about it. I wasn't one for going to doctors for the slightest thing, you see. Oh my wife, Janice, used to nag. "Do summat about yourself, you fat bastard," she used to say. Well, I just used to think me sight was getting worse because of my age. Anyway, I lost me job eventually. My sight had affected things that bad and so I thought I'd better book an appointment with the doctor, just to get Janice off me back. And – bang! There you are, sir. Type 2 diabetes with diabetic retinopathy. "Retino what?" I said. Well, I won't bore you with all the rest but anyway it involved a shed load of tests, medications and insulin injections and I'm squeamish about needles. But I guess the diagnosis came too late in the day, as it were. Getting circulation problems in my feet, now, too. But enough of all this depressing stuff. This is me, now. But I've been finding I like doing art. Relaxes me and takes me mind off things.'

'God, that's tough!' said Dora. 'Friend of mine had Type 1. Not much fun.'

'It's a bummer. But that's why this community stuff is so

169

good. Gets you out of your shitty situation for a bit of respite, see. How did your drawings go?'

'Jeez. That was hard. Not looking forward to getting the paint all down me pinny, next, either!'

Stacy laughed. 'You're so funny Dora!'

Marjorie took Dora to one side before they went back to try the delightful task of trying to paint with a blindfold on. A thought had struck her and she needed to express it. 'You know, sweetheart, you're a lovely lady and I just can't understand why you're bothering with all that Botox gunk. You don't need it.'

Dora turned on her. 'Bloody hell, you sound like my old mum! That's the one thing I hate about old people. They think they can say what they like to anyone just because they're *old*! Please keep your opinions to yourself.'

'Good grief, there's no need to be so crabby! I wasn't being nasty. I'm only trying to give you a bit of advice,' Marjorie bit back.

'Oh and who are *you* to tell me what I should or shouldn't be doing? You know, just because *you've* made an assumption about why I've done something a particular way or why I look a certain way doesn't mean you've got it right!'

'But you'd look so much better without it. Can't you *see* that?' Marjorie said, trying to reason with Dora.

Outraged at Marjorie's insensitivity Dora stepped forward.

'As it happens, Mrs Holier than Thou,' Dora said, jabbing her finger repeatedly in Marjorie's shoulder. 'I'm not actually going to do it any more because my mother – like you – keeps nagging me to stop. The only reason I did it in the first place is because I'm fast approaching fifty and I want what everyone else wants – to look pretty and be line-free. And, as the world can see, it's all gone wrong, which is crap because it's made me feel very insecure. And now, thanks to you, I feel even worse!'

'What the hell's going on here?' Eva shouted, working her way in between the two women. Stacy's hands were at her mouth and Raymond was shaking his head.

'Bloody hell, Marjorie,' he said. 'You've already apologised for your irregular behaviour at one of the other meetings, saying it wouldn't be happening again, and yet here you are causing another fracas. What's going on with you?'

Looking around her at the shocked faces, Marjorie burst into tears; great big, heart-wrenching sobs. She pulled away from Eva and found her way into the toilets, slamming doors as she went. Nobody understood her; it was all going horribly wrong.

Chapter 18

Marjorie lowered the lid on the disabled toilet and sat down. She covered her face with her arms and bawled. But she knew she wasn't just crying for what had happened with Dora.

She'd forgotten what Dr Baxley had said about taking a moment before speaking out against other people's ideals. She knew she'd dealt with Dora in the same way Oliver dealt with things all his life – blustering in where her opinion (and his opinion) was not sought. Marjorie wished she'd found a way to deal with Oliver over the years. If she'd succeeded, her relationships, going forward, wouldn't have been as difficult as they were now. It seemed as though life threw up harsh consequences, whatever she did. Tutting at herself, Marjorie realised she hadn't given it a moment's thought as to why Dora might have felt she needed to use Botox or other methods in order to look younger and prettier. *And yet I use make-up every day to enhance my own looks*, she thought. The only difference between their decisions had simply been that Dora had chosen a drastic course of action to enhance her looks, which, unfortunately, hadn't worked out for the best. But by

Dora's own admission she was already rectifying that problem. Yet Marjorie had stepped in critically, before she'd even known what was what, to judge poor Dora the way she'd seen fit. Why oh why hadn't she stopped herself from speaking out, like she managed to do with Stacy last week?

Marjorie shook her head. 'I'm a fool and I was wrong. I didn't know the full story.'

Before Marjorie had met Gracie's new boyfriend, Steven, she'd been ready to judge that situation too quickly and critically, she realised now. Gracie had told her Steven was wonderful but Marjorie had needed to find that out for herself. Marjorie had even been wary about his job title, which had sounded made-up to her. He was a quantity surveyor.

'A what?' Marjorie had said.

'Basically, he works out construction costs for building projects,' Gracie had explained.

Steven had been very polite and respectful of her daughter, on the afternoon she'd invited him and Gracie to join her for lunch. Gracie told her how she'd seen him at the station, always getting on another train to go elsewhere. Their eyes had met and they'd both smiled. Then she'd been in the station café earlier than usual one morning and suddenly there he was. He'd approached her and told her how he'd seen her on the platform and had always wanted to speak to her but didn't know how to start the conversation. They'd laughed, Gracie said, because they'd both been thinking the same thing. Steven had been holding Gracie's hand as she'd told the tale of how they'd met and Marjorie had seen the sincerity and love in his eyes. And then she'd known as instinctively as her daughter had, after meeting him that first time, that he was 'The One' for her lovely Gracie. Somehow, it seemed not to matter that they'd only been dating each other a few weeks. Marjorie just knew something felt right about their relationship.

Everybody's situation was different, Marjorie realised, although people were basically the same. Lots of things were going on around her at that moment; lots of things and lots of situations she was learning from, even though she was still getting so much of it wrong.

But she'd understood something about herself today.

It hurt where Dora had just prodded her and it felt like the nudge she needed to instil in herself that, from today, she really was going to learn to keep her thoughts to herself. She'd make no more comments that could be misconstrued; no more giving people 'friendly advice, for their own good'. Clearly they saw their own situations differently to Marjorie and she had to learn to leave people to their own devices and let them make their own decisions about what was right or wrong for them. It didn't matter how things turned out for the people she'd been trying to help. Their actions were the only ones that counted to them. They'd always only do what they saw fit; rightly or wrongly. That's how life was. She understood that now.

Marjorie sniffed, miserably, and then got some toilet paper and blew her nose.

Stacy had told the others she'd go and see if there was anything she could do to help Marjorie. So she stood outside the disabled toilet, waiting for Marjorie's sobs to subside as she knew they would eventually.

She leant on the wall with her arms folded.

She could see that people were so complicated. They had lots of problems. Dora had already admitted that perhaps she'd treated the older woman a little harshly but then she'd already had her own mother going on about the Botox injections not working out for her. Eva had said she couldn't believe two older women were having a bust-up in the community centre for no particularly good reason at all and said she'd needed to have a 'stern' conversation with them before they went home today.

Stacy'd had enough of her own rows of late too. Perhaps she'd been very naïve when she invited both her parents and Peter and Marvin to lunch that day. She'd hoped it might bring them all together because she knew how discriminatory her father was. She cringed at the thought of how it all went horribly and embarrassingly wrong on that score.

Her father had seen Marvin put his arm around Peter and he'd gone mad. He'd yelled at everyone – yes, all of them – saying that no one knew how to conduct their lives any more and it was high time they had someone back in power like Enoch Powell (whoever he was) who stood no nonsense. Then he said he was going to wait in the car for his wife and that she'd better not be long or he'd leave without her.

Luckily, her mother had ignored him and told everyone she was staying and that they were going to enjoy their meal and catch up with everybody's news.

'Don't worry about it, Mum-to-be,' Marvin had said. 'We get this sort of thing a lot. Shouldn't be any discrimination these days but that's how life still is sometimes. We're going to get married either way and we'll invite you all to the wedding. Whether Dad-to-be comes or not is up to him but you'll all be welcome!'

Stacy loved Marvin. He made everything seem better. And at least she'd reconnected with her brother again. She'd been invited to their place, the following weekend, and she was really looking forward to that. But she'd been disgusted at her father. Luckily he'd waited for her mum but, apparently, they'd had strong words afterwards.

Stacy could no longer hear Marjorie's cries but she could hear water running and Marjorie talking to herself now. She wondered whether to knock or just wait until she came out. Knowing everybody was waiting for some response in the art room, she had just lifted her hand to knock when the door suddenly opened and there was Marjorie with a rather red face.

'Um. Hi, Marjorie. You okay now?'

Stacy had made Marjorie jump, standing in the doorway like that.

'Eva wants to talk to you. Well, not just you. But she wanted me to come and get you anyway,' Stacy began.

'Yes, well I'm not coming back into class, love. I just want to go home now, thank you.'

'That won't be happening for the moment,' said Eva, striding up to Marjorie. 'Dora's confessed to her role in all this and so I'd like you to come back in so we can just have a quick chat.'

Reluctantly Marjorie walked between Eva and Stacy back to the room where Michael was chatting to Raymond and Dora was sat looking very sorry for herself. Dora was the first one to speak, however.

'Okay I'll say sorry to prodding you like that but I got mad at what you said.'

'Thank you, Dora,' said Eva. 'Well, everyone. This situation got a little out of hand today and this is why I say to leave all your worries at the door when you come in here. Life is shitty enough without bringing it into class with you. The whole idea, here, is to give you some time out from all that crap. Not indulge in it further. So have you learned anything today, Marjorie, apart from how to draw with a blindfold on?'

Marjorie managed a little smile. 'I've given myself a strong talking-to, so you don't have to.'

'Well, that's good. Now is there anything else you want to say, Marjorie?'

'I'd like to explain myself to Dora. Well, to you all in fact. I think sometimes we forget that other people have problems too, different problems, even though we're all basically the

177

same. We're all looking for love and acceptance in life. Some of us have never had that, you see.'

'Ah,' said Eva. 'Right well, I can see this is going to get a bit deep and the class has all but ended, now. So why don't you have a little chat amongst yourselves and see if you can all come out of it a lot friendlier than you have been today? You can use the canteen if you wish. But I do need to get cleaned up in here.'

'Very tactful,' said Raymond smiling. 'See you next time then, Eva. Bye, Michael. You coming next time? I could do with you evening the numbers out.'

'Sure, pops. See you next time,' said Michael.

Chapter 19

'I'm not being funny, Raymond, but why are you staying?' said Dora, irritably.

He shrugged. 'You know, I believe you reach a certain age in life carrying all sorts of baggage with you. And that baggage can cause big problems for everyone around you, if certain issues haven't been resolved. And, correct me if I'm wrong, but I think that's what happened here today?'

Marjorie sighed. 'You're right.'

'So I'm going to stay because I think that in order for us all to move on and stay sane and friendly with each other and to, hopefully, continue enjoying what people like Eileen have gone out of their way to put on for us, we need to patch up the gaping holes. We all have our stories. I also have mine. But the other reason I want to stay is to make sure no one gets hurt or starts falling out again. Okay?'

'Fine by me,' said Stacy, sitting down. 'So who's going to start?'

'I'll start,' said Marjorie. 'Because I've started most of what's gone on since this thing began. But first I'd like to buy you all a drink from the drinks machine, if you'll let me?'

'Sure, well I'd like to try a hot chocolate if they've got that,' said Raymond.

Marjorie scrabbled in her purse to find enough fifty-pence pieces or equivalent for their drinks and the machine pinged for a while until they all sat with their drinks in front of them.

'So, hit us with it,' Dora said.

Marjorie had already realised that Dora could be brash but she wasn't going to let that rile her. Maybe somewhere, deeper down, there was a heart in the woman. But then maybe she'd also got her own hard story to tell.

'Well, I didn't know it at the time, and possibly something happened, later, to make him like it because he certainly wasn't like it when we first met, but my husband Oliver was a wife-beater. I lived with domestic violence throughout my life with him. But I did nothing about it at the time because I couldn't. I was afraid of him. I was afraid that if I did something he'd only come back at me harder and do worse damage than he was already doing. I lost our first child because of his abuse and I very nearly, um, I nearly died myself that day, too. It was a horrible time in my life but he had no remorse and he even harassed me after I gave birth to our only child, Gracie. He never hurt Gracie, fortunately. I'd like to think I would have found the strength to leave if he had. But she witnessed his continuous anger towards me, which was not pleasant. I suppose I'm very fortunate that she grew up to be well adjusted. Her first marriage didn't work out but she has met a wonderful young man who appears to adore her and is also, thankfully, mindful of my very close relationship with her. So I couldn't wish for a better outcome for my daughter. However ...'

Marjorie paused to take a sip of her coffee. Stacy couldn't meet her gaze. Dora looked stunned and Raymond was gently shaking his head.

'My outbursts have been two-fold. On the one hand, Oliver died about five years ago, so I don't have to live with all that any more but his actions turned me into a very bitter woman. I wasn't allowed to have my say about anything when he was alive and so I relish the freedom I have now to speak out about any injustices I see, as well as thinking it's okay to say what I feel about other things – like with you, today, Dora. I'm sorry I upset you but I was just trying to help. However, I can now see you didn't want my opinion. On the other hand, my daughter tells me she is about to move out of the flat we've shared for four years and I will be on my own again. That thought terrifies me. I find it difficult living by myself and I have hardly any friends. This is why I wanted the Afternoon Tea Club to work for me. I feel it's the only chance I've got left now to make friends. But all I've done is alienate people.'

'Oh apology accepted. I'm sorry too. I know you meant well, Marjorie. But I've got my own story, too,' said Dora.

'And do you want to tell us that story, Dora?' Raymond asked quietly.

'Um, well, not right at this moment – no. So tell your story or Stacy can tell us hers.'

'Stacy?'

Stacy looked solemn, thoughtful. 'Okay. Um, well, I was brought up on a farm with my brother Peter and my parents were very strict about what we could or couldn't do. We had to work on the farm all our lives from when we were little. Evenings and weekends and the chores got heavier as we grew up. Friends weren't allowed round and we weren't allowed to go to their houses so we never really learned to mix well. My dad didn't hit us or anything but he made us afraid of him. If we were disobedient we were sent to bed with no food. Old-fashioned stuff like that. And Mum and Dad never kissed us or cuddled us. So I've never had much love in my life. I used to have lots of cats, probably because I was craving some kind of comfort; but I had an accident recently, slipped off the kitchen worktop trying to get a cat down from above the units and had to go home to recuperate. Well, my dad got rid of my cats and sorted my flat out for me because it was filthy with cat poo everywhere because I just couldn't, um, I couldn't cope any more. But I've recently reconnected with my brother Peter and he's got a lovely boyfriend Marvin who he's going to marry and I put on this lunch for everyone so they could all meet up and hopefully be friendly because, well, my dad's homophobic and a racist. But my dad went mad and said I was useless. I know I can't do anything right but I just want to be loved really. I don't have any friends. And I don't have a life, apart from my job in the library. And, anyway, that's my solace.'

One silent tear glittered down the young woman's face as she'd told her story. Stacy's story broke Marjorie's heart. It was clear how isolated and lonely she'd been all her life. And yet when Stacy had tried to reach out to her, in desperation, Marjorie had been nastily dismissive. That thought pierced Marjorie's conscience and she immediately put her arms around Stacy and held her.

'There, there. I'm so sorry for all your troubles, sweetheart. I'll be your friend, if you'll have me?'

'We'll all be your friends, Stacy. Won't we, Dora?' said Raymond.

'Oh yes, of course. I think that goes without saying,' Dora said with a sniff, looking uncharacteristically teary.

'Well, th-thank you everyone,' Stacy said wiping her face with her sleeve. 'That makes me feel a b-bit better now.'

Dora sighed. *My God! The trials some people have to endure*, she thought. But now Dora felt ready to tell her own story.

'Okay, well I've had a blessed life to a point,' she began. 'My family created their own little empire of hotels near London. Hen & Stag Hotels—'

'No way!' exclaimed Raymond, his eyes suddenly wide. 'One of my friends had a stag do at one of those, once. Crazy places. Crazy behaviour. Had a ball there, he did. Said it was better than Benidorm!'

'Hmm. Well, they wouldn't have been my cup of tea but it all worked out brilliantly as my family's business. They were sold off some years ago, after my father died, and then my mother and I ran the Arts & Crafts Hotel we've got in the Cotswolds for a while. It's never been my preferred line of work, although it's where I've ended up. But we're just on the verge of selling that now and moving down here to be with my Aunt Philippa who lives up the road from here, actually. It's where we're from originally. So due to my parents' successes in business, I've always lived a carefree existence. But I've never really known what I wanted out of life. I will admit that this is partly because I never wanted for anything. I've never married. I've never really been a home bird. In fact, I ran around Europe and America for quite a few years in my youth. My mother called me a wandering minstrel. I suppose, looking back, I had a peachy lifestyle, despite everything. Yet my mother is one of those no-nonsense types of women, with an answer for everything, so she's never really understood people who trip and falter at the difficulties of life. So, anyway, I did and tried every-thing – kicking back against my parents wanting me to join their business, because it wasn't what I wanted at the time. But when my father died I came back to roost, proper. My brother Stuart runs a small hotel in Devon, so I go see him and his family, sometimes, when I feel the walls are closing in on me. Through it all, though, I've never actually discov-ered where I belong in life.'

Raymond nodded. 'So you had a blessed life to a point. But is that all?'

Tears watered Dora's eyes. Marjorie raised her eyebrows at that. What? The foxy Dora had a soft centre somewhere?

'Please don't be dismissive of me, Raymond. I know only too well how people can be suspicious of those they deem to have everything in life. No one, truly, has everything. I was bullied at school because the kids either wanted some of what I had or they wanted to punish me because of what my parents had when they, themselves – they told me as they pushed my face into the playground – had a lot less. What my parents had accumulated didn't, actually, make me feel blessed. It was a burden to me my whole life. On top of that my dismissive mother thought I should be grateful for what I had and contribute, when all I wanted to do was run away from it. So, because I've never put down roots properly anywhere, I – too – know what loneliness is. I have no real friends either, to speak of, except my best friend Jodie, who's stood by me through thick and thin.'

'I don't think he meant it like that, though, did you, Raymond?' Marjorie said quietly.

'I'm sorry, Dora. I didn't. I just got the feeling there was, um, something else you needed to say.'

Dora nodded. 'Well, yes, there is. But every story needs background info, Raymond. We're all a product of the lives we lived before this point, aren't we? In other words, you won't know about me, until you *know* about me. So, um, what I've never told anybody – what I regret never telling my father before he passed away and what I certainly regret having never told my mother – is that, during those years I met the only love of my life. Oh, I had some fun and met plenty of men, I can tell you. But there was this one guy. And I, um, I kept his baby—'

'*His* baby? Oh God, Dora. It sounds like there were others?' said Stacy.

'Well, I'm glad you said that, Stacy, and not me!' said Marjorie carefully.

'I was thinking it, too, ladies!' Raymond admitted.

'Well, okay, I will admit I made some mistakes in my life. But who hasn't? That's the next part of my story because becoming rather promiscuous was part of my kicking back at everything my parents stood for – not that I'm totally blaming my folks. They deserved what they'd worked very hard to achieve. It's just that I was kicking back at the *product* of their success, if you see what I mean? And I was certainly kicking back at everything that had undermined me: my mother, the kids at school – oh, you know – everything. Well, Dad made us our fortune, so I didn't really need to work. But Mum made me work in our hotels, starting at the bottom, cleaning toilets and everything. To keep things real, she said.

'Eventually I went to secretarial college and then got a job with a leery boss who couldn't keep his hands off me! I had a two-timing boyfriend and, well, I'd just about had enough at that point. I wanted to explore; see the world. I got pregnant virtually straight away. And I'm sorry to say I had an abortion because I didn't want that kind of responsibility. And I certainly didn't want to be a single mum, when I didn't know who I was or where my place was in life. But with Andy? Well, I met him in a bar in Greece and we really hit it off. And, long story short, when I fell pregnant I kept her. Looking back, I did it because I wanted something from him – some part of *him*. And I know that sounds selfish. But I wanted to keep him close because he sort of got me when no one else had. Plus, he was a good sort, or so I thought.

'Anyway, we came back, settled down around his neck of the world, Kent way. I never told my folks I was back in Britain. I wanted to see if I could actually make a go of things and then prove to my mother she was wrong in thinking I was useless. So me and Andy stuck at it until after Lauren was born. He got a good job, so I stayed home and looked after our daughter. But after her first birthday we started bickering. Unfortunately, I'd been battling postnatal depression, which Andy didn't seem to understand, and the relationship faltered. He had a fling with an old girlfriend who'd been throwing herself at him for weeks, he told me. Guess she thought she'd be in with a chance being as we weren't married.'

Dora heaved a sigh and a few more tears dripped off her chin. Raymond passed her a tissue.

'Never in my wildest dreams did I think he'd have a fling. I thought we were so happy; so tight as a little family unit. I was starting to believe that this could be my place, with Andy and Lauren as the pivot of my world. But his actions tore me apart and knocked my confidence; I was gutted and just didn't know what to do. My mate Jodie told me to forgive him; men are weak, she said. Her chap had done something similar and she'd let it slide and they'd made it beyond that.

'So we muddled along for a while but he'd destabilised me. I felt uneasy and it hurt, real bad, knowing he'd not considered my feelings when he went with her. I mean, I know this sort of thing happens, sure. But I really thought we had something special and untarnished. Yet he'd done it when I was battling my worst with the depression – I couldn't even leave the house to see my doctor. I'd lost interest in things and he hated having to deal with Lauren whilst he was so busy at work. I had no energy; I couldn't concentrate on anything. Sometimes I couldn't even change her nappy for hours on end and she'd cry, incessantly, in her cot. In short, I was an irritable mess. And he wasn't supportive at all.

'Granted, he told me the fling had been a mistake. Apparently, he'd been out on the slash with his mates, got pissed and she turned up with her own special brand of comfort. "I'm sorry," he said. "We'll work this out," he said. And then it happened again, about six months later with someone else! I was absolutely gutted. Obviously he didn't care about me for it to happen a second time. I felt he'd purposely gone out and found another woman because he still couldn't cope with my condition, which seemed to be getting worse due to the stress of the situation. And perhaps he couldn't. But I was furious and mentally drained!

'So I hit the roof and stormed out the door, leaving Lauren with him because I was so deep in my depression I knew I wouldn't be able to look after her properly. I went to Spain to drown my sorrows. I couldn't stay with him, worrying it might happen a third time and worrying about Lauren living with all that grief and angst around her. You put your trust in men when they make their promises and then they shit on you. Sometimes a person can only take so much rejection!'

'I had postnatal depression with Gracie. It was not pleasant and it was something I had to deal with by myself, as well. Oliver wouldn't lift a finger. But to be honest I think it terrifies most men,' said Marjorie.

'But I'm sure your family would've helped you,' said Raymond softly.

'Not necessarily,' argued Marjorie. 'When I went to my mother for help with Oliver she told me to get on with things and deal with the fact that life could be unsavoury. It's not a given that families will help each other out. It wasn't in my case, anyways.'

'I agree,' said Stacy. 'My parents didn't love me and Peter the way I think they should've. I think their actions alienated us and made our own socialisation very difficult.'

'Exactly! I've realised nothing is guaranteed in life, Raymond,' Dora said. 'The whole thing would've given my mother the ammunition she needed to say, "I told you so."

Plus I'd left Lauren with her dad. He'd got a good job as a property negotiator in an estate agent's near Canterbury and his mother lived nearby to babysit. So I knew Lauren would be properly cared for and loved. I thought everything would be fine and that one day I'd go back when I was more together and confident and then we'd work out how to bring her up between us.

'Well, I got some help and I did go back for her third birthday and to see how I felt about things with Andy, but he'd got a new girlfriend by then – Dariana – and they were engaged. Plus Lauren was clinging to her and didn't seem to know who I was, and his mum, Pat, was there and she told me to leave because I was confusing Lauren. She told me they were all happy now and didn't need me. I was mortified. But I could see how my reappearance might be confusing for Lauren.

'So I took off again, with a view to dealing with it all later. But then I got wrapped up with the family business because my father wasn't well and when he died I stayed with Mum to help her out, initially. But then life suddenly took over. I suppose on the one hand I was hoping that by working with my mother I could forge a better relationship with her. I didn't believe that telling her about Lauren would help things, at that point in time. So I put my quest, to be part of Lauren's life, on hold, whilst I worked things out. I sent birthday gifts and letters over the years as well as a cheque for £1,000 on her eighteenth birthday and a big explanation about things. But the cheque was never cashed.

'I've tried ringing Andy and his mother over the years. I got through to Pat once and she said, "Just leave it, Dora," and put the phone down on me. He wasn't on any of the social media sites, back then, although I've recently discovered he's now on LinkedIn. But I didn't want to go back and cause a scene in front of Lauren or poke around in her life, upsetting her, so I've stayed away. I was hoping I'd come up with a better plan to sort this all out – long before now – but things simply never worked out that way. However, I've recently hired a private detective to see if he can find out as much as he can for me about how she is and how she's doing. I guess all I want now is to know that she's happy with her stepmum and not too mucked up because of what happened. I mean I'm sure she's fine. But I just want to *know* she's fine. Families eh? They can be a mess.'

Marjorie reached out and took her hand. Dora let her and looked into Marjorie's face and gave her a teary smile.

My God, thought Marjorie. *She's keeping the truth from herself, more like. She misses that child far more than she's letting on. But if I say anything she'll say I'm speaking out of turn again.*

'Yes, Dora. Families can certainly get into a mess,' Raymond admitted. 'My story is very simple but my son and family don't know the truth, either. Okay, so where to start with this? Ah, from the beginning, I guess. Right, so my wife Dianne was of Jamaican descent and initially we faced opposition from both sets of families – stick with your own kind, they both said to us, like in *West Side Story*; it's less complicated that way. I think my father was more worried about what the neighbours would think. But at the end of the day love is love. It's one of those things, like the weather, you can't control. Anyway we got married and we had a son, Simon, and then he went on to marry Jo, his childhood sweetheart, who is white. They have twins. Our families, eventually, were okay about things but it took a while.

'Anyway, Dianne and I had a wonderful family life together once we retired. But then a few years back we discovered Dianne had breast cancer. We were all devastated, of course, fearing the worst. My wife used to be a nurse and was a naturally caring and loving person, so her personality was perfect for the job of caring for the sick. But my God, we couldn't believe she had cancer herself. It's one of those things you think other people get and never for a minute realise it could happen to you. It was Stage II cancer with a three-centimetre tumour. So we discussed treatments with the doctor and she had a lumpectomy followed by radiation therapy. My son and I went with her for her first round of treatment and, oh, she was gracious and thoughtful about what we were all going through, without a thought for herself—' Raymond broke off to compose himself.

'That's terrible,' Stacy said quietly. 'My auntie died of breast cancer.'

'Ah yes, love. Cancer can be a terrible thing. But my wife didn't die of cancer.'

Stacy gasped and Marjorie and Dora exchanged questioning glances.

'Good Lord, Raymond. So what happened?' said Marjorie.

'Well, after treatment she'd not been at home long when we were having this stupid – completely bloody stupid – argument. She was talking about booking holidays for the following year because she'd been told if her treatment was successful and she didn't need further targeted therapy she might be able to have some quality of life, providing the cancer hadn't spread further. But I was saying that we had to be realistic about what she'd be able to do following the prognosis with her doctor. "Oh God, Raymond," she said, "let's worry about things when there's actually something to worry about." Of course, when I've sat and thought about that argument, I think she was also trying to cover up her fears by carrying on as though nothing more serious *would* happen. You're fine until you're not, as it were. Yet who's to say how any of us would react if we were diagnosed with a disease like that?

'Anyway, she was becoming tetchy with me and then she suddenly jumped up. "Oh, I'm fed up of all this," she grumbled. "For God's sake, Di," I said, "just sit down and rest." And with that she went stomping off into the hall and got her jacket off its hook. Then she turned to me and said, "I know you mean well, darling, but I'm fed up of resting. I just need to go out and get some fresh air. Look, I'll see ya later." And with that she opened the door and marched down the garden path to the gate. "Come back here, you silly moo," I shouted after her. "Nope, I'm going for a walk," she said cockily, opening the bloody gate!

'And then the next minute – oh God – then there was just this sort of dull bang. I couldn't place the noise at first. I just stood there, wondering what on earth was going on. Then I heard a siren. Then I seemed to wake up and I bolted down the path. And then I saw her. She – she'd – oh God! She'd been run over by a hit-and-run driver who was being chased by a police car. He'd mounted the pavement and caught her and then kept on going, hitting parked cars, all the way down the road.'

The colour had drained from Raymond's face. For a moment he seemed to be staring at his drink and then he clasped his head and rocked back and forth.

Stacy's hand was over her mouth and she was obviously trying not to cry at the *enormity* of what Raymond was telling them but little bleating sounds were escaping. Marjorie put her arm around her again. *How horrible for Raymond to witness that!* Dora just stared at Raymond. Everybody stopped drinking their drinks. A cleaner came up to them, and said the community centre was closing and could they vacate the premises, please.

Together they rose, as if in a daze, leaving their paper cups on the table and moving quietly out of the building, into the car park. A light breeze was whipping up crisps packets and dust, nearby. And they stood there dumbstruck at Raymond's account of his wife's demise. They felt empty of response.

'If I'd stopped her,' Raymond said suddenly, as if they were still in the community hall. 'If I'd just put my hand out and grabbed her arm to stop her ... But I'm not a grabbing-arm type of person. And she was simply being her occasional off-the-cuff self. But look where it took us! At the time I'd have done *anything* to get her back for a few minutes more – even *with* her cancer – just to have had a bit more time to hold her and tell her we'd sort it all out together. And then, on top of all that – *on top of that* – the bloody doctor's report said they thought they could've managed her cancer with hormone treatment! So she could've lived for *even longer* than any of us had expected. Well, I couldn't believe it. I don't usually swear but life is just totally bloody unfair and crap sometimes.'

Then his hands went to his face as his features crumpled again and his emotions suddenly swelled back to the surface. 'Oh it's so unfair! She never hurt anyone, yet look what happened to her,' he wept, standing there, next to the cars.

Then completely overcome by his dreadful memories, he drooped forward as his floodgates really opened. Luckily, Dora and Marjorie caught him, just before he fell.

Chapter 20

'Pass it to me! C'mon, kick it over here!' shouted Marcus as Troy was showing off his football skills, dribbling the ball around any obstacles he could find: park benches, dogs, a woman wheeling a pram. When he did finally kick it, it went slightly off course due to the erratic breeze.

'Oh, watch out for that old man. Look out, mister – oh no!' Marcus cried, as the ball hit an elderly man on his shin.

'Are you okay, old fella?' called Troy, scratching his head.

'Yah, I'm okay. Haven't played footie in a while though!'

'Well, come on then. Join in!'

The old man chuckled, placed his walking stick on the ground and then made a tremendous effort to position his right leg to kick the ball back and Troy was hooked. He and the old man had a gentle little game between them until the old man put his arm up to signal that he'd had enough.

Despite the fact it was rather chilly and neither of them wore jackets, Eileen was sitting on a bench next to her mother in her wheelchair, watching her sons' antics.

'Look at them, Mum. Oh, what a brilliant day! Thank you

so much,' she gushed throwing her arms around her mother's neck and kissing her.

'You're completely welcome.'

It had started off brilliantly too. She'd awoken groggily in bed that morning, on hearing unfamiliar noises downstairs. She'd blinked and looked at the alarm clock, 7.45 a.m. Strange. There weren't usually any noises at this time in the morning, until she got her boys up. She could hear metallic scraping, raised voices and her mother's occasional lilt as though she was having a conversation with someone. Those were not the normal sounds Eileen expected to hear any time, least of all today.

She'd been having a much-needed lie-in and taken the day off because today was her birthday. Her boss always gave his staff the option to do that if they wanted to. So she'd told her boys she'd be having a lie-in that morning. Her usual working day started with her wakening at 6.30 a.m. and getting the boys lunches sorted out, having her shower, helping her mother out of bed and getting her into the shower and then into the wheelchair, followed by making everybody breakfast, while either putting a wash-load on or doing some cleaning, so she didn't have to do it later when she came back from work. Eileen was an organised routine type of person and her morning routine was always the same. So usually she never had a lie-in, but her added workload of getting the Afternoon Tea Club off the ground had caused extra administration and meant overtime, even though she had Taynor's help. It made her colleagues laugh that Eileen always maintained the same routine, each day, whether it was her birthday or not. Even on her birthday she'd do all her chores in the morning and then she took her mum for a drive somewhere in the afternoon. When her sons came back from work the four of them would go to her favourite restaurant in the evening.

Some might call that boring but Eileen knew it would always be lovely. She didn't like to risk doing something new on special days – any other time of the year, yes. But not on birthdays and Christmases. She also always liked to have Christmas at home. And it was the one time of the year she allowed her mother to pitch in and cook their turkey dinner, quite simply because her mother did it best.

So that morning at 7.46 a.m. Eileen was utterly astonished when, just as she was thinking about going downstairs to find out what on earth was going on, her bedroom door opened and Troy came in with – goodness – *breakfast* on a *tray* with a single red rose in a rosebud vase she didn't even know she had!

Her mother would clearly be downstairs somewhere as her boys weren't allowed in the kitchen to make anything by themselves. She'd witnessed their efforts once before. Spilt flour on the counter tops and floor as well as sticky pools where an upturned honeypot had dribbled down the units because Troy had flicked water at Marcus and then a fight had ensued, resulting in her putting her foot down about any further attempts to do *anything* in the kitchen apart from tipping cereal into a bowl, adding milk and letting them eat it. But how had her mother got out of bed and got into the wheelchair by herself? The whole thing was most odd.

She started to ask that very question of Troy but was met with, 'Come on, Marcus. Hurry up!'

And then behind Troy came Marcus with a lovely bunch of flowers that had a label on them saying, 'Happiest Birthday, my darling daughter xx'. He also held a huge parcel under his arm, which he then placed by the side of her on the bed. The label on that read, 'Best wishes Mum, from Marcus and Troy xx'.

'Eat your breakfast first, Mum, and tell us how much you like it because we cooked it specially for you!'

Eileen started laughing. 'I wish— God, you two are so funny!'

'Okay, we thought you'd say that; iPad, Marcus!'

Marcus's iPad sprung to life and showed the two of them in the kitchen under her mother's direction, making the gorgeous scrambled egg and smoked salmon on toast she saw before her, without everything landing all over the place or on the floor. A cafètiere she'd also never seen before, with steaming coffee, sat on a napkin on the tray.

'Where'd you find these things, boys?'

'We bought the cafètiere and the tray and the bud vase. The tray is spongy underneath so it can sit on your knees or whatever. We will admit that Gran pointed us in the right direction with all that lot. We've been having lessons with

Gran, you see, while you've been working overtime. Especially for your birthday. C'mon, Mum, eat your breakfast or it'll get cold. Isn't that what you're always telling us?'

Eileen tasted the scrambled eggs half expecting them to taste too salty or to be thin and watery. But they were *perfect* and so were the salmon and the coffee. Her boys sat on her bed and watched her delighted features getting brighter and brighter.

'We've also done all the cleaning and put a wash-load on, too.'

'You've done *what?*' Eileen cried spluttering her food out again, envisaging all the colours bleeding into each other. That was a thought too far.

Troy almost laughed his head off. 'We're not entirely hopeless now. Gran taught us loads. She said it was time. Keep watching the iPad. It's all on there!'

'Mother, *please* eat your breakfast,' Marcus demanded. 'And then you can open your presents!'

The large parcel on the bed contained all of Eileen's favourite toiletries and a box of chocolates. Maybe the chocolates mightn't have smelled of perfume if the boys had wrapped their gifts separately but Eileen wasn't going to say anything about that.

Then they gave her an envelope.

It was for a weekend stay for the four of them on the Isle of Wight. None of them had holidayed anywhere since their father's disappearance over three years ago. Time off from work had always been used up lazing around the house or going out for nice meals. Not jetting off anywhere, although they wouldn't need a jet to go to the Isle of Wight.

'Well, we're earners now so we decided to do this for us all. We deserve it, don't we. And they'll even take Gran with the wheelchair and there's an island trip on one of the days. Good huh?'

'Come here, my darling boys,' Eileen said, with tears in her eyes. 'Have I told you how much I love you both, recently?'

'Aw, Mum!'

So that afternoon they'd driven to one of the parks, taken their father's old football he used to kick around with them when they were all little and had an impromptu game of footie. Eileen's mother threw the ball for them, pretending to be the goalie and they laughed and hollered and screamed with excitement.

'You paid them, too, didn't you?' Eileen whispered to her mother on the way home.

'How did you guess, love?' her mother smirked.

Classroom 4A had not been easy to find.

The directions the receptionist had given them, downstairs, were not accurate. Some of the elderly Afternoon Tea Club members had gone up in the lift but, unfortunately, had gone up one floor too high and were wandering around, beginning to panic, until Stacy found them. Then Stacy asked directions from a chap who looked like a caretaker and he showed them where to go. He unlocked their classroom and eleven hopeful students piled in and looked around, in awe of the computers and notices pinned to the walls. The classroom was on the first floor and had great views of the college's landscaped grounds.

'This is nothing like I remember being at school. Didn't even have calculators. Had to do adding up in our heads dint we, Hilary?' said one elderly lady.

'Oh yes,' said Hilary. 'And we had to write our times tables out by hand. Do you remember all that? This is amazing in here, though, isn't it?'

'Oh yes. Even my grandson says he's impressed that a sixty-eight-year-old man gets to come to college to do computer studies!'

'They look complicated things to master, though, don't they with those buttons there?' said one lady, tentatively brushing her fingers over the keyboard. 'And nothing's happening.'

'Well, the computers haven't been switched on yet,' Stacy explained, noting the wide-eyed worry etched on some of the elderly students' faces. 'The tutor will explain everything to you. Everything's easy when you know how to do something.'

'Welcome, everybody!' cried the tutor, as she breezed in behind them. 'I'm Miss Broughton and I'm so pleased you could all make it here today. Did you find us okay?'

Nine women and one gent exchanged doubtful glances but didn't say anything. Stacy sat down in front of one of the computers.

'Right, so I'll just tick off your names – roll call, if you like – and then we'll need to do the fire drill and I'll show you where we'll be going for refreshments later. Okay. Let me just switch your computers on first. I thought the caretaker was going to do that for me but I have a sneaky feeling he might have gone for a quick ciggie instead!'

Stacy smiled at that.

When they ambled back into the classroom, after the fire drill, and sat in front of the computers, Miss Broughton then went round setting notepads and pens out in front of everyone. The LCD computer screens had already blinked into life.

'Well that has eaten into some of our allotted time for this class, so let's get started, post haste. First of all, let's see what you all need help with today. How many of you have used computers before but just want a little clarity? Perhaps I can go around the class and ask you each in turn what skills you hope to acquire in these lessons?'

One elderly lady put her hand up. 'I've never used one, love. Fancied it, so I could prove to my grandkids that I'm not completely from the Dark Ages.'

'I'm a carer and have no use for computers. But as it was being offered I thought I'd come along and have a go at it,' said the lady who always wore a pale grey trouser suit to the Afternoon Tea Club meetings.

'So is that about the same for all of you?' asked Miss Broughton.

'Well, I switched one on once but I wouldn't know how to do it again!' said someone.

'Ah, well,' Stacy began. 'All I really need is some help with this new mobile I've just bought. I'm having some problems with it but I don't have time to take it back to where I bought it and sort things out. Plus I'd also like to learn about macros.'

'Macaroni did she say? Well, my old dad was Italian. He could've shown her how to make *that*, easy enough!' said the old gent and the class fell about laughing.

'No, she didn't say that,' said another lady. 'She said nachos. My grandsons, Neil and Brent, they like nachos—'

Mrs Broughton tried to bring the class to order by coughing loudly.

'Oh, you need a butter ball for that cough, love,' said one of the ladies. 'My mother was good at making those. You scoop out a bit of butter on a spoon and roll it into sugar and then dip it into vinegar. Greases up the throat a real treat it does!'

'Well,' said the lady, tapping the buttons on the keyboard to try and make it work. 'I must say I'm really going to enjoy learning about these new-fangled computers, once we can get them started!'

Chapter 21

That Monday, at work, was hard going for Stacy. She'd got a cold from somewhere, although she couldn't remember anyone sneezing over her at any of the classes she'd attended, recently, nor even at the supermarket when she went on Saturday. Or perhaps she got it from someone on the bus. She laboured through her list of priorities for the day in a bit of a daze because she was worrying about everything, especially the wellbeing of her cats. She put some books back in the wrong place and then her colleague couldn't find them. She couldn't concentrate on anything demanding so she decided to walk around and tidy the shelves instead. No brainpower needed for that.

'Stacy!' her supervisor hissed coming up behind her. 'Please try to sniff more quietly. All we can hear is your cold reverberating around the library.'

Sniff more quietly? How could she do that?

Life was so stressful at the moment. She'd been completely stunned by her friends' shocking revelations a week last Friday. The whole afternoon had been most revealing and totally upsetting. She'd mulled the whole thing over with a glass of shiraz at home, later that evening.

How on earth could Raymond go on living after blaming himself for his wife's death? And how could Dora live with herself after giving up her daughter? But the bloody boyfriend had set the wheels in motion for *that* to happen.

Stacy completely understood testing families and errant boyfriends. Both had caused her grief and made her feel crap, too.

And poor Marjorie. That woman had had an absolutely *dreadful* life in Stacy's eyes. No wonder she spoke out of turn, sometimes. Stacy was starting to understand what made people do the things they did in life. Yet who was she to berate people for the choices they made?

It seemed like everyone was struggling with their lives. If only her parents had encouraged better socialisation with her and Peter's school friends instead of preventing them from joining in with village life as youngsters. She'd turned to her cats for companionship and Peter had got as far away from his strange family as possible. At least Peter had made a new, happier life for himself with Marvin. And from speaking to Marvin, Stacy knew he had accepted her brother without putting restraints on his life, the way their parents had tried to do. She could see how Marvin would be the making of her brother.

Stacy sneezed again.

Where *had* she got her cold from? It had started just before work, this morning, with a runny nose. And it was still summer too! Or was she simply run down? Probably after all the stress she'd been under this last month. She hoped to be well again by the time she visited Peter and Marvin next weekend. That was something worth getting excited about because Marvin was going to come and fetch her on Saturday morning and then drop her back late afternoon. Her mother had said she'd make the same visit one day, too, but not just yet. She'd said she was going to try and talk some sense into their father, first, because he definitely needed to change his ways.

But Stacy was also plagued with guilt about the mess she'd got into with her cats. She hadn't slept properly since they'd gone. It was still so strange to not hear their familiar meowing all day and every day. Guilt also forced her to look up the charity, in her tea break. However, contacting them was not a straightforward process. She tried the phone number on the website but a lady wanted to take her details and said someone 'will call you back'. She'd waited all morning but no one had rung. Then she'd tried emailing her questions but by the end of the day, no one had rung back or emailed. And, being as there was no address on the website where she might be able to go and see her cats she decided she'd call into one of their charity shops to see if they could help her make a start tracking her cats.

Stacy rang her boss, the following day, to say she wouldn't be in work because her cold had worsened. Well, it wasn't exactly a lie because she really wasn't feeling any better. But she needed the day off in order to go to the charity shop. She was going to ask them if all her cats had been housed with new owners yet.

She took the bus and told herself she'd do a bit of food shopping on the way back, so it wouldn't be a wasted journey if she discovered they'd all been housed. And if they'd been housed she was going to buy some comfort food at the supermarket and curl up in front of the telly for the rest of the day.

Stacy stepped inside the Cats Protection charity shop, and went to the counter where a cheery young girl was serving.

'Hi there. My name's Stacy and a few weeks ago my father brought my eight cats into your organisation for rehousing because I had an accident and couldn't look after them. So I'm just here to see if they've all been rehomed and if not I'd like to take Melanie back home with me cos she's the nicest. So could you ring your bosses and ask them to let me know what's happened to them? I just want to make sure they're all right, you see,' she told the girl behind the counter.

'Um well that's not something I can do, unfortunately. What happens is that we have a bank of fosterers who house any cats we get until we can rehome them. So they'll either be looked after by a foster carer or will have already been rehomed. So I can't help you any further than that, I'm afraid.'

'But could you just give me a telephone number or email address so I can contact someone directly about this? I've not had much luck getting through,' Stacy persisted, starting to fret about how her animals would feel at being pushed from pillar to post, with no one giving them the specialised attention they needed or had been used to.

'I'm sorry I don't have those details, but we've got a website and a Facebook page and everything you need will be on there.' The girl smiled encouragingly. 'Good luck.'

Stacy left the shop downhearted. She thought they'd have known instantly about her cats. Surely eight cats coming into their care, in one go, would be a memorable event? The only thing the girl had said that made Stacy feel marginally reassured was that at least someone would be looking after them in some capacity. Just like her mother had said they would.

She sat on a low wall and googled Cats Protection again and then she ended up sending them another email. Perhaps her persistence would pay off.

Well, cats or no cats – cold or no cold – she was going to buy the largest strawberry cheesecake she could find and sit in front of the telly and eat the *whole* thing when she got home.

No one got back to her about her cats until the middle of the week when they replied by email and told her that her cats hadn't been in a very good state when they'd collected them from her flat. But they'd now been properly vaccinated and microchipped and were awaiting new homes. Due to the state of her flat and the cramped conditions they'd had to endure they said they would not likely give her the opportunity to rehome any of their cats in the future.

She couldn't believe it. Stacy had blanched, completely mortified. *Oh, what must they think of me?* How horribly embarrassing! She'd probably even be blacklisted by other cat charities now. She hadn't meant to upset everyone or keep her cats in the environment they'd endured. She'd tried to do her best by them all but the situation had simply got out of hand. Couldn't anyone see that?

She was annoyed with her bloody father, too. He said he'd taken the cats *to* them. Or perhaps he'd been too busy to do that? Damn, damn, damn!

A sob escaped her throat. Why was life so unbearable?

Black thoughts made her retreat even further into herself so she rang work and left a message to say she'd be taking another day off to deal with her cold, which actually seemed to be getting worse by the minute, not better.

'It's all the stress,' she groaned to herself.

By Friday she'd had to ring her brother and cancel her trip.

'I'mb sorry. But my cold is worsth than I'd expected.'

Peter said he understood and that they could always arrange another weekend or maybe she could come for a visit at the same time as their mother. Stacy said she would ring home and then let him know when that would be. Then she switched her mobile off and pulled the plug on her landline. She went to bed and curled up and cried herself to sleep.

Why was nothing working out for her at the moment?

Chapter 22

The cupboards were practically bare.

No amount of moving tins of peas around or a full pack of flour, which she could see was out of date, or mouldy dates and glacé cherries, pickles, sauces and all the rest of the rubbish she'd thought would be a good idea to try once she was able to do supermarket shopping, made any difference. Quite simply, there was nothing suitable to eat for lunch.

Her cold was now so bad that her face was swollen and her nose was red from the amount of toilet paper she'd resorted to, now that she was clean out of tissues. Even her bones seemed to ache. There was no paracetamol, no cough mixture, no tinctures, no nothing to alleviate her symptoms. She daren't ring her parents in case they whipped her back home again and she definitely did not want that. Well, somehow she'd have to go down to the corner shop and get some supplies. But there was no way she could go out looking and feeling like this.

What to do?

The only other option was to go begging at somebody's door to see if they had a little soup or something. If she'd done a full week's shop she wouldn't be in this predicament. But she simply couldn't carry a full week's worth of shopping bags on the bus. She always had to do her shopping in stages. That's why the corner shop was always so handy.

Tutting to herself and wrapped in her dressing gown, pink fluffy slippers on her feet, Stacy shuffled out of the kitchen, down the hall to the front door of her flat and then stepped out into the corridor, wondering whose doorbell to ring first. But then suddenly, horror of horrors, she heard the door close behind her, with a little click.

But her key was inside!

She couldn't believe her bad luck. What the hell was happening to her, of late? Everything but *everything* was going wrong! Why did no good luck ever grace her life? Or rather *why the hell hadn't she put the key in her pocket?*

She clearly wasn't thinking straight with her cold, with everything else going on around her. She banged on John's door. No answer. She banged again. No answer. Damn! She padded down the corridor to the next flat along. The internal light still hadn't been fixed and now the lift was out of order too. What a complete pain for people having to bring shopping up the stairs. *Somebody needs to play merry hell with the landlord about these things*, she thought, angrily.

The doorbell at the end of the corridor tinkled but no one answered. She thumped on the door. Bang. Bang. Bang. Still no answer. Where was everyone, today? Maybe they all had busy interesting lives, unlike herself. Plus being a Saturday wouldn't people be doing their shopping or be out with their kids? And maybe John was at a football match. It seemed that everyone in the whole wide world had a life, apart from her.

Tears seeped out of her eyes and slipped down her swollen cheeks. She sat on the floor and curled her arms around her head and wept noisily. She'd been doing more crying of late than she'd done since that night she'd curled up on her colleague's sofa when she'd left Mike. She realised she could be in the corridor for hours before anyone turned up.

And after what certainly seemed like hours and hours, she heard a voice.

'Good grief. Stacy, is it?'

Finally, someone! And there stood John, his arms full of grocery shopping, which he plonked by his door as he rummaged around for his key.

'I locked myself out, John. Was going to see if you had some soup cos I'm p-poorly and can't get down to the sh-shops,' she said as fresh tears began to fall.

'Oh, well! You'd better come in then. I've just done my shopping so I'll be able to feed you and then we'll, um, we'll see what we can do about your door. Up you get then.'

He helped her to her feet and then looked at her, with raised eyebrows.

'You look rough!'

Stacy nodded, not meeting his eyes and shuffled into his flat, her slippers flip-flopping down his hall, as he held the door open for her.

213

As she sat down on the sofa, Stacy looked around his lounge.

It was a far cry from what she expected, following the day he appeared at her door smelling of stale armpits. The place was completely clean and organised. He, on the other hand, wasn't. He had a great clump of hair on top of his head that was as unruly as her own used to be, even though it was clipped short at the sides. He looked scruffy and his unshaven face was patchy. He wore a smoky-coloured T-shirt and grubby green-coloured jogging bottoms that were rather too big for him. And yet his flat was orderly and neat. What a strange contrast!

She sat there, unspeaking, as he put his shopping away, humming to himself and made her some soup. Packet soup would've been fine, but no. He'd concocted the most wonderful soup she'd ever tasted out of fresh vegetables, his own stock and fresh herbs. They sat down at the lounge table to eat.

'That was delicious, thank you,' she'd said afterwards. 'That's the best soup I've ever tasted!'

'Well, I do like cooking you see. A little hobby of mine. Would you like some more?' he said.

'Is the Pope Catholic?'

She'd had three bowlfuls, along with a crisp French baton and butter. The whole thing was so warm and comforting she didn't really want to go back to her own empty flat, even though it was nicely redecorated now.

While she was eating her soup John tried her door with

one of his credit cards. In the end he had to call a locksmith because his card, which he said had opened his own door once or twice, didn't work on Stacy's. 'Not enough of a gap,' he said. She realised the locksmith call-out might cost her dearly but at least she'd get back into her flat and, in the meantime, she'd had some nice lunch. Plus John had given her a few bits from his own shopping until she felt well enough to replace it.

It was the nicest thing anybody had done for her in a long time.

Marjorie groggily pulled her bedroom curtains back to reveal a foggy, slightly damp morning. It was also how she was feeling. She'd received a phone call she hadn't wanted yesterday. Plus today was the day Gracie was going to leave her and move in with Steven. It had come round so fast, since Gracie initially told her that's what she'd wanted to do, after Steven asked her. Marjorie knew she'd have to stop herself from grabbing her daughter and screaming, 'No! Don't go!' It felt far too soon for her to be dealing with the enormity of her daughter leaving, way before Marjorie was ready for her departure.

So last night she'd squirrelled a large glass of neat vodka into her bedroom, to help her cope with the two incidents she was facing. She'd knocked the lot back in a few large gulps. But she'd never been a drinker, so the alcohol hit her hard. Hence her hangover this morning.

The other shocking incident had been the phone call from Lou's son, Derek, to let her know his mother had just passed away.

'Massive heart attack, Marjorie. Well, she was overweight. She'd had a couple of little ones a few months back.'

'Oh God, Derek. I never knew.'

'No one knew. It was only from speaking to her doctor I found out myself. She was good at keeping things to herself, my mother. Didn't want to worry us I suppose. Look, um, she's got loads of photos of the two of you back when you were nippers and nights out and whatever. If you'd like a few I'll have them packaged up for when I see you at the funeral. Could you, er, *would* you like to say a few words at the funeral?'

'Oh, yes, of course, Derek. We've been best friends since forever. I loved your mum like a sister. Oh, I'm so upset. It's such a shame, Derek.'

When she'd put the phone down Marjorie had cried for Lou and raged that Gracie would also be leaving her very soon. Life was positively unbearable, sometimes.

But Marjorie would also admit, to anyone who asked, that Steven had been very helpful with the transition that meant Gracie would be leaving her that day. He'd said she could ring them at any time day or night, if she was worried about anything or needed anything or was ill. And she could come and see them or stay with them whenever she liked. He said he'd do whatever he could to help make the change as smooth and pain-free as possible. Gracie had left the lease in her own name for the time being and told her mother that she'd come over every second weekend to take her for a big food shop, so at least they'd still have regular contact and Gracie said they could go somewhere for a cup of tea and a piece of cake afterwards. That was reassuring inasmuch as Marjorie couldn't drive and had been wondering how she was going to manage the shopping by herself, even though there was a corner shop nearby.

So some aspects would, thankfully, remain the same after their parting. Plus she was happy in the flat they'd been living in, so she had no thoughts of upping sticks to follow Gracie or move elsewhere. Yet clearly there was no other option but to accept things as they were and get on with it. But, oh, poor Lou. She'd not seen that coming. They'd been friends since Miss Ellmere's class at primary school. They'd done everything together – nights out, first boyfriends, the works. Nearly eighty years of experiences together!

So even though the vodka in her belly had aided sleep, when she'd finally slept – despite all her nagging worries last night – it had caused a huge headache that morning. She daren't tell Gracie about the vodka because she didn't want to upset her daughter by admitting she was unhappy about her imminent departure and *totally* upset about her best friend's demise. She would speak to Gracie later, in depth about all that, when she'd come to terms with it all herself.

Before Steven's arrival, later that morning, Gracie's bags were packed and ready in the hall. But the sight of them had caused

Marjorie to recoil in both fear and realisation that this would be the final severing of the special relationship between herself and her daughter, even though she knew they'd be seeing each other on a regular basis. A tear escaped down her cheek. *Oh, Gracie!* Marjorie really couldn't imagine what it was going to feel like living without her daughter by her side each day. Life would never ever be the same again, without her. She could feel the onslaught of tears, threatening to turn into a torrent of grief, as she busied herself getting their breakfast ready.

Marjorie had told herself she would not behave like this because Gracie would be feeling the strain, too. She'd tried to replace sad thoughts with happy ones but it hadn't worked. She wiped a tear away with the back of her hand. *Mustn't let Gracie see me like this. Mustn't.* Yet she knew this breakfast would *properly* be their last meal together as mother and daughter because within the next hour there would be *three* of them in this relationship, even though Steven was truly lovely.

'Hi, darling,' Marjorie said as brightly as she could muster, placing scrambled eggs and bacon on the table for them both as Gracie walked through the door and sat down for her breakfast.

'Hi, Mum,' Gracie said equally cheerily, but it sounded false.

Marjorie sniffed, miserably, as they sat together to eat. She was not a good liar. Her daughter's imminent departure felt like the elephant in the room. Gracie took her hand.

'You okay, Mum? Look, I know this is hard for you, especially with what's just happened to Lou. I'm really sorry she's gone because you were such great friends and it makes it even harder for you having to cope with both of us leaving you one way or another, I guess.'

'Yes, it is, love,' she whispered, her head bowed so Gracie couldn't see just how upset she really was.

'It's hard for me too, actually,' Gracie admitted. 'Deciding to move in with Steven wasn't a decision I took lightly either. I mean, I just never thought anything like this would ever happen to me. A few months back I was even pooh-poohing the idea of meeting someone new, wasn't I? But I guess that's how life works sometimes. Stuff happens when you least expect it.'

Marjorie teased her scrambled eggs around the plate until they were too cold to eat.

'Yes, it's very hard for me, darling, even though Steven seems just wonderful. And I do understand that life moves on for everyone. But I was just thinking, what if I have to go to the doctor or there's an emergency or whatever? I don't know what I would do about all that.'

Gracie took a deep breath. 'Well, Mum, you know you can ring us with whatever problems you might encounter. But I suppose you'll just have to get the bus to see the doctor for ordinary things that aren't emergencies. I mean you'll have to do some things by yourself like you had to do when Daddy died. But if there's anything else you can't manage by yourself just ring us first and then we'll work it out together. Look, you know I'm always on the end of the phone, apart from school hours. But you can always leave a message any time and I'll get back to you as soon as I can.'

'Uh-huh okay. But are you *really* sure you're doing the right thing, sweetheart?' Marjorie persisted. 'I mean you've only really known each other a few weeks.'

Gracie sighed again. 'I know, Mum. But it feels so right. We can talk about anything. We like similar things. He's gentle and caring whereas Harry *always* had an eye for a pretty girl. And like you say, time marches on. I'm forty-eight at the end of the year. Plus we'll be living closer to where I work so that'll be a big help. That train journey twice a day was a nightmare, especially when they had strikes and I had to get all those buses. And you can come to stay with us whenever you like. Look, Mum, I know it's a lot for you to take in at the moment. But I really do think everything will work out just fine for us all, if we just give it a go.'

Marjorie had nodded then. Everything her daughter said made sense. They had to let go of each other in order to see where the future took them. It was time. Marjorie took a deep breath and reached forward to give her daughter a long hug.

'I love you so much, you know, darling. And I guess I know you'll be all right. I'll probably be all right, too, eventually. And I'm here if things don't work out for you, you know. And Steven is just lovely. But I'm, well, I'm just being your mum and still looking out for you. Right well, enough of all this! Let's finish up here and get ready to say goodbye then!'

'So have you found anywhere yet, Dora? Have you even been looking for somewhere else to live?' Philippa asked, as she helped her sister, Yvonne, through the door with a bag of bath towels and bed linen.

Dora had driven her mother down to her Aunt Philippa's with Yvonne's final bags and belongings to help move her into her sister's annex that weekend. Dora was staying the night and then driving over to Devon to see her brother Stuart and his family.

This time, the changes going on around Dora hadn't felt as energising. Probably because, this time, it truly was the end of an era for her family's business. Her mother had just struck a deal with the woman who'd shown interest in the Arts & Crafts Hotel in the Cotswolds. It was the last of her father's hotels to be sold. And once her mother was settled in with Philippa there would be nowhere else for her to run home to; so now she would have to find her own bolthole. Dora knew this would be a daunting new experience for her. She'd not had her own proper address since leaving Andy and Lauren years ago. It would feel odd to have her own front door key, once again.

'Not properly I haven't, no. I want to make sure Mother gets sorted and settled first and then I'm shooting off to stay with our Stuart for a while.'

221

'Oh, you're such a wanderer, Dora! I don't think you'll ever settle down, will you? I mean, excuse me for saying this but you're halfway through your life with nothing to show for it. Having fun is one thing. But everything gets boring after a while, no matter what you do. I was a bit like you as a girl, you know. But there's something amazing about putting down roots, getting to know people, having folk over for dinner, being with people you can rely on. Stuff like that. You might remember we moved about a bit with Nigel's job. He was one of those sales reps. They kept sending him off to work in different areas, which was a bit of a pain because we had to move home each time, too. Anyway, I'm happy to be properly settled now. And me and your mum get on great so it's going to be good for us to reconnect again.'

Dora nodded, crossing her arms.

She was fed up with trying to justify her lifestyle to everyone, even though she was at another crossroads in life. Oh boy, she'd had a fair few of those! But what to do next? She'd saved enough to go travelling again. But was there really anywhere else she fancied jetting off to? She'd been to most places. Well, she'd been everywhere she'd wanted to go to, anyway. Was there even anyone from all those years travelling she could meet up with again? Probably not. The few people she'd met on her travels were seasoned travellers themselves. But she was sure they'd have all settled down somewhere by now. Should she wait and see what her inheritance entailed once payment for their hotel arrived? Ah but she got on well with Stuart's wife, Hazel, so maybe she'd wait until she arrived at their hotel and then discuss everything with them.

'Yes well. You're right. I have to do something, of course. But I'm not really sure where I want to hang my hat, if truth be known. Not so sure I want to go jetting off again, either, because I've done all that. But I'll have a chat when I see Hazel. She's a canny sort with her feet firmly on the ground. Anyway, come on, let's get Mum settled and put the kettle on, Auntie, I'm parched.'

Chapter 23

As the weather chose to be very windy and a few degrees cooler than the last few weeks, Marjorie had decided to occupy the void Gracie had left by having a good old clear-out. She felt she had to do something productive! She couldn't simply sit down and cry at the emptiness and misfortune of her life, now that Gracie had moved out. She'd decided she wasn't going to ring her daughter for a few days. She knew she had to give Gracie space to breathe and time to settle in with Steven, without feeling guilty about what was happening to her mother. And by having a good clear-out, Marjorie could start to get the flat ready for her own full-time occupation and bring in things that were to her own taste and comfort.

So that first day she cleared and cleaned the flat. She couldn't remember the last time she'd done what she termed 'a good honest day's work'. But she intended to occupy what used to be her daughter's bedroom because it was larger and brighter than her own. So she changed the bed linen and moved her own little bits and pieces from the smaller room into the larger one. Marjorie felt pleased about doing all that. She left three black sacks of rubbish, unwanted items and food past its sell-by-date in the kitchen ready for taking down to the bins later. She was a little out of breath and certainly very tired that first night, so she had a soak in a hot bath and slept without the fitful tossing and turning she'd experienced of late.

On the second day she decided to remove the black bin liners to the bin shed, outside, and struggled downstairs with the bulky bags because the lift was out of order. But when she reached the bottom she realised that she didn't know where the bins were actually kept. Gracie had always done that. So she left her rubbish by the stairs while she went out into the car park. No bin shed there. So where did the binmen collect the household rubbish from then? She found the cycle store but there were no bins there either.

She could feel herself beginning to panic. Well, she'd have to find out where it was because she'd be doing it on a regular basis. She started to walk slowly back up the stairs when she spotted someone coming down.

'Oh excuse me, deary, I'm Marjorie from Flat 11,' she said a little out of breath. 'Can you point me in the direction of the bin shed? My daughter moved out recently so it's just me and I've just realised that because she used to do the bins, I've no idea where to put the black sacks.'

The man smiled. 'Sure, I'm Terry from the second floor, Flat 16. I'll show you. They're down here by the cycle store. On the other side actually. You probably wouldn't notice it at first glance. There, see. Oh and just shout if you have any other problems. I'm an electrician by trade and pretty handy with most things.'

'Phew, well thank you, Terry,' said Marjorie, relieved. She was glad she'd met him. He also loaded her black sacks into the bins for her.

That evening she rang Gracie. She hadn't wanted to ring her this early into their separation but she was feeling lonely and she'd had a very trying day.

'Hi, darling! Just thought I'd ring to see how you're doing? Oh, you've already settled in? And he's making you feel really welcome. Oh, I'm pleased about that. Me? Oh, well I've had a jolly good clear-out but I was wondering ... You see there's still medicines in the bathroom cabinet. Ah, you don't need them. Okay. And I was looking at the boiler to see where everything is. The hot water is set for – okay, I'll leave it where it is, then. That's good. Well, I think that's about it. I've met one of the neighbours, Terry from Number 16. He helped me find the bins for the rubbish and he says I can call on him for any problems I might encounter, so that's reassuring. So, um, apart from all that, how are you feeling about things, darling?'

Gracie sighed on the other end of the phone. 'Well, it just feels so strange being back here in Dorset, knowing I'm probably going to bump into Harry at some stage. But I'll jump that hurdle when I come to it. I'm far more together now than I was back then. Harry used to enthral me when I was younger. But it feels so right being here with Steven, now. He's got this lovely little two-bedroom cottage with a copse of trees at the bottom of the garden and a little brook running through it. It's gorgeous, Mum. Can't wait for you to see it. Anyway, we're off out to sample local restaurant delights. So we'll speak soon. I'm pleased you're settling in and meeting the locals. Lots of love. Bye, Mum.'

Marjorie was surprised and a little saddened that there were only eight people at Lou's funeral: Derek and his wife and son, herself, Lou's brother, another friend and two neighbours who used to pop round and check up on Lou periodically.

'—and so to conclude. Lou was my best friend and confidante for over seventy-five years and she helped me when I was living through some very unhappy times. I don't know what I'd've done without her, in those days. And she never shied away from saying what she thought. It often got her into bother, though. But that was my L-Lou – I'm sorry, just give me a minute. Gosh, this is hard. I'll, um, I'll really miss her. She was my last and greatest friend. You're in God's care now, Lou. Sleep tight!'

Tears streamed down Marjorie's face as she took out her tissue and dabbed at her pink teary eyes. She then gathered herself and moved slowly from the lectern, as Derek mouthed a heartfelt 'Thank you.'

Marjorie wasn't only weeping because it was the end of an era for her and her best friend. It was also the end of the safe closeness she'd had living together with her daughter for so

227

long. Gracie had already been gone five long days. Oh, Marjorie had busied herself doing the things she'd needed to do. She'd even forced herself to take the bus into town for a mooch around. But it wasn't the same as when her daughter had been at her side. Yes, she realised, she *had* spent long periods by herself whilst Gracie was teaching at school. But it didn't feel the same; it wasn't the same. She always knew Gracie would be back by the end of the day, when they lived together, and they'd have dinner and cosy chats into the night, unless Gracie had to mark the children's exercise books.

Yet despite the strange noises she'd noticed now she was living alone again the silence sometimes seemed deafening. She'd cried herself to sleep last night, worrying about everything but it had made her face puffy this morning when she'd wanted to be more presentable for Lou's funeral. She knew she had to get to grips with this. Hundreds of people found themselves alone as they got older. She knew she would have to learn to accept it.

Derek gave Marjorie a little parcel at the gathering afterwards. They'd just gone to a nearby pub to have sandwiches and a few drinks. Marjorie would have laid out a much nicer spread for her dear old best friend. But it wasn't her place to do that. Nor was it her place to say anything. She was getting better at holding her tongue, these days. *Thank you, Dr Baxley.*

She sat and opened the parcel and the first photo that fell out was the first primary school photo they'd had taken together. A fresh wave of tears then assaulted Marjorie as the memory ricocheted her back – back before Oliver, back before Gracie, back to times of laughter and childhood happiness in a playground in a Bournemouth school; seeing who could do the best handstands against the school wall, or hands crossed twizzling around, or doing needlework. Times were very hard during the Second World War years, according to her parents, but as children she and Lou never really noticed that. They were evacuated to Bournemouth when the bombs started dropping, because the port of Southampton was strategic to the Luftwaffe. But to Lou and Marjorie those times were full of naïve childhood adventures, despite what the adults had to endure.

Yet shouldn't old age bring the promise of idle days; safely wrapped up in the knowledge that I'm secure and loved into my twilight years, with the care of my family around me? Why, now, am I having to worry about where to put the rubbish or how to get to the doctor's if Gracie can't take me? And why, now, did my one and only best friend have to leave this world when I'm lonely and needed her most? Marjorie thought, her face buried in her hands.

Why, now, had life suddenly become so challenging?

Chapter 24

The day of the coach trip to Bournemouth had been put back until the last week of September, due to Taynor being off sick and Eileen going to the Isle of Wight for the weekend with her family. The previous day there'd been a downpour but it had cleared to give the day trippers lovely blue skies and an enticing temperature of nineteen degrees for their day out.

The coach had dropped them off by the lower gardens on Westover Road and everyone had padded down through the pine trees, delighting at the little squirrels, into the gardens below.

When Raymond had spotted the sea, he'd shouted, 'Last one in the sea buys drinks at lunch!'

And the crowd had yelled raucously and taken off as fast as their legs or walking frames and walking sticks would carry them. Some were tottery. Some couldn't stop laughing. Even Michael had made the coach trip and he was wheeling as fast as he could with a whoop and a holler, his helpers trying to keep up with him, shouting directions if he was veering off course. 'Left, left not right! *Left*, Michael!' Others helped each other as best they could since they were ALL determined to, at least, reach the water's edge even if they didn't go in.

'Oh, it's so champion to be getting out and havin' some fun for a change!' someone had cried.

Marjorie, Stacy and Dora had linked arms and were just taking their time, looking around themselves, drinking everything in: the aquarium, the pier amusements, people still out and about enjoying the September sunshine and eating ice creams. They could almost see as far as Poole Harbour entrance in the distance to the right and almost make out the Isle of Wight to the left.

'Never been to Bournemouth,' Stacy said.

'Really?' said Marjorie, incredulous.

'Might have told you, we went up north, once when we were kids. To Mablethorpe, near to where Dad's family are from. But I don't remember it. We were never taken anywhere else though. You've been everywhere, though, haven't you, Dora?'

'I have, love. Everywhere. And it was fun whilst it lasted. But anyways, are we going to dabble our tootsies in the English Channel or what?'

'Oh yeah!' screamed Stacy, taking off after the others. She kicked off her sandals when she got to the beach and ran through the sand to where Raymond and some of the others were already paddling and laughing, near the pier. Then everyone started splashing each other and squealing in delight.

'Child's play!' scoffed Dora, as she rolled her jeans up to her knees, tentatively put a foot in the chilly water and then chuckled as she happily kicked the water about with the others. Marjorie smiled at her. It was rare to see Dora looking as happy as she was today.

Even on the coach journey to Bournemouth the atmosphere had been one of abandoning one's problems at the door of the bus, like Eva was fond of saying, and then everyone joining in with songs like 'The Wheels on the Bus' or 'Summer Holidays'.

Michael's wife, Janice, was here with him, too, chatting to a group of people, when Marjorie approached them.

'When was the last time you went on the beach, Michael?' Marjorie asked softly.

He shrugged and sighed. 'When I was a kid I think. But I must say being here, knowing the pier and the gardens and the sea are all around me is great. I can smell a bit of the sea air too. We don't get away much the wife and I. So this has been a real treat. And it's marvellous they've allowed my helpers to come, too.'

'Yes, well, what if we get your helpers to get you onto the beach, so you can wriggle your fingers in the sand?'

Michael's wife widened her eyes. 'Oh, what an incredible idea, Marjorie. Oh, yes let's, Michael! We've never sat on a beach together, have we? Right. Summon the troops!'

So the two carers Michael had been allowed to bring with him lifted him out of his wheelchair and placed him down on the sand where he sat with Janice, and they laughed and joined in with the rest of the group's enjoyment down on the beachfront.

'Wow ... sand!' Michael exclaimed, picking up handful after handful of it and letting it run through his fingers whilst his wife laughed and laughed. Marjorie took a photo of them as they shared a kiss and sent it to Janice's phone. Then she took a couple more of them both larking about, just for good measure.

'Oh wow. That's cool of you, Marjorie. Thanks so much for that.' He grinned. 'Do we look good, Janice?'

'Oh it's brilliant, Michael. We haven't got many photos have we? I'll get them framed. It'll be a lovely memory.'

'Right, guys,' Eileen called, clapping her hands. 'Who's for lunch?'

A few people said, 'NO!'

Everyone else yelled, 'YES!'

'Right, so we're going back the way we came and then it'll be a short coach journey to the hotel we're having lunch in. Yes, please go back through the gardens to where the coach dropped you off. He'll be back there. Have you all got towels to wipe your feet and whatnot?'

Everybody had something or found something to wipe their feet on.

'So how's life with you, Marjorie, since your daughter moved out?' Raymond said as they ate their fish pie, cauliflower and green beans. Their first course had been a large bowl of roast tomato and red pepper soup with bread and butter.

'Well, it's only been a few weeks but was very hard for me at first. I kept ringing her, probably because I was very anxious and unsure of things. I mean she usually put the rubbish out. But *where* did she put it? She had a special medicine cabinet but did she need any of the things that were still in there? Stuff like that. Bits of non-essential stuff that becomes essential when you can't find or can't do something, you know?'

Raymond nodded, chewing his food carefully in case there were any tiny fish bones in it, although they'd been assured there weren't.

'Same for me when my wife died. She'd done *everything* before. So it was like starting from scratch for me too. I guess I'm like most blokes. The wife takes over and does tasks because they are more efficient at doing things that seem to either take us ages or we don't want to do. It is very hard learning to live by yourself again. Lonely too. Plus you notice strange background noises you never heard before. Have you noticed that?'

'Oh yes, Raymond. I couldn't sleep at first wondering if someone was breaking in all the time or whatever, even though I have lived on my own before. But even before I moved in with my daughter I knew one day circumstances would change for her. It's just that as the years went by I started getting settled and comfortable with the idea of it just being me and her. But, well, everything happened so fast once she'd met

Steven. I suppose I'd envisaged a scenario whereby she met someone and went out for at least a year before they got married. That way I'd have had plenty of time to get used to the idea and prepare myself for her leaving. But she's only really known Steven a couple of months now and they've already moved in together!'

'Ah, but didn't you say she was in her late forties?'

'I did and yes, you're right, I was always encouraging her to get a move on with things. So it's my own fault – I hold my hands up! I should've kept my mouth shut.'

'Life is difficult, though, Marjorie, whatever choices you make.'

'I agree. But from today I'm doing a little experiment. I've decided I'm not going to call her if I get stuck with something or have a query. I'm going to make do and mend, as my dear old mother used to say. In fact I'm not going to call her for at least five days to see if I can finally start to cope being on my own. To be honest I bet they're thoroughly fed up of me calling. I heard irritation in her voice the last time I rang.'

'Or why don't you ring me, Marjorie?' Raymond suggested. 'After all, friends should help each other out, shouldn't they? Then she won't need to worry so much. I reckon she's probably worried sick about you. She must realise that *her* choices are affecting your happiness and that must be a huge burden on her shoulders.'

Marjorie sighed and pushed her plate to one side. A waiter,

hovering nearby, scooped it up and arranged her dessert spoon and fork either side, in preparation for her pudding.

'I think you're probably right, Raymond. It's very selfish of me to keep ringing her. But if you really don't mind, I think it'd be much better if I rang you next time I get stuck. Thank you for your kind offer.'

'So how're things with you, Dora?' said Stacy taking a sip of water. 'Has that detective chap found anything out about your daughter? Or have you made contact with her yet?'

The long table they were all sitting on was in the process of being cleared so the diners could have their pudding of Eton mess or jelly and vanilla ice cream.

'Yes, well, I've had a phone call from Tony, the detective chappie. I wanted to see if he could contact my daughter with a view to me possibly meeting her, being as Andy and his mother won't let me see her. And, failing that, my main concern was to find out if she'd received all the letters and whatnot I sent her, telling her my side of the story, in case Andy told her something different. Anyway, he's been monitoring her movements to try and get close to her. And a couple of days ago he waited outside a bistro where she was meeting friends for an evening out and he made contact with her there, as she was leaving. She said she didn't want to meet up with someone she had never known and especially didn't want to meet up with someone who'd done the things I'd done and also abandoned her – whatever that means. The answer was

236

also "oh" when he asked about the letters because she told him she'd never received anything from me. She wouldn't tell him *why* she didn't want to meet me but it might be that she's been hurt by all of this, of course.' Dora paused and took a long swig of the red wine she was drinking. 'You see, this is why I wanted to meet her! Because I just don't know what Andy has said about me over the years. He could've told her something that painted me in a dim light for all I know.'

'Do you think the detective guy told you everything Lauren said?'

'What do you mean, Stacy? Tony Gallagher used to be a family friend, so I'm sure he'd've done right by me. So I have to believe what he told me.'

'But I've seen those programmes where people meet up with their long-lost relatives. They always want to meet them. Or they're at least curious.'

'Ah! The programmes always show you the ones who *want* to meet up with their relatives. Not the ones who don't want to. And some don't, apparently. Anyway, I've lived without her this long. I guess if she ever wants to come find me there are ways and means, even though I've moved about quite a bit.'

Stacy wasn't so sure that Dora felt as dismissive as she sounded. She must've been very hurt that her daughter wanted nothing to do with her. *She's probably acting as if it doesn't matter, to hide her disappointment*, Stacy thought. *That has to be it.*

Puddings had been served and everyone was eating quietly.

It was gone 2.30 p.m. when they'd finished their lunch and teas and coffees. Some people looked sleepy. A good meal always made Raymond feel sleepy, he'd told Marjorie.

'Don't think I'll be going shopping now. Could do with a kip if truth be told. Oh the joys of getting old!'

'Well I wouldn't mind having a dash around. Anyone fancy coming with me?' said Stacy. She hadn't managed to get any new clothes sorted out for herself yet and it would be a real treat shopping somewhere she'd never been before.

'Well, before everyone goes off every which way,' said Michael. 'I'd just like to say thank you to Eileen and Taynor for setting this trip up for us. You've all made us feel exceptionally welcome and it's been absolutely bloody great. Excuse the swearing. But it has. Janice and me don't get to have holidays. Neither of us drive. And we've not got kids who could drive us anywhere. So this has been an absolute blast. So thank you for that. And a big thank you, also, to Marjorie for getting me and Janice down on the sand. Oh God. That sounds bad! But my wife has got a couple of fantastic photos of me and her enjoying our day out, now. Something to show our mates and her parents. So thanks for that, too, Marjorie. Thanks, guys!'

He started clapping and everyone joined in. Marjorie went red.

'You're a motivator,' Raymond whispered to her. 'I think you're starting to come into your own, now, my dear. So you can allow Gracie to have her new life because I think yours has just started again, too.'

Chapter 25

Raymond was standing, sipping a glass of red wine, lost in thought, gazing out of Marjorie's lounge window that overlooked the bird table in the communal yard. Lights were on in ground-floor flat windows, highlighting the bird table, reminding him of Dianne. The iPlayer was on low, crooning out tunes from the Sixties. He couldn't remember the last time he'd been invited to a party on a Friday night. Simon had dropped him off and said he'd pick him up at any time, later on. Marjorie had filled her dining table with all sorts of M&S nibbles, which looked deliciously tempting. The décor was restful with soft tones of cream and beige.

The doorbell had rung and Marjorie was welcoming Dora into her flat and asking what she'd like to drink.

'Oh, red wine if you've got it. It's my go-to tipple for any celebration,' Dora said with a smile. 'Nice place you've got here.'

'Thanks. I'm starting to like it now I'm getting used to being on my own. It's on a good bus route for town and near to the community centre, which is great.'

The doorbell had been abandoned and someone was

knocking on Marjorie's door for all they were worth; loud, banging thumps!

Marjorie yanked the door open in alarm and there stood Stacy in a flattering pale grey jumper and black jeans. Stacy was certainly starting to look a lot better than when they'd first met. She no longer looked slightly odd and manic and even her hair and clothes seemed to have arrived in twenty-first-century Britain.

'Are you all right?' Marjorie asked her.

'Oh, Marjorie! You simply wouldn't believe it, would you! I've been bursting to tell you since you invited me to your house-warming party but I thought I'd wait. You'll just never guess – oh hi, Dora, Raymond. Gosh, I might as well tell you all. Well, you and I, Marjorie, we live in the same block of flats! There! Incredible, isn't it? I'm on the second floor. And here you are on the first!'

'What?'

'It's true, Marjorie. I've simply come downstairs to your flat. So after we've eaten I'd really like it if you'd all come upstairs to my place for coffee and chocolates, if you want? How weird is that? Ha, ha! It's incredible, isn't it?'

Dora and Raymond exchanged glances.

'It's bloody bizarre!' said Dora, taking a swig of her drink. 'Goodness, Marjorie. This wine is slipping down a real treat. Is it Italian?'

'I think so, yes. Well, Stacy, that's a complete surprise, I must say. I've only met a couple of our neighbours in all the

240

time I've been here. There's that lovely man on the second floor. Think his name is John and his neighbour Terry, who's been most helpful – oh, they're on your floor, then! Right, well I've prepared a buffet for you all so just help yourselves as and when you see fit. Plates and napkins on the end there. Hope there's something you all like.'

Raymond beamed. 'Well, it all looks quite delicious, Marjorie. I do like those curried vol-au-vents and, oh look, I like those chicken satay things as well. You have been busy.'

'Yes, well, I've been dying to fill this flat with some friendly faces since Gracie left, you see. It's been quite lonely even though I've been finding out about things as I've gone along. You've helped too, of course. But I suppose these things take time, don't they? But I'm getting there now. And it's marvellous to be able to watch all my favourite TV programmes, like *EastEnders*, when I feel like it. It wasn't Gracie's cup of tea. So that's a bonus.'

Stacy giggled.

'That's what I've always loved about living by myself. I can do *anything* I want. At home my parents were so controlling it got stifling and then I was scared in case I said or did something wrong and Dad would yell. So it suits me being single,' said Stacy, helping herself to a bit of everything off the buffet table and piling her plate up. 'I know it doesn't suit everybody, though.'

She sat on a chair by the table and became very engrossed in her food. The doorbell rang again.

'Oh, hi, Eileen. Hiya, Taynor. So pleased you could make it. Come in. Yes, I'll get you a drink but help yourself to the buffet and please sit anywhere.'

Eileen laughed. 'Oh, that's funny. You sound just like I did when you all came to afternoon tea on that first occasion, do you remember? Everyone looked baffled and I was telling them they could sit anywhere. A good few months have ticked by since then, haven't they? Oh thanks, Marjorie, I'll just have an orange juice, if you've got one. I'm driving. Taynor, do you want a very small white wine or some juice? Thank you so much, Marjorie.'

'Hi, Eileen. It's lovely to see you here,' Stacy said.

'Actually I don't usually accept party invites but then I thought, why not? None of us would've met if it wasn't for the Afternoon Tea Club, would we? And I've never been to a house-warming party before. So there you are. I haven't been out in a while. I'm usually torn between family and work, as you can imagine.'

'That's right, Eileen, so it's lovely to see you out of work, as it were,' said Raymond smiling. 'Anyway I hope your bosses appreciate the terrific job you do for them. We certainly do. Our lives were very predictable and actually quite empty until we saw that flyer, I must say.'

'Yes, well this is what my mother said, you see, Raymond. And with the turnout for the Bournemouth trip and the afternoon tea sessions, my bosses can see this is the way forward. We'll be having a meeting just before Christmas to adjust some of our plans, according to the take-up of the activities we've provided and we also want to catch up with everybody to see how they feel it's all going. We'll probably touch base with you all every now and then for that reason. Then we won't get stale you see,' said Eileen, chewing on a chicken satay skewer.

'Good idea. So are there any changes to be had yet?' queried Raymond.

'Ah, well, one of the computer courses doesn't seem to be working out,' said Taynor. 'We don't know if it's because people don't like to be doing it on a Friday or feel they don't need both classes. So we might just do that once a month or alternatively change the days. But this is the sort of thing we'll discuss with everyone to see what they want to do going forward. But just to let you know because I'm so excited, my husband and I are expecting our first child!'

'Oh congratulations!' gushed Marjorie. 'How far along are you?'

'Only about four or five weeks and we've decided to be happy with whatever we're graced with, so the grandmothers are already knitting white or pale lemon onesies so we won't be caught out either way. We're going to call him Danny, after my dad, if he's a boy or Adele if she's a girl. So it's going to be very easy.'

'When's your baby due?' said Dora.

'Well they gave us the date of 22nd April or mid to end of April. A spring baby. We're thrilled.'

'Oh, it will be truly wonderful,' said Raymond wistfully, remembering his and Dianne's joy at discovering she was pregnant with Simon. 'We only had the one but he was a complete delight!'

Marjorie noticed that Dora seemed to be drinking a lot. She wondered if she was thinking about Lauren, with all the talk about babies. Perhaps now was time to switch the topic of conversation.

'So do you get much time for your own family, Eileen, with the amount of work and organising you have to do for every-body else?' Marjorie asked.

'Well, I've got two boys, although they're hardly boys any more. Problem is they're in their early twenties and still at home. They say they'll go when they each find the *perfect* woman to marry. But let's be realistic – I'm probably stuck with them for life!'

That made everybody laugh, even Dora. Marjorie could see that everybody got on so well. It was as if they'd been friends for years. People like Eileen and Taynor clearly had the knack of bringing an unrelated group of people together in a way that encouraged blossoming friendships.

After they'd eaten they took up Stacy's offer and traipsed up to her flat where she'd laid out mugs for tea or coffee and petit fours that she'd bought from M&S. The interior layout was an exact replica of Marjorie's. But it had a more eclectic feel about it. The table had four very different chairs around it. The curtain in the lounge was a cheesecloth-type drape, swept back across the window like a swag and secured with a brass holdback. There was one two-seater low-backed black leather settee with a colourful throw and a multi-fabric armchair, laminate flooring and off-white-painted walls. They all thought it would make a great party room.

'Okay, Dora, here's your tea with milk and one sugar,' said Marjorie, helping out. 'Eileen, did you say no sugar with your coffee?'

'I did, thanks.'

By the time the clock had ticked over to 9.30 p.m. everybody had started saying goodnight and thanking their hosts for a wonderful evening.

'Until we meet again,' Raymond said dramatically, kissing all the ladies' hands to the sound of giggles, especially from Dora, who looked as though she was just starting to enjoy herself!

'Thank you all so much for coming.' Marjorie smiled at everyone, as they collected their jackets from her flat.

As Dora walked towards the door Marjorie stopped her.

'How are you getting home?'

'Not far. Two streeths away so I'm walkin',' she slurred.

'No, you're not. Anything could happen to you. Go sit in the lounge a minute while I say goodbye to everybody and then you're going to be having a large glass of water and sleeping in my spare room. No arguments!'

Dora didn't surface until gone 10.00 a.m. the following morning and when she did appear, her face was creased, one eye was

245

bloodshot and her hair, normally in a bun, was loose and straggly around her shoulders. She looked teary. And she looked a lot older than forty-nine, in Marjorie's opinion. However, Marjorie was proud of herself for not saying a word about any of it!

'I'll do toast for you because you need to eat something. I used to fancy toast the next morning, after a bender, when I was in my teens,' Marjorie said with a smile.

'You? Never!'

'Just because I'm an old bird doesn't mean I haven't lived. In fact, I liked it when my Oliver was down the pub and pissed off his head because he'd come back too drunk to take a swing at me. Usually he'd crash on the sofa or in the hall where he fell. I'd know if he wasn't back by around 9 p.m. that he hadn't fallen out with anybody. I'd also know it was safe to get his vodka bottle out and have a couple of little sips of it, myself. Being as it was his drink, I topped it up with water afterwards and he never seemed to know.'

Dora grinned. 'Okay I'll have a couple of pieces of toast. White bread please and, um, yes, a large glass of water might help, too.'

'Good. Right so, er, what's happening with you at the moment? Sorry I didn't get much chance for a natter last night. Parties are like that though, aren't they? You only get the chance to have a few words with each person.'

'Well, my mother has finally sold the hotel. There were a few hiccups regarding right of way down one side of the

246

property that somehow hadn't even been picked up on when we originally bought it. So we thought the woman might pull out over that. But it's all gone through now and we've been paid. That's the main thing. So now my mum lives with my Aunt Philippa a few streets away from here, actually. But how funny! You and Stacy, neighbours!'

Marjorie nodded. 'Must say that was a bit of a shock. But I've noticed Stacy seems to be coming into her own a bit more now, since her accident. And I think she's benefitted from touching base with her parents again. She needed to do that. But from what she says they're not a very loving family.'

'Unless they show it in other ways?'

'Yes, could be. Her father sorted her flat out and that can't have been cheap.'

The toaster pinged.

'Right, well, here's your toast, madam. And I've got honey or plum jam. Either of those suit?'

'Great, I'll take the plum jam please.'

'Okay. And what about you? Where are you living now?'

'Well I'm going to be staying at my friend Jodie's for a while. But I'm staying with Mum and Philippa at the moment because Jodie's on holiday. And you'll be pleased to hear that I've already made a start looking at flats around Southampton.'

'So we could *all* end up being neighbours then?'

Dora nodded, smiling. 'Now that would be funny! But I've started meeting people, like yourself of course. My family is originally from around these parts, as you know, anyway. And it's something that's starting to feel right for me now. Like my mother says, I can't be a wandering minstrel all my life.'

'No, I suppose not.'

As Marjorie chewed her toast an idea popped into her head. 'Well, Dora, now it's just a thought, this. But I have an offer for you. Would you like to stay in my spare room rent-free while you get yourself sorted out? I know you have friends and family but sometimes that sort of thing doesn't work out. You don't have to answer straight away. But it would also be a little company for me, although you can come and go as you please, of course. Might just give you some breathing space. It's only an idea and I won't be offended if you say no. But just have a think about it, okay?'

Chapter 26

It was a crisp Sunday morning at the beginning of October and Marjorie was humming to herself as she was finishing tidying the flat. She was quite enjoying living by herself these days and didn't need to keep ringing her daughter for advice about everything now she had Raymond on the end of the phone. Plus there was usually something going on with the Afternoon Tea Club. So that was a bit of a lifeline for her. And she'd found she was quite good at drawing, like she had been as a youngster. In fact, Eva had been very encouraging with all of them now they were able to dump their worries at the door before entering the class. And the results were speaking for themselves since even Dora's chimneys no longer looked like giraffes!

'See? You can ALL draw now! You could draw before, of course. But your nerves got in the way,' she'd told them last time.

Marjorie, Raymond, Dora and Stacy still went to the drawing classes. It was something they enjoyed doing together. Other people had joined and then left. But the four of them were the mainstays. In fact, Marjorie had started drawing on a regular basis when she was at home, alone, with nothing much else to do. She hadn't continued with the painting, though. It hadn't really been her thing. But she knew Raymond and Michael still went. It was great for the both of them having a bit of man-time together.

After a bit of practice she'd managed to sketch the outside bird table with a couple of blue tits pecking crumbs that she was going to show Eva the next time she went to class. She'd been to town and bought a couple of new pencils. She'd asked the shop assistant to advise her which were the best ones for how she wanted to draw the birds. It had taken her a couple of days doing the rough sketches before tackling the finished picture. But she'd thoroughly enjoyed doing it. And she was thrilled she'd finally found something else that she could do when she was home alone in the afternoons. And if Eva sang her praises she was going to attempt a vase of flowers next!

She'd just put the vacuum cleaner away and switched the washing machine on to do her bed linen when the doorbell rang. And there, much to her surprise, stood Dora with a cabin-size suitcase.

'I know it's been a good few days since you asked but my ox of a mother has been getting on my nerves. So the answer's yes, if you'll still have me?' Dora said, with a smile. 'Just for a few weeks until I find my new home.'

Marjorie's jaw dropped open. Well, after her and Dora's rocky start she hadn't really thought Dora would have taken her up on her offer. But since that day at the community centre they now had a much better understanding of each other. So why not? Dora was obviously happy with the offer, otherwise she wouldn't be here. But Marjorie looked down at Dora's bag, puzzled.

'Is that all you've got?'

'Well I'm a traveller, through and through, Marjorie. I have no furniture or anything of that nature. At the hotel we lived in the owner's flat, which was fully furnished from the get-go. So I've never had to buy that sort of thing. And I don't have any knick-knacks of any description either. Wherever I've gone I've always travelled light. So all I have is just a few items of clothing. I don't have any long dresses or fancy evening wear because I never go anywhere fancy. So this is me.'

'Well, come on into your new temporary home then! Oh, but just one thing: I'm off to my daughter's in the next hour because it's her birthday. I'm quite excited because I've held off going to see where they live until now. I wanted them to have some proper time together before I came trotting along. But her lovely boyfriend Steven is taking us out for Sunday lunch and he's coming to fetch me any minute now. I can't wait! But let's get you settled. So, this is your room through here. It's a nice bright room. The bathroom's there. I did my Saturday shop, yesterday, and the fridge is full, so just help yourself to whatever you fancy. There's a spare drawer in the bathroom you can use for all your toiletries. I'll be out until about 5 p.m. today. Have you got my mobile number?'

'Yes, you gave it me at your party, remember?'

'Okay grand. Right, so can I make you a cuppa whilst we're getting you settled in?'

Stacy was pacing the room. She was not one for biting her fingernails but both her forefingers were now bitten down to the quick and she was randomly biting her others.

Her mother's cryptic voicemail message was: 'Prepare yourself, Stacy. We're all going off to see Peter and Marvin for lunch today. Dad and I will pick you up around 9.30 a.m. so get ready and be waiting. Oh and I've smoothed things over with your father, so please don't worry.'

That message could mean anything or it could mean nothing but Stacy did not want to spend any time in her father's presence if there was going to be an almighty row when Marvin and her father came face to face later that day. She also didn't want to spend time in their car for a couple of hours en route not knowing what to say; not sure if something might start him off thinking about things and then a huge argument ensuing between them all.

She couldn't stand the uncertainty of it so she rang her brother.

'Peter?'

'No, it's Marvin. That future sister-in-law? Oh hiya, Stacy.'

'Hello, Marvin. Look, um. My mum said we're supposed to be coming over to yours for Sunday lunch. Is that true?'

'It is, sweetheart. Apparently your mum has, what she terms, "sorted your father out", whatever that means.'

'Yes, she can be cryptic sometimes, which is worrying. I must say, you're taking this very well, Marvin. But I'm sure Peter's told you about our family, by now, and you certainly know from last time what Dad's like?'

'Uh-huh. Look, don't worry. Pete and I have spoken about this at length. I know he's as worried about this as you are. But the reality is that there are homophobic people out there. Always will be. Now, I don't like it any more than you or Pete, but sometimes in life you have to acknowledge that we're not living in a fairy story where everything will always work out okay. Pete and I have encountered prejudice before and we have to accept that's the way it will be for some folk. However, we try to avoid trouble whenever possible. And we know it's naïve to think you can do exactly as you please in life. Life doesn't work like that. But anyway, this is a first step towards some sort of acceptance, I suppose. So, look, we'll see you later and see how it all goes. But, sweetheart, it's not your bad if it doesn't work out.'

'Okay. Thanks, Marvin.'

Well, that felt better. The nail chewing could stop. She'd done her bit. Peter was so lucky to have such an understanding partner. Even so, she was still worried as to what would happen at their door. How would her father actually greet Marvin?

Her doorbell rang at 9.35 a.m. and her mother was standing on the mat.

'Your father's outside, so are you ready?'

'Look, Mum. Come in a minute. Now, exactly what is going to happen here? What's happening with Dad? He was furious last time. I mean I don't want this visit to be awful, too, with everyone tippy-toeing around, you know. I feel it's all my fault for putting you in that situation when you came to mine last time. But I wasn't being awkward towards Dad. It was to try and get everybody to come together to try and understand each other.'

'I know that Stacy. Look, okay, let's have a quick chat, before we go. Let me tell you about how things have been. You might understand a little better then,' her mother said with a sigh. 'Right, so I have lived with your father for a long time. We met at a barn dance in the old village hall. He seemed a warmer person then but he was never very affectionate. I have foregone a much better social life to be his wife and work the farm, even though I knew I would inherit it, eventually. But farming is not an easy life. It's well known that you make sacrifices to live and work on a farm. The hours are very unsociable, for a start. My family struggled with it all their lives. And your dad and I struggled in the beginning, continuing with their animals and then it not working out and changing over to arable farming, which could've been a really risky move.

'I went through a period when I certainly wanted to give up. And things weren't always easy between Jerry and I, but then most couples experience conflict and problems. I even wanted to give up and try a life without your father. Yet I had the two of you to consider and I couldn't just up sticks and leave because where would we have gone? Anyway, around that uncertain time for us the price per tonne of crops dropped, so your father was working harder than ever to compensate. Then we laid old Jack off, because we couldn't afford to pay him. Do you remember him? And then my mother died. And then weeks later your father's parents died in that car crash and he was gutted. So I knew I had to stay and help him cope with all of that. But they were very testing times for us!

'And then Peter walking out of the door, the moment he turned eighteen and then you, a few months after your eighteenth told me something. I knew your father's stern ways and – yes, if I'm honest – my lack of empathy hadn't motivated you both. It had sent you both out of the door. But, my God, I was lost without you both. Oh I buried myself in my daily activities, not sure whether to think about leaving again or not. And then my father went into the nursing home and I was given power of attorney. And that finally meant I had some control over our future. Previously, he'd pulled the strings, regarding the farm. But we've had a lifetime of that farm and, after the two of you left, I decided I didn't want it any more. I wanted my father to sell it so we could move to a little cottage near the sea, but we didn't quite have enough savings for that, so we had a long talk about things – including my wanting to leave. But he persuaded me to stay and I decided to carry on. I stayed with your father and we saved hard. I will admit that I was saving so we could *either* retire together, if that's what we decided when the time came, or so I could leave and be by myself, without your father, Stacy.'

'You told me some of that before, Mum. But I didn't know you wanted to leave Dad.'

'I know. But what I hadn't told you is that I really think I *would* like to live in a little cottage, and have a different, more enjoyable kind of life with holidays and days out to see my children and, hopefully, their own families when they eventually marry and settle down. But I'll do that by myself, without your father, if he cannot conduct himself in a more affable way. Does that surprise you, Stacy?'

'Yes, a little, I suppose. But I certainly hope he doesn't blame me for starting this all off about Marvin and stuff?' Stacy said, suddenly feeling guilty and wondering if her father might have a go at her later about the problems he felt she was causing.

'No, love. This is about my relationship with your father. Our relationship as a family unit has suffered because of the problems between your dad and me. But it was only when your grandfather went into that nursing home that I felt empowered to act, you see. And when you came back to us after your fall and we got chatting, and when I reconnected with Peter again and met Marvin, *that's* when I realised my children should no longer suffer because of your father and I. However, I can finally admit, now, that we've not been great parents and I do apologise for that, Stacy.'

'Okay, Mum. But if you bought a cottage near the sea,

somewhere, could I come and stay with you? And could we have more get-togethers with Peter and Marvin? Like a proper family and without walking on eggshells all the time?'

'We could do all of those things, Stacy. But listen, getting back to today. I've told him I'm giving him this one last chance to be civil to my boy and Marvin. And he knows that if he isn't – if one hurtful word comes out of his mouth, today, in any respect – I've told him I'm going. He's such a stubborn man, yet we could have such a wonderful future if he got his act together. So I'm hoping today will turn out fine for everybody.'

'I really hope it works out, too.'

'Right, well, now you know what the situation is between us. So let's go, Stacy, or he'll wonder what we're doing.'

Stacy closed the door to her flat with a click. Despite what her mother had said, and even though it had made her feel better about things, she was dreading what her father might say to her when they got to the car. She actually felt a little sorry for him. Did he really know what he'd put the family through because of his own lack of empathy? They'd never spoken to each other except for his instructions to them as children. They'd never asked opinions of each other, never discussed their likes or dislikes or garnered any views about politics or anything at all. They were like strangers. Yet where would he be if her mother left him? How would her father cope with that?

As they approached her father's old Toyota, Stacy could see

he wore a frown. She couldn't remember ever seeing him with relaxed features. No wonder he had hard lines all over his face, although some of those lines were from squinting in the sun when he'd forgotten to wear his hat, whilst working in the fields.

'What took you so long?' he grumbled.

'I forgot to pick this up,' Stacy said, thinking on the spot and then holding up the bottle of red wine she'd got for Peter. 'So we had to go back.'

Her father grunted but seemed to accept her excuse.

Stacy didn't feel compelled to make small talk whilst they drove along because her mother took care of that. Plus she'd chosen to sit behind her father so she wouldn't have to make eye contact with him in the mirror. The car's interior smelled musty and the seats were worn at the edges. Everything about her parents was worn and tired, Stacy realised.

But she was so relieved it was Peter who opened the door to them when they arrived at his flat. He must've seen the look of relief on her face, as he hugged her because he whispered, 'Don't worry about it all, sis. We've got this,' before turning to their parents. 'Hi, Mum, Dad.'

'Wow, it's beautiful, Peter!' Stacy said breathlessly, as she walked down the wide hall to the lounge.

Their flat looked like something straight from the pages of a slick home magazine. The kitchen, lounge and dining room were open plan, opening onto a balcony with distant views of the sea. The walls were a soft aquamarine; the kitchen units and the two large sofas were cream. There was a turquoise throw over one of the sofas and maple-veneered floorboards. Shelving incorporating a desk area and huge TV was along one wall; a colourful Turkish rug graced the floor.

'Good grief,' Stacy's mother gasped. 'It's amazing. I love it. Oh I'd love something like this when we move.'

'You're moving then?' said Peter, surprised.

'Hope to, love. Time for a change. Time to move on.'

Their father had shaken hands with Peter at the door because his wife had nudged him in encouragement. He'd walked slowly into the property, looking around himself, nervously. Stacy knew he was half looking around in case Marvin jumped out at him, larger than life.

'Um, Marvin will be here soon. He's just been to see his mum,' Peter almost whispered. 'Go have a look around. There's two large bedrooms and two bathrooms, similar sort of décor. Marvin's the interior designer. It's his trade you see. I'm the computer buff.'

'Well, I can see he's very artistic,' said their mother, walking around in wonder. Their father cautiously sat down on one of the sofas. He looked out of place in his tweed suit. Peter went to sit next to him.

'Hi, Dad. Pleased you came. Um, I know this is hard for you. But I just wanted to say that this is the way it is, you see. We've, um, we've had various reactions over the years. So it's been hard for me and Marvin, too. But we're all trying today and I know this is going to be uncomfortable for you.

259

But I must say I'm pleased you made the effort. So thanks for that, Dad.'

Jerry said nothing. He just sat with his hands in his lap, looking at the floor. Peter had said his piece. There was nothing else he could do. But just at that moment, the front door swung open and Marvin waltzed in with a bag of groceries, followed by a small plump woman in a fitted black dress, short dark hair, hooped gold earrings, a broad smile and a twinkle in her eye.

'Hello, hello!' she sang. 'I'm Marvin's mum and I thought it was high time we all met, being as we're all going to be related by marriage soon, eh? Ha, ha!'

She took the groceries off Marvin and shooed him out of the kitchen area.

'Told them I'd do the cooking. Well, they can probably cook but they prefer to go out or get takeaways. Not the way I'd conduct myself. High calories don't suit my waistline, as you can see! Right, so is anyone going to introduce me? My name's Bella. Oh and I can see you're Jerry! Well, Jezza, you're going to have to loosen up and start accepting what's happening here. These two boys love each other and they're getting married, whether you like it or not. It was a shock to me at first but what can you do? It's the way of the world, old man. You gotta take it with a pinch of salt. Drinks anyone?'

Well, Jerry's face was a picture!

His jaw fell to the floor; his cheeks flared red. Stacy's hand shot to her mouth. *Was he going to explode?* Her mother seemed to be trying her hardest not to burst out laughing at the breath of fresh air who was this astonishing, wonderful woman in front of them.

And then Stacy knew, in an instant, that Marvin's mum was going to be the best thing about Sunday lunch that day!

Chapter 27

'Bye, Marjorie. I should be back in a couple of hours. Yes, I'm going to have a look at that cute flat I told you about with the two bedrooms. It's a couple of roads over from the community centre. Close to Mum and Philippa. Close to you and Stacy. Crikey, we really *will* all be neighbours! Too close for comfort did you say? Ha, ha. See you later.'

It had been really nice having Dora stay these last few weeks. She was very easy to get on with and cleaned up after herself, as well as helping with anything else that needed doing around the flat. She'd cooked on a couple of occasions too. Marjorie had sampled chicken teriyaki as well as Indian potato curry, perfectly warming for the frosty month of November. Dora's friend Jodie had been around for a meal with them and then they'd gone to the pub, afterwards, for a glass or three. Jodie was a right laugh. She'd been married a couple of times and had a son who lived and worked as a teacher in Australia.

'Yes, I flit between the two countries, each year. Wish he'd get his ass back to Britain and get settled down to be near his old mum, though. But kids, huh? They do what they do. Dora says she'll come over with me next year and we're going to play tourists. That'll be much better for me than hanging around his place awaiting his return from work each day!'

'I know that feeling,' said Marjorie. 'My daughter's a teacher, too. But she's met a lovely chap – in fact they've just gotten engaged! – and they've moved away. It was hard for me to settle without her at first. But Dora's helping me get over that. Oh that reminds me, I haven't rung my daughter for a couple of weeks! That's a new record for me.'

It was true. Dora had helped her a lot. She even showed her how to change a light bulb. And whilst that might seem a silly and easy thing to do, to some people, Marjorie had never changed one before – she didn't even know there were differences between the bulbs or the stems and whether they were dimmable or not. Then, between them, they mastered the central heating system instructions as well as the hot water tank. In fact, Marjorie hadn't rung Gracie for any reason whilst Dora had been staying with her.

And then, just as Dora left the flat, as if on cue, the phone rang. It was Gracie.

'Hi, Mum. It's me. Haven't heard from you in a while, so I'm just ringing to check everything's okay. Dora still there?'

Marjorie chuckled to herself. Yes, it somehow felt good to be self-sufficient again. And if Dora took the flat nearby she wouldn't feel lost and lonely any more. Oh, it was nice that Stacy wasn't far away either but youngsters didn't have the same aches and pains and anxieties as she and Dora and their friends. It was different. Yet Marjorie had even come to realise it *was* possible to maintain a friendship with someone young enough to be her granddaughter.

'Oh, Gracie, everything is wonderful, darling. But, you know, if I hadn't met all the lovely people at the Borough Community Centre I doubt if I would think everything was fine at all. Now that's a sobering thought, isn't it. And yes Dora is still here and I'm pleased she is. We're getting on like a house on fire, which has been great for me and I've even been out and about with her and her friend Jodie. I'm starting to come into my own, darling, and not before time either, I might add. How are you and Steven? Set a date yet?'

'Yes. Ish. Well, I'd like a spring or a summer wedding. So we're just looking into all that. Think Steven would like us to get married somewhere exotic like Mauritius. Not by ourselves. Just immediate family. How would you feel about that?'

'Oh, darling, that would be lovely. I've not been away in years. Good grief, I'll need to renew my passport, though. I've hardly ever used it. I used it once when Oliver and I went to Italy before all his nonsense and then, again, when we won that trip to Paris.'

'Right, well you'd better look into updating it then. And I've told Harry about us all. I bumped into him in Waitrose. He's starting to put on weight and his hair's going grey. But he had yet another young thing clinging to his arm. He'll never learn, Mother. What a shame, really. But I'm totally happy with Steven, so that's that.'

'Okay then, Gracie. Look I must go. My mobile's ringing!'

'Okay then. Bye, Mum.'

'Bye, darling!'

Marjorie tapped the green phone button.

'Hello Marjorie Sykes here?'

'Hello, Marjorie. It's Raymond here. I'm just ringing to see how you're doing now? I haven't done much with the community centre recently because I've been doing a bit of DIY outside with my Simon. We've had those three steps removed and replaced with decking. So it's only one step down into the garden now. Much easier for me. Oh and I bumped into Dora the other day and we had a natter. So how are you getting on living together?'

'Well, it's been just delightful really, Raymond. I do enjoy having the company, even though it's only a temporary arrangement until she finds her own place.'

'I'm very pleased for you both. And she seems a lot brighter too. Right, well the other reason I'm ringing is to ask if you'd like to go out for a little meal with me? Oh and I don't mean as a date, before you start panicking. I mean a friendship thing where two friends simply go out with each other. There's a wonderful little pub near where I live and I could pick you up and drop you back afterwards. Would you like to think about it and give me a ring back? I'm free every night apart from Fridays, once a month, when I babysit for the grand-children.'

Good grief! Marjorie could not believe it. Nobody had asked her out in a very long time. But Raymond had stressed it wasn't a date. It was just two friends meeting up for food and a chat. A bit of company. She thought back to how angry Oliver got when she even glanced at another man. She'd rarely lifted her head up to appraise anything or anybody when he was around.

She even felt a little embarrassed at being asked. What if they didn't get on for some reason? How embarrassing would that be when they bumped into each other at any of the activities laid on by Eileen? But no, she mustn't think like that. How often had Gracie told her to rejoice in the fact that men did approach her from time to time and show some interest, even if it was only a smile.

But Marjorie knew she was a different person now to who she'd been with Oliver. She was even a different person to who she'd been when she was living with Gracie, a matter of months ago. The community centre friends she'd made and subsequent outings and parties had changed her. And, together with Dr Baxley's encouragement, she felt a lot more confident than she'd ever been in her whole life before. Why only yesterday Dora had dubbed her gregarious!

So, yes! Dinner between friends sounded absolutely wonderful.

'Are you still there, Marjorie?'

'I certainly am, Raymond. Thank you for asking. I'd love to go for dinner with you. Any night would be perfectly fine. Just tell me when you'd like us to go.'

Despite the wonder of supermarkets, Stacy still needed to buy bulky or heavy items like toilet rolls or cartons of milk from the corner shop because struggling on and off the buses with them and then having to carry them home was too problematic. She'd tried it at first because she had a proper shopping bag, albeit rather old. But a week ago it had split as she was getting off the bus; tins of tomatoes and beans plopping onto the pavement, rolling under the bus and then she had to shout for the bus driver to stay put until, red-faced, she emerged from the task of retrieving everything. Never again! It wouldn't have been a problem if she'd had a partner in her life, she'd suddenly thought; someone to shoulder the heavier loads like these. It was the first time she'd thought like that, about actually wanting to have someone in her life. There hadn't been anyone since Mike.

She'd seen him once, a couple of years ago. He was busking rather badly on a street corner in the middle of town. His hair was long, lank, unwashed. She'd stood near some onlookers listening to him for a while. His guitar needed tuning and there weren't many coins in his cap. Thinking back, she remembered the first time he'd touched her. She'd been mesmerised, smitten. Yet he'd looked old and dishevelled when she saw him again; his sexy swagger had left him. The people drifted away. His eyes rested on hers temporarily and then he'd looked away. He hadn't seemed to recognise her. Or maybe she'd never meant anything to him.

Stacy wondered if she had another cold coming on. She felt chilled to the bone, even though the shorter days of November tended to be chilly and damp. She'd put her gilet on and wrapped a huge scarf around her neck for the short hop to the corner shop during her lunch hour that day. Luckily it was only a ten-minute walk away, less if she jogged, which she'd taken to doing now it was colder. So she'd have just enough time to make the private phone call she needed to make today and sort a few other things out. She did need to buy milk first, though. She said 'Hi' to the girl behind the counter. It was the same girl who'd been there since Stacy moved into her flat but they'd never shared more than a hello or 'that'll be such-and-such a price'.

Searching the shelving for anything else that might take her fancy whilst she was there, Stacy spotted the old lady with the cricked neck. Mrs Michaels. The way she moved, with slow concentrated progress, the wire basket cocked on her arm, and the laboured way she had to angle her head to look at goods on the higher shelves, made Stacy feel sorry for her.

'Hi there. Do you need any help?' Stacy asked the old lady, kindly.

Mrs Michaels smiled wearily. 'Oh, hello, Stacy. No, I've got what I came in for. I'm just looking to see if there's anything else I fancy.'

Stacy smiled. 'Yes, I do that, sometimes.'

'You'll be pleased to hear, I'll have all the help I can get now. They're taking me away soon.'

'Taking you away? Whatever do you mean?' said Stacy, alarmed.

'Oh, I've got a place in a nursing home, so it'll be a lot easier for me now. My daughter has finally managed to sort it all out for me. So I've just come in to get a few last bits for me and my Tibs and then they're going to be clearing everything away, selling some of it, I should think. So I've got a few days left and then I'll be leaving.'

'Oh,' said Stacy, wondering what would happen to herself when she reached old age, with no family looking out for her.

'You don't know anyone who'd take my cat do you? He's a sweet little thing. He's no bother. He's an indoor cat. Didn't you say you've got some cats?'

Stacy's heart missed a beat. Taking people's unwanted cats in had got Stacy into the mess she'd found herself in before. She did miss having a little fluffy face or two greeting her when she got home from work, but she wasn't going to start all that again. No way. Life was much better now she didn't have to be at the beck and call of all her animals. She'd actually started enjoying the ordinary bits of life that seemed to come naturally to everyone else: shopping, watching TV, going for walks. She felt so free; she was even enjoying working in the library again and bringing home books to read, something she'd not had time to do in a long time. It's how she wanted to continue living her life. She smiled at Mrs Michaels.

'I used to have cats but they all got too much for me. I had eight of them.'

'Oh, well that's rather a lot to handle. That's too many.'

'Yes, it was crazy really. Anyway, I'm sure your daughter will find somewhere for your cat. It's been nice bumping into you here in the shop from time to time. And I hope you have a really nice time in the nursing home. I'm sure there'll be lots of nice new people to meet in there. Take care. Bye for now.'

'Bye then, love.'

Stacy picked up two one-litre cartons of milk and made her way to the checkout.

Walking back to the flat she was wondering what she should do about Christmas lunch. Should she invite her parents to hers? She might. She smiled to herself as she recalled Peter and Marvin's Sunday lunch, after Bella breezed in. That woman, Stacy had known, was not going to take any crap from anybody. Bella had busied herself carving the roast pork after her initial outburst and Stacy's father had just sat there, looking as if he was about to say something but no words passed his lips. Now, whether that had been her own mother's influence or whether he'd realised Bella would eat *him* for lunch, if he spoke out of turn, Stacy was not sure. But he'd been surprisingly civil throughout their meal – even managing to answer questions put to him by Marvin – shock, horror!

At the end of the meal he'd even shaken Marvin's hand and said, 'Bye then, son.'

Halleluiah. Job done!

Peter and Marvin had rung her later that night, immensely thrilled it had gone so well. She didn't tell them that when her parents had dropped her back at her flat, she'd got out of the car and gone round to her father's window and indicated that she wanted him to wind it down.

'Just wanted to say, Dad, that I have been frightened of you most of my life and I hated you when I was little because I don't feel you treated either me or Peter right. But you stepped up when I had my fall, sorting my flat out, and you also stepped up today and did something that I will forever be proud of you for. We had a great time at Peter and Marvin's today and that was because of you.'

Then she had leaned in and kissed her father's head. As she pulled back she saw that there were tears in his eyes. But he still said nothing. Maybe he didn't know what to say.

At the foot of the steps to her flat Stacy changed her mind. She popped the milk on the bottom step, tore her scarf off and went racing back to the shop. She could see the old lady ambling back home, clutching the small number of items in her plastic carrier bag, as usual.

'Mrs Michaels? Hello, Mrs Michaels? It's okay – I'll take your cat!'

Chapter 28

Stacy felt so much better. It was only one cat after all. She vowed to herself that she definitely would *not* get any others. But she did miss having some company after her others were taken away. Plus she was helping Mrs Michaels who would have worried about where her cat was going, just as Stacy had worried about her own. No, she was doing a good thing. It would be a new start for both Tibs and herself. There, she hadn't needed a partner at all; she'd just needed another furry little body to cuddle from time to time. And, best of all, she knew she could still have a life with Tibs. Yay! It was a win-win.

She got back to her flat with her milk and had just stepped through the door, when she was tapped on her shoulder. She nearly dropped the milk in fright.

'Bloody hell, John. Will you stop creeping around? Gave me the fright of my life it did. What do you want now?'

She was so angry her face felt hot. She took after her father in that respect.

John just stood there with his ruff of hair, baggy jogging bottoms and an unpleasant body odour wafting around him.

He frowned and then thrust a bunch of letters into her hand and turned to go.

'Delivered to me by mistake in case you're wondering,' he snapped, going into his flat and slamming the door.

Damn! Stacy thought. *Maybe I was a bit harsh.*

She closed the door and had just put the milk away and removed her gilet when her doorbell rang.

She glanced at the clock. She had to be back at work in approximately two minutes. Should she answer it? What if it was Marjorie needing assistance with something?

She opened her door and there stood John, his hands on his hips.

'Just for the record, what is your problem, Stacy? You're so rude, sometimes. And I do not deserve that. I have gone out of my way to be respectful and help you whenever I can and all I get is you bad-mouthing me or screwing your nose up at me, in disdain. What's wrong? Do I smell bad or something?'

'Well, yes, since you mention it, you do. You're always lolling around in dirty, smelly clothes. Have you no self-respect? Don't you possess a shower or bath, huh? Do you even work? Now, I don't have time for all this. I'm late for work as it is. Oh and by the way, since we're getting everything off our chests, I just want to let you know that I'm getting another cat. Yes, a *cat*. Something else I'm sure you'll enjoy moaning about. So if you don't mind—'

She'd wanted to slam the door in his face but let the door close itself, instead.

What was it about her next-door neighbour that really annoyed her? She couldn't quite put a finger on it. He *had* been kind to her when she was ill ... but he'd also dropped her in it, telling her parents about her cats. Yes, she'd certainly been miffed about that. But the fact he rarely seemed to wash irked her too.

It had been respect all the way for Marjorie.

Raymond had picked her up in his car, coming around to the passenger side and opening the door for her to get in. She beamed. He was the perfect gentleman. He'd also done the honours, once they'd parked at the pub, by holding the heavy pub doors open for her as they entered the building and found a table.

'Booking's under the name of Raymond Nichols.'

'Yes, sir. That'll be table twenty-six, over there.'

Clinking glasses sparkled in the subdued lighting of the bar; a log fire crackled and roared in the huge grate. People smiled, lulled or numbed by alcohol, by the ambience and just by being with people they cared about. Marjorie felt cosy and cared for. It was something new for her. Raymond certainly was a true gent.

'I do like your outfit. Is it new?'

Marjorie glanced down at her burgundy and pink print dress with three-quarter-length sleeves, and black belt, the skirt just below her knees. It made her feel very feminine along with her new patent black shoes with kitten heels. She'd deemed it perfect for any social outings, especially since the year had just ticked over into December.

'It is actually. I haven't treated myself to anything new in years. I used to shop with Gracie. This is the first time I picked something out by myself.'

'Well that colour certainly suits you,' Raymond said smiling.

They both chose the Hearty Chicken and Bacon Stew with root vegetables. It had a perfectly wintry-sounding name. They followed it with Amaretto coupe, which was a rum-flavoured mousse with Amaretto biscuits, chocolate sprinkles and cream. They took their coffee by the fireside. There was no need for an outpouring of chat as they knew quite a lot about each other already. And it was just perfectly pleasant sitting side by side in the glow of the fire, as their evening ebbed away.

'Do you know, I can't believe how my life has changed since meeting everyone at the Afternoon Tea Club. It's been a real winner in my book,' said Raymond.

'Well, I certainly agree with you there, Raymond. You and Dora have helped me no end. I'm a lot happier and far more confident than I used to be,' said Marjorie, sipping her coffee. 'Oh, and one other bit of news – well, no, two bits actually. Dora is buying the flat she went to see and is probably moving in just after Christmas. She says we'll all be invited to her own house-warming party. And she's got her fiftieth birthday coming up a week on Wednesday. She's having that at the community centre and we're all invited, along with her family and friends and apparently everybody else as well!'

'Everybody else?'

'Well yes. She's inviting all the other people who want to come from the Afternoon Tea Club, apparently, because she says without the Afternoon Tea Club her life would have been very different. And she's going to put on a buffet so there's something for everyone and they can help themselves. So that's two engagements we've got around Christmas; isn't that nice?'

Stacy left work early so she could collect Tibs from Mrs Michaels.

'Or we could leave it until the weekend if you like?' Stacy had suggested, earlier in the shop.

'No, love. I have to get used to living without him so it would be much better for me to prepare for that now. So can you come and get him later?'

'Of course. Look, it's a real shame we didn't do all this sooner but would you like to come back to my place, so you can see where he'll be living and we can have a spot of tea together?'

Mrs Michaels had grinned a crooked toothy grin.

'Oh yes, I'd like that, deary. I never go out anywhere!'

The old lady said her daughter didn't visit very often being as she was a solicitor in London and extremely busy. Mrs Michaels' flat was handily a few houses or so along from the corner shop. She lived in a small converted one-bedroom flat on the first floor of a house. There was no lift. Stacy supposed it was the best thing for Mrs Michaels that her daughter was taking her to a nursing home. At least there'd be no chance of her falling down any stairs and not eating properly now.

After they'd brought Tibs back to her place, Stacy made a cheese omelette with avocado salad for their tea. She'd googled 'healthy meals for the elderly' and decided that was her best and easiest option. Fortunately, Mrs Michaels said she wasn't allergic to any of the ingredients and tucked into the food with relish. She patted her stomach afterwards.

'That was the best meal I've had in a long time, deary. Thank you so much for that, Stacy. And what do we think of this place, eh Tibs? It's really nice isn't it? Look at you climbing all over the furniture and sniffing under things. I hope you don't mind all that, love. You might have to get him a clawing post though.'

'Oh that's perfectly okay, Mrs Michaels. I'm used to that kind of thing. He can do whatever he wants and he can sleep wherever he wants, too. He's here to make himself at home. Oh, look, he's curling around my legs. Ah, I think he's made himself at home, already, don't you? That must put your mind at rest.'

'Oh, it does, love. It does. Um, could I use your loo before you walk me back?'

'Of course. The bathroom's next to the kitchen.'

The doorbell rang just as Mrs Michaels was locking the bathroom door. Stacy snatched it open and there stood John –

or was it John? Stacy didn't recognise him. The smart man in front of her was wearing a tuxedo, his hair had been cut and the delightful odour she could smell on him was clearly aftershave of some sort.

'Just to prove to you that I do scrub up sometimes. And I wanted to tell you a bit more about me—'

'Crikey, John – look, I really don't have time for this. I've got a guest—'

'You've certainly got attitude. That's one big problem you've definitely got.'

He pushed his way into her hall, as she stepped back in shock and he closed the door behind himself.

'So the reason I smell sweaty in the mornings is because I work out and then I go have my shower. I'm into keeping fit. I need to be fit for my job. And the last few times you've seen me in my scruffs is because I'm helping my mate Terry, who lives at the bottom of our corridor, to move out. He's moving in with his girlfriend and I've been helping him move his stuff. I've taken holiday leave to do that for him, I might add. Because I do nice things for people. Oh and did I mention I'm a policeman? That's one of the reasons I need to work out most days. So I can chase criminals! And the fact I moaned about your bloody cats is because sound travels in these flats and I could hear every word you yelled at them and every meow and howl they made. And I'm not putting up with any more of that kind of crap, let me tell you, when I'm working shifts. So as long as your new cat doesn't make any annoying sounds we just might be able to get along a wee bit better – oh!'

John looked down. Tibs was winding himself around John's legs. Stacy heard the toilet flush and moments later Mrs Michaels appeared.

'Oh, hello, love. Are you going to introduce us, deary? Oh, look, Mr Tibs loves you too. This your boyfriend, Stacy? Don't mind me. Nothing like a bit of healthy arguing, is there? It's the making-up part I used to like best. Hope you're coming with us for my walk home. It's a nice brisk night out tonight.'

Chapter 29

It was late. They'd just finished an impromptu game of Scrabble and had cheated like mad! Now they were drinking hot chocolate, with a tot of brandy in it, like Dora used to have when she lived in Spain. They sat in their dressing gowns, sitting either end of the settee, Dora with her legs curled up, Marjorie with her legs crossed. Dora was smirking.

'So come on, Marjorie. Out with it! Did you sleep with Raymond?'

'No, I bloody well did not,' puffed Marjorie. 'That's not what Raymond and I are about. The date, if you can call it that, was actually very nice. It felt ordinary or perhaps that's not the right word. Raymond is easy to talk to, as you know. So it just felt like a natural, comfortable progression of our friendship. We've already decided to go on the London trip but – oh stop, Dora! I can see your face. We *will* be sleeping in separate rooms. I don't actually see us as girlfriend and boyfriend. But it's just so wonderful to be taken out by someone again. Courting we used to call it. But I don't think it's even that. Anyway, never mind about me. Now, what about your flat?'

'Oh, it's just perfect for me, Marjorie. And it's just big enough to have the occasional party and I fancy doing that. Two good-sized bedrooms. An eat-in or party kitchen, so that's good. And a parking space. I don't have my own car yet but Mum says she might give me hers.' Dora grinned.

Marjorie had noticed how much more relaxed Dora was now since she was starting to sort her life out. Her face was almost Botox free and she swore she wasn't going to be doing that any more. Her mother and Philippa would be coming to her fiftieth birthday at the community centre and Dora was going to try and introduce them to as many people as possible.

'They'll never remember all our names!' Marjorie laughed.

'Probably not but they'll get to see that I have done something about making new friends. It'll make my mother happier knowing that. Plus she said she'd wanted to see what our get-togethers were all about. Philippa says she wouldn't mind joining the club and even wants to have a go at the computer course, so there you go. I've spoken to Eileen about my birthday and she was saying they were going to do a Christmas bash for the Afternoon Tea Club but since the community centre is fully booked in the immediate run-up to Christmas, she asked if I'd be okay if they held the meeting before my party. Then, afterwards, we would carry on with my festivities. She said, if I agreed to that, they could pay half of the meal costs. I thought that was quite good of her. But what do you think? Do you think it'd work out?'

Marjorie shrugged. 'As long as you don't mind, I don't see

that it matters. You're holding your birthday bash with people we've mainly met because of Eileen and her mum, anyway. So in a way you're sort of indebted to them. And if you hadn't met the people from the Afternoon Tea Club, you probably wouldn't be having the same kind of birthday party.'

'Yes, you're completely right. That Afternoon Tea Club has been the making of me, I have to say. I was still drifting along, wondering what to do about things, without it, and now I've got everything because of it, including all my new and wonderful friends. Without all of you it'd just be me, Philippa, Mum and Jodie! Very bland, apart from Jodie. So I'll tell her I'm okay with it then. She said they wouldn't be taking up much of our time.'

'Right, well, being as we're on the subject of birthdays, my fiftieth birthday present to you is—'

'Oh God, Marjorie, I don't have any need for gifts at my age. I've got everything I need or want but I'd really like it if you could help me out by just coming furniture shopping with me, at some point, for my new little pad, as this will be my first time, ever, shopping for furnishings. Could you do that?'

'Well, that's a given, Dora. But I *do* want to give you something for your fiftieth. And I hope you don't think I'm being outspoken here—'

'As if, Marjorie!'

'But I'd like to pay for us both to go to one of those health spas for the day, finishing off with you getting your hair cut shorter with a few highlights at a hairdressing salon. Now that alone will knock at least a decade off you. A chin-length bob would look fantastic on you and be so much easier to manage rather than styling it into a bun every day. What do you think?'

Dora screwed up her face. 'Well, I will admit something to you, dear friend. I was pissed when you told me about my pink lippy months ago and yet I never wear it now, you know. You were right, back then – it did make my problem with the Botox stand out. I looked proper dreadful. And, you know what? Yeah! I'd really love going to a spa with you. I used to do that a lot when I was younger. And that's another thing I haven't done in years. So, yes. Love to. Plus I've already been wondering what to do with my hair and I like the sound of a bob. Nice and simple. Mum's paying to have my teeth whitened. So I should look pretty amazing with all of that. So thank you, Marjorie! Thanks heaps!'

With tears in her eyes, Dora got up, put her mug down and threw her arms around Marjorie.

'In fact, thanks for *everything* you've done for me. You're a real friend.'

Simon turned the TV off. It was that time of night. Raymond had nearly fallen asleep in the armchair, after his brandy. They'd been chatting about the grandchildren and the mischief they, laughingly, got up to.

'Dianne would have loved all this.' Raymond had grinned,

looking at the latest videos of his family's exploits on the iPad. It didn't matter what they did or where they went, it was the amount of giggling he was happiest to see. Simon often brought his father back to his place for a meal and sometimes a sleepover and they spent a lot of time reminiscing.

'So how's that girl you're seeing?' Raymond asked.

'Ah. Bit like those dates you had recently. Didn't work out, Dad. Some you win, some you lose, eh? Can't get all het up about it, though. Have to move on to the next one, don't I?'

'Take your time, son. There's no rush. You've got all the family you'll ever need. It's just that I think we all need a bit of companionship towards the end of our lives, don't we. The Afternoon Tea Club helps with that. It's why I like going. You meet all sorts of people there. I'd love you to come along with me, one time, and meet some of my friends. Or I might throw a little party myself, one day, like Marjorie did, and introduce everyone to the family. They're kind people. You'd like them.'

'Sounds good, Dad. And if you fancy having a party I'll rope everyone in to help. Be quite enjoyable, I would think. So how was *your* latest date, then?' asked Simon.

'Well, it wasn't a date as such, son. It was more the meeting of two similar minds for a very enjoyable evening out. No one can replace your mother and I wouldn't want them to. But Marjorie's had her share of problems too. So it was really nice spending some time with her. At least she didn't go to the ladies and then disappear on me!'

'Sorry, dad. Coralia did apologise to me about that but she

explained it away by saying it wasn't a match made in heaven. It's a bit awkward being as I still have to work with her. But what's done is done, I guess.'

'It is, son. I'm fully over it, anyway. And Marjorie is really nice. She's the perfect person for me to see from time to time, so I hope you're okay about that.'

'Yeah, I am, Dad. Whatever makes you happy; just like you say to me. Plus you can love your friends, I guess, without it being a passionate affair and, yes, I'd like to meet all your friends, one day.'

'Hi, Mum. Everything okay? Yes? Good. Well you must be having a good time, judging by the fact I never hear from you any more?' said Gracie, with a hint of sarcasm in her voice.

'Oh, very funny. But we both know I had to get on living by myself again. Well, actually, it's more a case that I've *started* living again, thanks to the Afternoon Tea Club. I've got a fantastic new group of friends. We've been out and about all over the place together. And because of the art class I've recently drawn a picture of the bird table and got it framed and it now hangs over the mantelpiece in the lounge. My tutor said it was excellent, as you'll see next time you're over. And I've even been out on a date night!'

'My God, you've *what*?' said Gracie, incredulous.

'Yes, one of the gents took me out for a lovely pub meal recently. But we're not dating, per se, sweetheart, so don't worry. Anyway, love, are you ringing about Christmas?'

Gracie took a deep breath. 'Yes and no. Well, actually, yes I am. We'd like you to come stay with us for Christmas this year but we might be trotting over to see Steven's folks in New Zealand the following year. Is that all right with you, Mother?'

'Of course it is, Gracie. I really don't mind sharing you, now. I'm getting used to it. I wasn't happy about it at first, of course. This whole experience has taken me completely out of my comfort zone. But it's been such a grand, enlightening time for me. So whether I'm on my own or whether I can muster some of the troops for next year we'll both have grand Christmases whatever we choose to do, Gracie.'

'Okay then. Well, that's set my mind at rest. I was a little worried, you see.'

'Darling, we both know that sometimes our paths will cross, now you're going to be marrying Steven, and sometimes they won't. I've been so lucky to have you in my life on a daily basis. Lots of parents never get the chance to hold on to their children for so long. I love you no matter where you are in the world. That bond between us will never be broken, wherever we live or whenever we die. Please be reassured about that. And never feel guilty about taking your chances in life or snatching up your dreams whilst you still can. I only want you to be happy. And I'm starting to feel very happy with my own new life, too.'

'Okay, Mum. I'm so pleased for you. Well, actually, I'm relieved you feel like that about things because I was really worried you wouldn't be able to cope without me. However,

I can see you're managing to cope just fine and you've got some wonderful friends, so that makes me feel much less guilty about having left you,' Gracie said quietly.

'Darling, I think we both felt guilty about things. I even felt guilty for imposing on you for so long. But I couldn't help that I loved living with you. I think, as women, we always feel guilty about *something*, don't we, sweetheart? Anyway, let's forget about all that. At least we've both found some happiness again. And that's the main thing!'

'Oh absolutely, Mother. So there's just one other thing I, um, was going to tell you later. But I'm so thrilled about it, I'm telling you now. Oh, Mum!'

'Oh, Gracie! You're not ...?'

'Yes, Mother! I'm two months pregnant!'

Stacy and John walked back from taking Mrs Michaels home. Stacy hadn't put Mrs Michaels right one way or the other about the non-existent relationship between her and John. The old lady was on a roll, yakking on about what a handsome couple they made and not to leave getting married too late because they'd want to have babies, of course. John hadn't dissuaded her, either, because what, at the end of the day, did it matter what Mrs Michaels thought? Let her have her fantasies if she wanted, thought Stacy. She was leaving the area in a few days' time.

A nippy wind had risen and Stacy was walking fast, with her arms folded, trying to stave off the chill that was penetrating her flimsy jacket. John had offered to give her his tux jacket but she had scowled and told him not to be so silly.

What a pair we must look, Stacy thought, as she walked by John's side. *He looks quite out of place here. Just like he couldn't find his way to some party.*

I can't wait to get this ridiculous outfit off, John thought. *But at least the mare at the side of me knows what's what now.*

Stacy virtually ran up the stairs, preferring not to take the lift, even though it was working again, as were the corridor lights. The last thing she wanted was to be stuck in that lift in such close proximity to John. No thank you! She just wanted to find Tibs and get acquainted with her new companion. But John grabbed hold of Stacy's arm before she could thrust her key into the lock. He was a little of out breath. Walking fast was a different exercise to lifting weights.

'Just a minute, Stacy. Are you really going to cold-shoulder me for the rest of your life? Is that how you think neighbours should act? And what about next time you get locked out of your flat or the boiler bursts or something?'

Stacy tried to shake him off. But maybe what he was saying made sense. Did her life really have to be one long battle with everything and everyone? She let out a long sigh, as she unlocked her door. Then she turned to face him.

'Look, John, I'm sorry okay? I've had a rough ride lately. You were right in the hospital when you noticed my family's, um, shall we say quirks? They were controlling and unloving beyond what is normal, all my life. Every birthday was just an ordinary day with only the four of us. No friends allowed. No parties. We were never allowed to go to school friends' birthdays either. It was like they were shutting us off from the outside world; alienating us from society. My childhood? Well, it was crap! We've recently found out my brother's gay. Not that it's a problem with me but it nearly caused my parents to split up, due to my father's ignorance. However, that just might have been smoothed over now. And the cats? Well, they were my bad, sure. Yet even that's been rectified now, um, thanks to you. But my first and only boyfriend thought he could share me with his mates. So you see I've not had good experiences with men. Any men. No one has ever loved me. That's why I guess I kept the cats. But in the end even they let me down – partly my fault, I know. This little one, though,' Stacy said pointing down, as Tibs's head appeared round the door of her flat with a meow, 'this little one seems a cut above. He seems to like me. He likes you too. So that's not such a bad thing. They say animals know the merit of man, so I guess that makes you an okay sort of guy.'

Stacy bent down and picked Tibs up. He meowed softly again.

'Ah, sweetheart. Are you missing your mum?'

Tibs sniffed Stacy's nose and then licked it. It tickled. She laughed briefly, glancing up at John. He was watching her in a way she couldn't work out. But he had the most beautiful green eyes.

'So, okay, I know I've been standoffish and horrid when you've been so nice to me. And I do appreciate what you've done for me. But, well, I just didn't know how to act with you. No one's been as kind as you have in a long time.'

Stacy sighed, cuddling Tibs and avoiding John's gaze, not sure if she was making any sense to him. But it suddenly dawned on her that she would like some human company after all. Perhaps it's what she had really needed all along.

'So, anyway, I was wondering, um,' Stacy began, not sure how to put what she knew she needed to say. 'Um, would you like to come in and have a drink with me, by way of an apology? I mean I know that might seem a bit forward but I think it might be advisable to get to know you a bit more. Just in case I get locked out of my flat, again, you understand?'

'Hmmm,' John said wryly. 'I thought there might be an ulterior motive for the drink. Well, I'll come in and help you sort Tibs out, if you wish. Get him settled and then I guess we could take things from there.'

'Things, John?'

'Our friendship, Stacy.'

Chapter 30

Marjorie's jaw dropped open as she and Dora approached the resplendent waterfront spa for their 'Relaxing, Rejuvenating, Head-to-Toe Pampering Day' as advertised by the spa's glitzy website. And from the moment they snuggled into their fluffy white robes and slippers amongst the restful Scandi-designed interior, they knew their day was going to be luxuriant like no other. The spa's attention to detail was clearly devised to both relax as well as astound its visitors. Sparkling bluish mosaics made the swimming pool feel exotic; dreamily fragranced creams, lotions and potions encouraged confidence in their anti-ageing claims; the massages and facials pumped and primed and freed the spirits of their clients; the delicious, immaculately cut and prepared sandwiches with bite-sized cakes on the afternoon tea menu with tea in squeaky clean white tea pots and cups was a pure delight.

'I'd forgotten how invigorating these places can be,' Dora said, breathily, as they lounged in the café area afterwards. She could see how her facial had ironed out some of her creases, temporarily, and her face still glowed from the experience.

'Well I have to say *this* afternoon tea is a zillion times better than the one at our community centre. But the community atmosphere is much better over there. So, have you enjoyed the first part of my fiftieth birthday gift? The hairdresser is booked for 5.00 p.m. so we mustn't be late.'

Dora's smile reached her eyes, which told Marjorie everything.

It felt good to have given Dora such a boost. Marjorie could see she'd been down in the dumps recently, probably more because of her impending birthday and what it meant for her. She'd also had a lot of changes of late to contend with and even though Marjorie felt they were ultimately happy changes, she realised her friend hadn't been happy about the detective's upsetting news that her daughter didn't want to know her. That must've felt like a stab to the heart, even though Dora had seemed to dismiss the incident. Yet as far as she knew Dora hadn't discussed it with anyone outside of their Afternoon Tea Club circle. Marjorie noticed that Dora kept her deepest feelings close to her chest. She'd even done that, herself, with Oliver. She kept all her thoughts about him locked away in a pretend box in her heart and only took those memories out when she wanted to dissect her feelings or come to terms with what happened. The only person she properly discussed Oliver with was her doctor. So she did understand Dora's reticence.

But then, life was never simple. Marjorie of all people knew that! Nor did you get your just desserts all in one go. Life seemed to deal out both blows and snippets of heaven whenever it saw fit. 'Ours is not to wonder why,' Oliver's mother used to say. Boy oh boy, thought Marjorie, she'd come a long way since those dreadful, debilitating days. Her own life, she was happy to note, was much richer and far more fulfilled now than she ever imagined it could be. And she was happy that she and Raymond could simply be friends when they went out for meals. Love was no longer on the agenda for her and that, to Marjorie, was absolutely fine. She had lots of new and wonderful friends now. Plus, joy of joys, she was soon going to become a *grandmother* – her most treasured dream of all!

At the end of the day Marjorie knew all her own prayers had been answered and she felt blessed.

She took another cake from the top of the cake stand and swallowed it in one go.

'Greedy pig!' Dora grinned.

And then they both fell about laughing their heads off!

Stacy got into the car and slammed the door shut. She stared at the man beside her. She'd felt very nervous about what she was going to do, prior to this moment. But she knew she had to do this. Somebody should have probably done it a long time ago. But that was neither here nor there. At least *she* was doing it now.

'I hope you've got this right because this is a biggy! I want no doubt that you've done your homework. That's what I'm paying you for, after all,' she said.

'Christ, I said it was all kosher, didn't I? Now buckle up.'

Stacy clicked her seat belt in place, praying today was going to work out according to her plan and then hung on to the edge of the seat as the driver squealed his tyres as he turned sharply and they sped off down the road. Stacy had practised over and over what she was going to say but she knew she'd only get one shot at it. It had to be hard, impactful, and leave everyone concerned under no doubt what was going on.

When they arrived at the house, Tony told Stacy to stay in the car while he did a quick recce. Stacy knew a lot hinged on this and began biting her nails again. She'd spoken to John at length about what she was going to do today. He'd warned her off, initially. 'And you can't just barge in. If you're not invited in, you can't go in, Stacy. It's as simple as that.' But he'd told her Tony knew the ins and outs of the law and as long as she followed his advice she would probably be okay, providing things didn't turn nasty. But if things became unpleasant she was to apologise and leave straight away.

'I don't want you doing this if truth be known,' he'd said. 'But I'm starting to understand how you need to do some of the things you need to do.'

She'd smiled at him. 'It'll make you a better copper, understanding crazy people like me.'

He'd given her one of his cosy big hugs then and she'd melted into it. They'd turned a corner in their relationship thanks to darling Tibs. He'd brought them together – reluctant hero and antsy girl. It certainly hadn't seemed like a match made in heaven at first. But something had clicked between them, and to Stacy's utter surprise it was working out.

Tony returned to the car. 'Right. They're all in there. Now, just to let you know, and as far as I know, there's no wife or girlfriend on the scene, in any respect any more, to make matters worse. Apparently he's been single for quite some time. So if you're going to do this, go for it now. They sometimes leave at different times.'

Stacy did feel a bit uneasy at that.

She clambered out of the car and straightened her jacket. She hoped her first words would put the cat amongst the pigeons and create enough of a disturbance to stop them throwing her out straight away. She'd practised what she was going to say and she'd allowed for various questions. But she would soon see how things panned out. At best it might open a line of communication between them all. At worst, well, even if Andy started a slanging match with Dora it had to be better than no response from them at all.

Stacy's mouth felt dry as she knocked on the door. She couldn't believe she was actually going to do this but she was so desperate to help Dora – she couldn't sit quietly and not make an effort, even if she tried and failed. She, of all people, knew that families made mistakes with each other. But she was halfway to putting her own family back together again. Even Peter and Marvin had thanked her for that.

She waited a few seconds, smoothing her jacket again nervously. She could hear them talking, inside the terraced house that belonged to Lauren's grandmother. Tony had already checked out the family's movements, when Dora had employed him, so he knew that Lauren usually went to see her grand-mother with her father on a Sunday afternoon.

Lauren's grandmother, a tall elegant lady with steel-grey curly hair, opened the door.

'Oh hiya. Sorry to bother you. I'm a friend of Lauren's and I've just popped round to see her with some news. May I come in?' Stacy began, confidently.

Lauren's grandmother shrugged and allowed Stacy to step inside. So far, so good.

'Friend of yours, poppet, with some news, she says.'

Lauren was the spit of Dora, Stacy thought, as the girl looked up from where she was sat with her father at a table. It looked as though they were in the midst of a board game. Her long curly hair was naturally blonde and she had a round face with laughing eyes. And Stacy could see why Dora had fallen for Andy's boyish good looks. He still had a full head of hair, also blonde, and was trim and slim. They were a very attractive family.

Right, Stacy. Just go for it.

'Okay, guys, I won't beat around the bush. So, Andy, did you ever tell Lauren why her mother left her? Have you told your own mother the true story?'

BAM! Yep, that hit the spot as the three of them reacted by blinking and staring, beseechingly, at each other.

'*What?*' Andy struggled to say, as he started to get to his feet. 'Who are you?'

His mother started to realise she'd been duped, too. 'You said you were a friend of Lauren's! You said you had news?'

'Well, yes, I think Lauren's old enough to take this news now. She's what? Eighteen or nineteen? That classes her as an adult. So let me tell you what the situation is between your parents, Lauren. Okay, starting from the beginning, your lovely mum belonged to a wealthy family who were engrossed in their hotel empire and couldn't understand why your mum didn't want what they had. After experiencing working in their hotels she decided she didn't want to work for them so she went travelling and then met your dad. Your dad and your mum moved in together, had you, and it was good for a while, she tells me. Dora finally had something that belonged *just to her* and she started to plan for your futures together. But, unfortunately, not long after you were born your mum experienced postnatal depression. Your dad probably couldn't deal with it, which is understandable because it can be very debilitating and stressful. But then your dad decided to have a small dalliance. Like men often do. Isn't that right, Andy?'

Lauren glanced nervously at her father.

'Now look here!' Andy finally snapped, jumping up. 'Whoever the hell you are, it doesn't matter what happened. The point is that Dora left her daughter. Dora *left* us!'

Stacy knew she had to remain calm. '*It doesn't matter what happened?* People don't leave each other for no good reason. Dora loved you, Andy. You let her down. Dora wasn't well and so she left Lauren with you because, at that time, she really couldn't cope with a young child whilst she was trying to get to grips with her illness, as you know, Andy. She even came back to try and work things out with you again on Lauren's third birthday but you'd met someone else by then and Dora didn't want to stress her daughter out further. So she left feeling insecure and let down all over again,' Stacy explained. She could see she still had time to get her final point across before Andy or his mother threw her out.

'But worst of all is that you never let Lauren see the letters did you? You never gave her the chance to get to know that her mum really loved her and only wanted the best for her.'

'L-letters? Did she send me letters, Dad?'

'She sent letters to both your father and your grandmother. And I'm guessing they've never let you see them, have they?'

Stacy allowed her words to settle for an instant. Andy's mum looked dumbstruck and she sat down again.

'So it was you who had the affair, Andy?' she said quietly. 'That's not what you told me.'

Stacy let out a nervous laugh. 'Let me tell you a story about families. Now I have a family, Lauren. Who doesn't? Families come in all shapes, sizes, colours and creeds. My parents let me and my brother down by squashing our spirits. They didn't even give us love. I won't go into all the nonsense about that. But believe me, I've realised there is no perfect family. Families make huge and grave errors with each other. That is how life is, Lauren. It's hard enough trying to make sense of your ruddy family without the extra crap that's piled onto you out there in the big wide world. *But* … Do you know what goes some way to making it all better?' Stacy paused to let her words sink in.

'*Love* is what can help make it better. *Acceptance* is what can help make it better.'

Tears started to prick Stacy's eyes as the depth of her own situation started to hit home. Her family was still so messed up. Things had started to improve but there was some way to go yet. She felt drained. She felt as though she was always trying to put people back together. But where was it getting her? She looked sadly at the small family in front of her.

'Your mum, Lauren. Your wonderful, funny, amazing mother sent you letters to try and explain her actions. She watched you from a distance hoping for a way in, hoping for the opportunity to finally be reacquainted with the daughter she has *never* stopped loving. All I'm asking from you, Lauren, is one thing – give your mum a chance. And to you, Andy, I will say this. All this started with *you* and what *you did*. So *you* really need to be the one to fix this.'

Was Stacy imagining things or was Andy nodding slowly? Lauren's hand slipped into his as she looked up at him, questioningly, with the same big blue eyes that Dora had. He wouldn't look at her.

'Okay I've said my piece. Now it's up to the rest of you to sort this thing out. But the other thing is this: it's your mum's fiftieth birthday on Wednesday. The address where we'll be having her party is on this piece of paper here. I'll leave it on the table. But I'd sincerely like it if you could *all* be there. By the way, Dora doesn't know I've come. She's a proud lady. Oh, and sorry for barging in on your nice quiet Sunday afternoon.'

Chapter 31

The evening of Dora's fiftieth birthday was blustery, cold and raining but it didn't matter one iota because everyone she cared for was there with her. Her mother and aunt and new-found friends and the rest of the Afternoon Tea Club were filing into one of the meeting rooms, at Borough Community Centre, chattering and giggling, for the end-of-year get-together with Eileen and Taynor before everyone went their separate ways, after Dora's party, for their respective Christmases.

It felt cramped in this new room and everyone was fidgeting because, in all honesty, they all had better things to do! They had their party frocks or suits on and simply wanted to party with Dora, next door, and drink something fizzily alcoholic. But when Eileen asked for some quiet, everyone did quieten down.

'Right now Taynor and I are so pleased to see everyone from the Afternoon Tea Club as well as new faces connected to Dora's fiftieth birthday party. I can already see that it would be safe to assume that everyone has gained something from what started out as an idea from my mother, who was bored with her afternoons of not very much to do. Would that be correct?'

People clapped, and there were cries of, 'Hear, hear.'

'Well, she's here again, tonight. So please welcome my mother, Veronica!'

'Yeah Veronica!' everyone cried.

Raymond had been roped in to help manoeuvre Veronica through the crowds to where her daughter and Taynor stood.

'Thank you! Thank you, kind people. Well, I never expected to get such a wonderful response to my suggestion that as you get older you still need something to do with your time. I've heard some wonderful stories that have sprung from the formation of the Afternoon Tea Club. People making new friends or finding old ones. It has certainly been an eye-opener and I'm so pleased to be here again today to witness some of these amazing unions – all of it because of one small sugges-tion. But now I'm going to pass you over to my daughter so we can get on with the business of the evening. Over to you, Eileen ...'

'Okay everyone. Right now let's get straight down to business and then we can be out of here, PDQ! So every-one's given me feedback regarding their courses, which is great. So with the computing and internet, a lot of you have already dabbled and now just need certain pointers. A few of you haven't tried it yet but want to learn but can't do both days. So we've decided to change the computer courses and just do the one afternoon on the first Thursday of each month, so we don't get mixed up with the art classes on the Fridays. And quite a few of you have signed up for swimming and that's doing well. The art courses are okay and everyone is also happy with the two afternoon tea sessions. Great. So, a revised timetable will be sent to everyone by the end of the year and we'll get the London trip arranged as well as the price for that and include it with your revised timetables.'

Eileen paused to shuffle through her paperwork. 'Now! We're compiling a new database of all your names and contact numbers so from next year anything new will be sent to yourselves directly via email or by phone. We do have a lot of your contacts already, of course. But please let us know of any changes to your personal details and please let us know if you have any other suggestions in order to make the Afternoon Tea Club an even better experience for everyone. So that's it, folks. Oh and just to let you know Taynor will be going on maternity leave in the coming months, in preparation for the baby she's expecting around mid to late April next year. So congratulations are in order since she and her husband will be having their first child.'

'Congratulations, Taynor!' people shouted.

Eileen chuckled. The people in that room were certainly a lot livelier than they had been at the first Afternoon Tea Club meeting. In fact, her bosses and the community in general had welcomed the whole concept with open arms. More and more people were starting to hear about it, now, and asking

302

about the kind of things on offer for their ageing and home-bound community.

'Anyway, back to the here and now. Before we totter in to enjoy ourselves next door, would anyone be prepared to come up to the front and tell me how they think the Afternoon Tea Club has changed their lives? I will be videoing this for my bosses – wave to the camera man in the corner over there – to prove how successful this whole process has been so far because, as a club, we are certainly going from strength to strength!'

At first no one said anything. Then Dora coughed and walked to the front to stand next to Eileen.

'Yes, I think quite a few of us have been changed by this experience, haven't we, guys?' Dora said looking first at Marjorie and then at Raymond and then finding Stacy, in the crowd, standing next to her new boyfriend, John, and then waving them over. They had also been changed by it, so they walked to the front of the gathering and stood next to Dora.

'I really didn't know what to expect when I came along. I don't think I came to the first meet. I was down here with my mother visiting my aunt when I spotted the flyer and came in for a nose. I had a life but didn't really know who I was and certain circumstances were beyond my control so I was pretty much in free fall. The people around me, whom you see today, caught me before I fell even further,' Dora said.

Marjorie took her lead from Dora. 'Yes, life has been a trial for me too. Same as a lot of people I shouldn't wonder because we all have our crosses to bear, don't we, folks?'

There was head-nodding and murmurs in agreement.

'So I've recently had to learn how to live by myself again and I will admit it has been difficult. I also know that I would not have succeeded in this transition if it wasn't for the new friends around me who I met because of the Afternoon Tea Club. Another thing I've learned is that it doesn't matter who you are or what age you are, you can still make friends. My two closest friends are different ages to me. The age gap between me and the lovely Stacy over there is fifty-six years and the age gap between me and my other friend, the wonderful birthday girl Dora, is thirty-two. I didn't think that sort of thing could actually work out. But it has. At one time I thought age mattered when choosing friends. But it truly, truly doesn't, folks.'

Raymond then nodded. 'I agree completely with what these two ladies have said because I was becoming insular after my darling wife died. I couldn't see any way forward. My son was a great help but then he had his own problems in life. But by meeting these people around us, I feel I have taken on a new lease of life. We go out for meals. They are supportive. They're great fun.'

Stacy, standing next to Raymond, also nodded. 'The best thing I've done in a long time was to put my fears of rejection aside and strike out, making the new friends I've made here. I had, literally, no one until I met them. They have helped me through my own very stressful and transitional period in my life. And so the Afternoon Tea Club must continue doing what it does best. It joins people together. And when people feel connected they also feel valued and when they feel valued, it gives them the confidence to reach out and accomplish anything they darn well want to do in life.'

Chapter 32

There was pink bunting, there were streamers; there were all sorts of different shaped and coloured balloons in a net above them. There were helium balloons with huge numbered fifties on them, the DJ was playing music from the 1960s – 'Sugar, Sugar' by The Archies was blaring out – and there were retro posters from advertisements of the day, fixed around the walls. The large buffet table was piled high with all kinds of fare from different eras, things like stuffed celery and cherry tomatoes, pigs in blankets, curried prawn vol-au-vents, chicken satay skewers, cold meats, a selection of cheeses, salmon mousse, salads, pineapple and cheese on cocktail sticks, bite-size sausage rolls, vegetarian as well as vegan canapés and little red flags on foodstuffs with peanuts and other allergens. Something for everyone, Dora had told the caterers. There was another table with all the drinks both soft and hard being served by the helpers, who usually only assisted with the afternoon tea sessions. Eileen had arranged that. And Dora's mum and Philippa had supplied thirty bottles of Champagne – yes the actual stuff, Marjorie was delighted to discover as she'd never tried real Champagne before!

A beautifully decorated white and pink cake took prime position in the middle of the table, in the shape of the number fifty. The helpers were telling people that everybody was going to be cut a piece of the cake whether they went home early or not and if they did leave early to come and find the servers so they could give them their cake.

'Oh but what a gorgeous spread!' Raymond said, his eyes almost popping out of his head, as they all filed in from the smaller room in the community centre, after their meeting with Eileen and Taynor.

'Ooh, it makes me hungry just looking at all that lot!' said someone else.

There was seating all around the edge of the room as well as tables and chairs if people preferred to eat at a table. There was even enough space in front of the stage, in case anyone wanted to dance.

'So introduce me to all your friends, then,' said Dora's mother, coming up behind her daughter with Philippa in tow. 'It would be nice to start with the people you included when you were singing the praises of the Afternoon Tea Club. Must say my sis and I wouldn't mind coming along occasionally. But it's just a hop and a jump from where we live so it'd be silly not to pop round occasionally, unless we're otherwise engaged by our travels. What say you, Philippa?'

'Well, I told you, earlier, that I wanted to try that computer stuff. I'm fed up of being left in the dark when people are talking about things like desktops and Chrome and COBOL or whatever. It's been a ruddy jungle to me. So I've just spoken to Eileen and now I'm on the next course, starting on Thursdays, I think she said, after Christmas. So it'd be nice if you'd come along to help me out the first time, sister dear. And I wouldn't mind making a few new friends myself. They tend to pop off all of a sudden when they get to our age, don't they, darling?'

'They certainly do. And d'you know what? I wouldn't mind having my ninetieth birthday here, next year, if it could be arranged. It's rather a nice venue for big parties, isn't it? Plus it's near enough to stagger back home afterwards, when we've had a skinful. Eh, Pippy?'

'Okay, well never mind about all that now,' Dora said. 'I'd like to introduce you to Veronica. Remember me telling you that she's Eileen's mum and she's the one who came up with the idea of the Afternoon Tea Club? Ah, well, actually I'll introduce you to her later cos she's chatting to someone else; so come and meet Raymond first. He's over there. Hi, Raymond. So, Mother, this is Raymond. He's one of the Fab Four as we call ourselves. And, Raymond, this is the Dragon Lady I've been telling you all about!'

Whilst Raymond laughed nervously, Dora slipped away and went to chat to Marjorie.

'Well, what a turnout. I feel like a queen presiding over my subjects! Must say my mother is completely surprised by all of this, I can tell you. She said earlier that she thought I'd come a long way in the grand scheme of things and that she's proud of me, no less. That's all we want in the end, isn't it? A bit of acceptance. A bit of love.'

'We all want that, yes, love. We don't all get it, though. But it's what we strive for. And what does Mama think of the new hairstyle and the teeth whitening she's paid for?'

Dora did a little spin, her arms outstretched, dramatically. 'Well just look at me! She loves both, as do I, my dear. She didn't recognise me at first, though. Walked straight past me in the reception! At least my aunt spotted me straight away and she was very complimentary I must say,' Dora said, giggling. 'Tell you what, though, you were completely right about the hair. It's knocked *years* off me! Much better than all that plastic surgery nonsense I was mucking around with.'

'Well exactly. And now the Botox has worn off I must say you really shine in that wonderful cocktail dress. That red goes terrifically with your blonde hair and you've certainly got the legs to pull in the crowds. So you must feel pretty amazing!'

'Well I certainly do. I feel dapper, I must say!'

They'd gone shopping together for their outfits. Marjorie hadn't found anything she really liked for Dora's party and, anyway, she wasn't one for buying lots of different frocks for different occasions. So she was in her burgundy and pink print dress she'd worn the night she went out with Raymond. It was going to be her go-to outfit for the winter months. But she'd decided to sort her wardrobe out and purchase some new items for when summer, and the prospect of lots more parties, arrived.

'Oh by the way, have you seen Stacy's new beau? He'd be rather fanciable if I was twenty years younger. Can't take his eyes off our Stacy though, I must say,' marvelled Dora.

'Oh I know! Isn't it wonderful that she's finally met someone decent? Ironically, he also lives in our block of flats and he's a copper, so he'll take good care of her. So that's her off our hands!'

'Yes but what about you and Raymond, Marj. I do think he has a soft spot for you.'

Marjorie shrugged. 'We're friends first and foremost. He's still in love with his Dianne, though. Always will be, so I don't think there's room in his heart for anyone else. Yet I'm completely fine with that. I've actually grown to like my own space now and just look at the four of us; the things we've done since meeting up at the Afternoon Tea Club; we're very different people to who we used to be! And I hope we'll always be friends because we've got so much in common now.'

'Oh yes, I completely agree with that, my dear,' Dora said hugging Marjorie. 'Oh look. There's Jodie!'

Dora waved Jodie over and the two hugged. Jodie had been away on a new cosmetics course.

'Wow! What the ruddy hell happened to you, old mate? You've lost twenty years already! So the new techniques I've learned on my course aren't going to be needed then? Gosh, you do look pretty amazing.'

'It's an incredible transformation, isn't it? And not a trace of Botox in sight!' declared Marjorie.

'Ruddy unbelievable. Who says you get craggier when you get older? It's a myth!'

'Hiya, Stacy. So how's everything going for you and the lovely John then?' said Dora, as Stacy walked over to join them.

'It's great actually, thanks, Dora. Took a while before I could let my guard down because of everything, you know? But we're very close now.'

'Oh, that's wonderful news, sweetheart!' said Marjorie.

'I know. It feels almost like a miracle. And, guess what, Marjorie, my mum and dad aren't splitting up after all,' said Stacy, glancing nervously at the door. 'She says she's going to give him another chance because he behaved impeccably when we went for Sunday lunch at my brother's and Marvin's place. Also Grandpa has told them to get rid of the farm and they're starting to look at cottages and flats to retire near the sea. And me and Dad have started getting along a bit better now. I went round and we had a long chat. He told me he'd always loved us but that he just wasn't any good at showing emotions like that. And we had a long hug, afterwards, which felt strange but it also felt good. So I feel as though there's renewed positivity with my family now. And I've got a little cat, Tibs. But don't worry I won't be getting any others! And Tibs loves John too,' Stacy added with a beautiful smile that lit up her face.

'Oh, that's wonderful news, Stacy. I'm really happy for you.

But are you all right, love? You seem a bit fidgety,' Marjorie said.

'Oh yes, I'm okay. It's nothing. Anyway, is there a gift table? I want to put my card on it.'

'Yes, well, I put mine on the table by the back wall. Everyone else put stuff there.'

'Okay, I'll see you later then. I want to introduce John to Raymond.'

Right, time to eat! Marjorie thought, and moved over to the buffet.

She smiled at the amount of food in front of her, then started piling things on her plate. She went to sit down at one of the tables and it reminded her of the first time she'd come along, at Gracie's insistence, to afternoon tea at the community centre. A lot had certainly changed for her since then. A lot had changed for the other wonderful people she'd met, too. Come to think of it, she was very happy with the way she was conducting her life these days. She chuckled at the thought of Gracie feeling ever so marginally piqued – but in a nice way – that her mother was standing on her own two feet these days. And happily so.

'Do you mind if I join you, Marjorie?' said a familiar voice. Marjorie looked up into the soft, kindly brown eyes of Raymond.

'Oh, of course, my dear. Take a seat. And I, um, I just wanted to apologise for that first time I refused you, Raymond. I was very insecure back then. When I was with my Oliver he made life very difficult for me if I spoke to other men, so at first it was a hard habit to break. Thankfully those times are a long way behind me now.'

'Oh don't worry, love. I thought something was amiss in the way you disappeared so fast. Anyway, we were all different people then. I've been speaking to some other people tonight and everyone's story seems to be the same. Life has changed for us all because of the Afternoon Tea Club. It's such a simple thing and yet it's been so impactful. Oh those pigs in blankets look nice. Haven't had one of those in years! Think I'll grab a few. Do you want anything else whilst I'm up?'

'Yes, a couple of the cheese and onion sticks, please. Haven't had those in ages, either.'

Marjorie glanced around herself at the other people at the party. A few of them were trying to get into the groove of 'Build Me Up Buttercup' by The Foundations. There was raucous laughter at a private joke, behind her. Yvonne and Philippa were chatting to a young couple. John and Stacy only had eyes for each other, although Stacy did appear nervous. Eileen and Taynor were finally sitting down after having done the rounds to see what everybody else thought about the Afternoon Tea Club. Taynor was carrying her pregnant bump high up, which meant it could very well be a baby girl. Pah, old wives' tales weren't always right. Taynor had said she'd be happy either way. They were all nice people.

Gracie had rung earlier and told her they'd set the date for their wedding, first of August. 'Not long after the baby's born.'

A summer wedding. *How lovely!* She'd certainly need a stomping new outfit for that, she thought beaming.

'And we're not flying anywhere for the wedding, Mum. We'll probably go to Mauritius for a belated honeymoon after the baby arrives. I agree with my doctor and don't want to risk any complications by flying, especially at my age. So we're going to find somewhere around here to get married. Steven has a few nice places in mind. So you don't have to worry about renewing your passport if you don't want to.'

That news had pleased Marjorie who'd been worrying about which suntan lotion to buy – she got blotchy if she sat in the sun for too long – and what sort of outfits she'd need to get for hot sunny climes.

As Raymond returned with their food, the DJ had put on 'Dizzy' by Tommy Roe.

'Oh, put those down a minute, Raymond. Do you fancy having a jig around with me to this song? It's one I always loved when I was a lot younger. Oh, come on! Don't look so terrified. We're allowed to make fools of ourselves at our age. Come on. Up you get!'

Raymond didn't do modern dances but he made an effort, one hand in the air and a little bending in time with the beat. It made Marjorie howl with laughter. They were joined by Stacy and John. And then Eileen appeared with Taynor.

'Oi move over!' shouted Dora, dragging her mother and Philippa into the dancing arena. 'Oh, come on, you two! You both know how to dance!'

'Cooee! Make room for a little one,' sang Jodie, her arm hooked through that of an elderly man, who looked as though all his Christmases had come at once!

Then someone got hold of Dora's waist and spun her round. She opened her mouth in shock.

'Oh my God, Stuart! Didn't think you were going to make it. Hi, Hazel. And Stephy. Yay! Well, give us a hug then. Ah, it's fantastic you're all here! You staying with Mum or what?'

'Yeah, sis. We're up for a few days so it'll be great hanging out with all the family. Haven't seen Philippa in a while either. And, wow, you look so different! Been on holiday somewhere?'

'I wish! But so pleased you noticed. Hairdresser and teeth whitening. I'd recommend it to anyone who wants to knock a few years off.'

'Great. Well it beats all that other muck you kept trying. You used to look like a ruddy clown!'

'So everyone keeps saying but things change, thankfully. Now go grab platefuls of food and get stuck in.' Dora grinned, hugging her brother for all he was worth.

Chapter 33

Dora broke away from the dancing to ask if the helpers would start putting glasses of Champagne or Buck's Fizz into people's hands before they started leaving early. Then she asked the DJ if he'd put some softer music on so people could start to relax and unwind before her Champagne toast.

A few older people had left early, but at least they'd been given their little pieces of cake to take home with them. Yet glancing around the enclave of her partygoers she could see most people were starting to tire.

'Crikey, I'm bloody tipsy now!' Dora told Jodie.

'Well, if you can't get pithed on your fiftieth birthday, me old mate, when can yer?' Jodie slurred. The elderly gent she'd dragged up to dance had complained his feet hurt and had gone to sit down.

'So true, my dear. Anyway, I think it's time for my toast. Right where's my mother?'

'I'm here, darling!' Yvonne said, coming up behind her, with a smile. 'Right are we doing this now?'

'Yes, we are. Everyone's seated so we won't bother getting

on the stage at the risk of falling off! How many bottles of Champagne are left?'

'Oh, about twelve I think.'

'Okay well we'll do this from over by the table then. I'm not dragging heavy bottles around the place.'

'Okay, darling. I'll bang the gong!' said Yvonne.

She grabbed a stainless steel server platter and banged it a few times with a spoon.

'Hear ye, hear ye, hear ye!' she cried.

Everyone looked round.

'*Mother!*' Dora hissed. 'Behave!'

Yvonne stuck out her tongue.

'Right, folks!' Dora began. 'Well I'd just like to say I've had an absolutely *wonderful* birthday, so thanks to all of you for that! And thanks for all your wonderful cards and little pressies. I've also lived a wonderfully interesting and chequered life, too. But we won't go into all that!'

'Aw, why not?' someone shouted.

'Because that would be telling ... But I'm here today, all the better for having met all of you. And that is care of Veronica's brilliant idea, foremost, as well as her daughter's brilliant idea of making it happen, second. So I'd like to present a bottle of bubbly to the team that is team Veronica and Eileen. And another bottle of bubbly to the team that is Taynor and what will be her new family sometime around next April, I believe. Congratulations, Taynor, but no sneaky sips until after the birth!'

'Hear, hear!' people shouted, clapping.

Eileen and Veronica exchanged surprised glances and even Taynor looked shocked as they came forward to receive their bubbly.

'Right, now I also have bottle of bubbly for the following people. And these people are my friends and family. Some of them are my new friends, thanks to the Afternoon Tea Club. But they are all people who have helped and supported me through my own journey whilst I found a bit more acceptance than I was getting in the world. So please come up for a bottle of champers and a big hug from me. Marjorie. Raymond. Stacy. Jodie. Philippa. And Michael, for being inspiring in our art classes. And last but not least for my brother Stuart and his family. I'm feeling very huggy and kissy today!'

Everyone piled up and plastered her with kisses and long hugs.

'Happy fiftieth, Dora!'

'Cheers, Dora!'

'Right now just one last thing, everybody. There's stacks of food left so please help yourselves on your way out and take whatever you'd like. There's nowhere for any of it to go apart from down your tums. There are doggy bags on the side by the drinks table over there.'

'Thanks, Dora!' everybody yelled, clapping.

Stuart stood up and took over. 'And finally. A toast to my little sister Dora. She's come a long way in life and our family and all her friends are extremely proud of her. So would you please be upstanding – well, that's for those of you who can make it, please be upstanding to wish Dora a very happy fiftieth birthday!'

'Happy fiftieth birthday, Dora!'

The balloons above them in the net were released, much to the delight and yelling and stomping of all the birthday guests. The DJ put on some easy-listening sounds.

Raymond smiled at Marjorie.

'Would you like to dance with me? A proper dance this time?' he said, standing up and offering his hand. 'I'm not keen on the fast ones but I don't mind slow ones. This one, "My Way" by Frank Sinatra, is an old favourite of *mine*.'

Marjorie stood and allowed herself to be led onto the dance floor. She turned to face Raymond and he put his arm around her waist and took her hand in his and they danced a perfectly comfortable waltz. Others joined them. Dora dragged her mother up and they danced together, their heads close, chatting about the things that mothers and daughters chat about.

On the second tune, Marjorie asked Raymond a question she'd been wanting to ask but hadn't dared. But she'd come to the decision that, whatever the response, she would be happy with that. She'd lived to a certain time in her life whereby any joy that came her way and felt like a bonus, *was certainly* a bonus. Besides, she'd been gifted so much just knowing this wonderful bunch of people. And her daughter would be married soon and then – joy of joys – she would finally become a grandmother! So she already had heaps to be extremely thankful for.

'Raymond. What have we got here, you and I?' she said simply, as they moved in unison to the music.

She didn't want to push things with him. But she didn't want to start having feelings for this man only to realise he couldn't reciprocate those feelings for her. She knew his wife's memory was still a strong contender for his love and she knew how his guilt for not preventing Dianne from leaving the house, that day, hampered much of what he thought and felt now. Possibly it would always prevent him from moving beyond thoughts of the past. However, she did understand his reticence since her own memories of Oliver had certainly put the brakes on her life for many years, after he died. But she was finally coming to terms with all of that now.

'Ah! Well, you and I, Marjorie,' he began, after a little pause. 'You and I, first and foremost, have got a wonderful friendship. It's a friendship I never thought I would have with a woman, after Dianne. All my friends were men before. But I think you and I *now* have something more than *just* a friendship, even though friendships are marvellous institutions. So if you're in agreement, Marjorie, I'd like to see where this thing takes us ...'

Stacy was sitting sullenly at one of the tables.

'I really thought they'd come, you know.'

John put his arm around her.

'You've done your best, Stacy. The rest is up to them. We can't predict what someone else will do. It's the same in my line of work. Everybody reacts differently to things like trauma, shock or bad news. Some people lose it and smash things up or hurt people. Others bury their head in the sand. Or maybe they've simply been discussing things and want to go and see her privately. That would be more likely, don't you think? Look, let's finish the Champagne and let's have one last dance.'

'But they don't know where she lives. I only put the address of the community centre on that piece of paper. And she's moving into her new flat soon so they won't know where that is, either.'

'Well, you've tried your best. Come on, Stacy. I want to have our first slow dance together here. Let's start making some of our own happy memories, sweetheart. Let everything else sort itself out.'

As the evening wore down, people started slowly drifting away. Dora hoped they'd have happy memories of her party. She'd wished them a happy Christmas and fun at New Year if they were going to parties. They all traipsed out around ten-ish with their food bags and happy boozy smiles.

'Thanks for inviting us, Dora. It's been wonderful!'

'Yes, thank you, Dora. We don't often go to parties!'

'You're all very welcome!' Dora smiled, happily.

The DJ had started putting his decks and equipment away

and Eileen and Taynor followed him out the door after hugging Dora and all her family and friends.

'Happy Christmas! Happy New Year! See you next year. We start up again from mid-January, so see you then. Bye!'

Even though Dora had told people to take as much food as they liked from the buffet table, there was still masses of it left.

'Hey, guys,' she said to her remaining crowd, 'Please take some more of this stuff. It's sacrilegious to leave it all here.'

Eileen had told Dora that the woman who locked up after parties would come at midnight so could Dora put any rubbish in the bins provided, ready for removal. Usually everything had to be cleared out by the partygoers but on this occasion she'd okayed it with the organisers for Dora to just do the clearing and leave their rubbish bags in the canteen. Marjorie, Raymond, Stacy and John and the rest of Dora's family had said they would stay and help clear up. And so they set to, putting jackets on the backs of chairs and rolling their sleeves up as they started the clearing process.

By 10.40 p.m. the last black bin sack had just been put in the kitchen and the chairs stacked in the corner of the hall. Raymond and even Stuart were pink-faced and perspiring.

'Remind me not to offer a full spring-clean at the end of the next party!' Raymond said chuckling.

The door connecting the main hall to the reception area, opened.

'Anyone want a balloon to take home, guys? Otherwise we'll have to go round popping them all,' Dora called out.

That made Marjorie smile.

'Um, I think I'd like a balloon,' said the voice of the girl who came in through the door.

She wasn't alone. Her father was with her and his mother was behind them. The girl's grandmother went straight over to the surprised but delighted Stacy and gave her a hug.

'Thank you so much! You were right, love,' she said. 'I didn't know the whole story. I do now.'

Dora stood staring, from one to the other, her mouth slowly opening in awe. Marjorie knew what was happening straight away; it was patently clear that they were witnessing the long-overdue reunion between her dear friend and her long-lost family. There was no doubt that Dora was Lauren's mother with her blonde hair, blue eyes, the same cheekbones. Dora's mother's mouth dropped open in shock too and she stared in complete disbelief at the scene being played out in front of her.

Stacy was so happy she burst into tears. John hugged her and whispered, 'Why are you crying, Stace? This is the best possible outcome. You should be so pleased.'

'This *is* me p-pleased!' she spluttered.

'God, I'd hate to see you when you're sad then,' he said with a smile.

'I think it's time we left,' Marjorie said to Raymond, quietly.

'What, love?'

'No, don't. Please stay. This is momentous for me. I'm sorry, Mum. I should've told you. But the time never seemed right and I never thought ... I really never thought this day would come. I'd hoped it would happen. But no, I never truly believed it would,' Dora said, looking across the room at her mother.

Andy looked around at everybody and then he suddenly moved forward. He went to everyone in turn, shaking their hands.

'Hi, I'm Andy,' he said. 'And this amazing young woman here is my – no – mine and Dora's daughter, Lauren. And we're, um, we're very pleased to meet you all, even though this is a little overdue.'

When Dora's mother had recovered from her shock she strode over to Dora, her eyes blazing.

'Why didn't you tell us? *Why didn't you tell us?* Your father would have *loved* her! Your father would have absolutely bloody *ADORED her*!' she yelled, bursting into tears. Then she abruptly turned on her heels and stormed out of the building, with her sister in hot pursuit.

Dora stared after her mother in complete astonishment; as did everybody else. She never imagined, for an instant, that her mother would react so aggressively to this amazing news. Her mother should've been hugging her only actual granddaughter for all she was worth! She'd been building bridges with her mother for years; always waiting for that one special moment when – she imagined – Yvonne would take her in her arms and tell her she loved her, no matter what she did in life. But, in that instant Dora realised her mother would never forgive her for this.

And that knowledge was too much for Dora to bear. Her head drooped forward and silent tears flooded her face, dripping off her chin as she stood there, crushed.

Stacy and Marjorie reacted, first, but Andy was nearest and reached out and scooped her into a tight hug.

'I'm so sorry about all this, Dee. It's all my fault,' he said hoarsely, wrapping his arms around her, feeling her racking sobs.

And then suddenly Lauren was there too, tears dripping down her own face as she reached out to hug the woman she'd recently been reintroduced to as her mother. 'It's okay ... Mum. It'll be okay!'

Chapter 34

After the commotion over the shock arrival of Dora's daughter, Marjorie and Stacy had busied themselves making teas and coffees for everyone. Then Marjorie and Raymond had left with Stacy, John and Jodie.

'We'll speak later,' Marjorie had whispered to Dora, giving her a big hug. 'It'll get better.'

Dora had walked up to Stacy and thrown her arms around her.

'Thank you so much, Stacy,' she whispered. 'It was a plucky thing you did for me and I will be eternally grateful that you did it. It's the best gift anyone could've given me, despite the, er, result. I owe you big time for this and love you heaps.'

The rest of the family were finally sitting quietly, pensively, around a table and sipping their hot drinks when Philippa brought Yvonne back into the room. Yvonne snatched herself out of Philippa's grasp and sat down at the opposite end of the table to Dora. Philippa sat next to Dora and gave her a hug. Yvonne sat rigidly, with her back to Dora, her arms folded. She was furious at this unbelievable turn of events.

She'd thought they'd almost become as close as sisters over the years. It was like a slap discovering the biggest secret Dora had kept from her.

And even though the heating was on in the hall the atmosphere felt frosty.

'So, Yvonne, I just wanted to say that this is not Dora's fault,' Andy began, breaking into the strained atmosphere. 'We certainly made mistakes and it is a bit of a mess. But we're here today to try and start putting things right.'

No one spoke.

Hazel held Steph's hand and had an expression on her face that suggested she'd much rather be somewhere else. Stuart was looking down at his feet, slightly shaking his head. Dora's lips were quivering as if she was about to start crying again. Her face was tear-stained with mascara streaked down one cheek. Philippa was patting Dora's hand and trying to shoot daggers at her sister who refused to make eye contact with anyone.

'I understand exactly how you feel, Yvonne,' Lauren's other grandmother said, finally finding her voice. 'I have also been led to believe something very different to the truth. I spent a lifetime thinking it was Dora who'd gone off with someone and walked away from Lauren and I'm not usually one to get mad at anyone—'

'Grandma lost it with Dad,' Lauren said with a small smile, interrupting the tension between the so-called adults. 'But I want to get to know my mum, now. I think I always did want to know her. I always wondered what it'd be like if we met.

And, um, to both grandmas, kids *do* keep things from their parents. And I wanted to say that parents do not always know us or know what's best for us. You may think you do and you may even *want* us to think like you. But everybody's different. And, Dad, you were wrong to do what you did. You weren't protecting me from anything by not telling the truth. You were keeping me from the truth.'

'Well.' Dora sniffed as Philippa handed her a tissue. 'I think that's the most astute thing anybody's said tonight. And yes, between us, me and Andy have certainly screwed things up. I will admit. But I do want my daughter back in my life. I *need* her in my life and if all of you here don't like that or can't accept that this thing has happened and move on from it, tough. I'm sick of worrying about every sodding aspect of my life all the time. Damn right I had no confidence before. The success of my family was a tough act to follow. I never did feel good enough in their eyes and so the decisions I made may not have been great at the time. But what's done is done. Can't we just move on from that?'

Dora glanced around the table. This time Stuart began to nod.

'Well, Mother? And screw your neck back in, you're not bloody perfect, yourself!' Dora snapped.

Lauren's hand shot to her mouth, to stifle the giggle at her mother's comment. And gradually everybody started to smile. That was the old Dora. Not standing for any nonsense!

'Bloody hell, Yvonne. You're so bloody immature sometimes!'

Philippa shouted, making everyone jump. 'Well, are you going to kiss and make up or what? It's way past our bedtime!'

Lauren got out of her seat and went to stand by Yvonne's chair.

'Um, I know you're really mad with everyone, Grandma – can I call you that? But you know what? I think once you've got used to the idea, you'll like it. We're all going to try and be friends with each other and I think once everyone gets friendlier it'd be really nice to have a proper family Christmas together. Maybe at Grandma Pat's this year or next year if you want?' Lauren said slowly. 'I think it'd be great.'

Andy raised his eyebrows.

This sort of thing hadn't been discussed. Lauren had been so distraught when Stacy had left that day. After she'd confronted her father about the truth, she'd stormed off to stay with friends, switching her mobile off with no word when she'd be coming back. Andy truly thought he'd lost his daughter for a while, there. Even his mother told him to, 'Get out of my house!' *Why did I let it all get so out of hand?*

His mother now glanced at him and nodded.

'I'm sure everybody's already made arrangements for Christmas, Lauren, even though it's a sweet idea. But we could easily meet up another time ...?' she said softly.

Yvonne sniffed and turned back to face her family. Her cheeks were glistening with silvery tears.

'Or, or what if we have a New Year's Day party around at

329

mine and Philippa's when we've all had a chance to mull everything over and get to know each other first?'

'Yay, Grandma!' Lauren giggled.

'Oh yes! That's a good idea,' said Andy's mum. 'New Year; new start for us all.'

'Right, so perhaps the best idea is for us to introduce ourselves properly and I think Dora should do that,' said Yvonne, without looking at her daughter.

Dora started to get to her feet, when Lauren jumped up and handed Dora and Yvonne a small parcel each.

'But first I'd like to give you these. They're your Christmas presents from me and Dad and Grandma. They're photos. We got a few together and marked on the back what year they are and where we were. They're all of me – well, a few of Dad and me. Dad and Grandma picked out the best ones for you,' Lauren said breathing enthusiastically; entwining her fingers, her eyes bright.

'Plus,' she added. 'I can do the introductions. We're Andy, me and Grandma Pat and I know you're Philippa, Grandma Yvonne's sister, and you're Uncle Stuart and your wife is Auntie Hazel and your daughter is Steph. We're cousins, Steph. There. It's done! Now can I have something to eat from the buffet? I'm starving!'

Stuart, Hazel and Steph who were due to stay with Yvonne and Philippa until Sunday morning, left early Saturday morning, after breakfast.

'You need to talk to your new family, Mother,' said Stuart. 'We'll be back at Christmas and we'll work it so we stay for your New Year's Day party. We still keep the hotel closed during Christmas and New Year, to give ourselves a good long break, so that'll work out perfectly for us. And I know we're supposed to be going out for dinner tonight but it's not as important as you spending time getting to know Lauren and her family. We can always do stuff another time. Anyway, we're off. Things to do. See you later. Bye, Mum!'

So Yvonne and Philippa cancelled their weekend plans and went to visit Pat and Andy at both their homes on the Saturday. Lauren said she was happy with the offer Dora made to go shopping for a gift for what had been Lauren's nineteenth birthday last April and they ended up having afternoon tea in the spa down by the waterfront, where she'd been with Marjorie.

'I really love the clothes we got today – thank you! Dad hasn't really got a clue and Gran, well, she thinks I should just wear sensible stuff all the time,' Lauren said, helping herself to an immaculately square-cut piece of Victoria sponge off the cake stand, which was crammed with a variety of bite-sized pieces of cake, as usual.

'You're very welcome, sweetheart,' said Dora, pleased she'd allowed Lauren to pick out what she'd wanted to buy, rather than trying to choose Lauren's clothes for her.

'I know I keep saying this but it's so strange, isn't it? I can't believe it, really. It's what I dreamed about for years. I missed out on heaps of things I couldn't do, like send Mother's Day cards or anything – but Grandma Pat helped me a lot. I was brought up by Auntie Dariana for quite a few years when I was growing up – one of Dad's girlfriends. And I got her a Mother's Day card once but she just looked at me as if I was nuts. And – oh, there's just so much I want to tell you!' said Lauren, her face flushed with excitement.

'I know! It's so funny, you know, because I was panicking thinking, how do you start a conversation with a daughter you've only just met, proper? But you make it very easy for me. You've got such a lovely personality. Your dad and Pat have done a marvellous job raising you, sweetheart. And you seem to be taking all this rather well. So do you – I mean, it might be too soon for all this – but do you forgive your father and I for *this*?'

Lauren shrugged. 'I don't know about that yet exactly. I think I do. I mean I know things get complicated sometimes. I've got friends whose parents split up and it was horrible and everything. And there's loads you can find on social media about all that – about relationships and how nothing lasts or things change, you know? Or maybe it's just easier to say, well, that's how it was with you and Dad then. And *this* is how it is now. I mean Dad's been great with everything, apart from this one big fat lie. But he even told me about periods and stuff, way before my friends knew about it all. But it's not the same as having someone, having *your mum* on your side, explaining stuff, even though Grandma Pat was good. And, Mum, I'd really like it if you could meet all my friends? They're dying to see you.'

Dora laughed nervously at that. Wow, critical teens. She couldn't wait for that experience! She wondered what they'd all think. She'd probably be miles older than some of their mums. But she couldn't start worrying about things like that now. It was part and parcel of her new life with Lauren. But, in another way, how lovely to be welcomed back – no, the best bit was that she was happily being *accepted* back into the open arms of her little family, without question.

Marjorie yawned as she stood in the kitchen in her dressing gown as she put toast in the toaster. There was no other noise in the flat apart from the kettle boiling. She hadn't seen Dora since her wonderful birthday, last Wednesday night, but Dora had texted to say she was staying with her mother and Philippa, whilst they sorted everything out. They all had so much to catch up on, since the arrival of her beautiful, estranged daughter. What a massive, marvellous life change Dora was facing because of a risky but selfless act on Stacy's behalf. It was probably the last piece of the jigsaw that had been Dora's life. She'd feel complete now, Marjorie thought, but she sighed. It wasn't long until Christmas and afterwards Dora would be moving into her own new flat. And then, sadly, Marjorie would be on her own again.

That thought left Marjorie feeling a little deflated. She'd

worried about Dora leaving just as much as she'd worried about Gracie moving on. But as she sat down to eat her toast with a generous helping of honey she smiled. Coming and going. Living and dying. It wasn't all bad. At least she had some pretty amazing friends now and they'd always be there for her, even though they were going through their own challenging phases.

Hey, Marj, her inner voice was yelling, *this is life! And, anyway, Christmas is just around the corner and you haven't done any shopping yet!*

She knew all the shops in town would be full of Christmassy glitz, carol singers and good cheer. She could put it off no longer! It was time for that now. And she knew she was going to do it by herself, without well-meaning friends or family around her. It would be one of her new experiences because in the past she'd always done it with Gracie. Yet she was totally comfortable with that thought. Raymond had said they'd meet up again after Christmas and she was completely fine with that too. She definitely wanted to step back and think about everything, over the Christmas period, especially about her relationship with Raymond. *Slowly, slowly, catchy monkey.*

Yet, she was itching to know what happened after she and the others had left Dora with Lauren that night. On the one hand, she wanted to give Dora the space she needed to sort out her family life but she was curious to know how it had all panned out. If Gracie had confessed to having a grown-up daughter somewhere Marjorie knew she'd have blown her top with a slanging match, at the very least!

So just before she left to catch the bus to do her Christmas shopping in town she rang Dora.

'How's it all going?'

Marjorie heard a long sigh on the other end of the phone.

'Crikey, Marjorie! I'm still trying to come to terms with it all. It was very tense at first after my ox mother threw her wobbly. Plus I'd given up on the whole thing, as you know. I mean probably at some point I'd have thought of another way to get through to her. But, of course, I didn't know that Andy had lied about what happened between us, although I suspected he might not have been completely honest about things. Anyway, Lauren gave me and Mum some photos; the years we missed out on. I've been looking through them and bawling my eyes out. But I'm just about to go out with her again today. With my daughter. Oh God, that sounds weird. Nice but weird. We want to catch up on things without the rest of the family getting involved first. Mum can come to terms with it in her own good time. God, was she mad! I've never seen her so angry. But I think she rues the fact that Dad didn't know. He'd've adored her as a baby and she was a beautiful baby, Marjorie. So, yeah, me and Andy messed up big time over that! But what's done is done. I'm just thrilled Lauren is taking it all so well. I can see she's going to be another strong-willed family member, so that should be interesting! We haven't hugged properly or anything yet. So it does feel a bit odd. But I also feel as though I'm going to suddenly wake up from this amazing dream and it won't be real! I'm going to meet up with Andy, tomorrow, for a cup of coffee and a long chat about things. We're all going to take things slowly. But how're things with you and Raymond? Saw you having a very slow dance with him that night. Nudge, nudge, wink, wink?'

'Well yes. I will admit that things are progressing. We had a little chat and it seems that he sees us as more than friends. Not lovers or anything. Oh no, not that – I don't think I'm ready for that. But a little affection in my life would be most welcome. And we're going to a dance on New Year's Eve. So I suppose you could say we're an item. But, just like you, we're taking things slowly. We've both got our families to think about, as well, of course. So we won't be introducing each other just yet. Anyway, go have a super day with your wonderful daughter and we'll catch up soon.'

Chapter 35

Gracie had always been a good cook and this year's Christmas Day luncheon was no exception.

Steven's cottage was cosily warm and quaint. All the windows were leaded, and the rooms had low ceilings and cream-painted walls. Stable doors with latches, exposed floorboards and a roaring log burner took Marjorie back to another era, one of more time-honoured values. The kitchen had tiled backsplashes, traditional cupboards and with a cream Everhot range cooker, instead of the gleaming glass and the stark shininess of today's modern kitchens. It felt much more welcoming. The two bedrooms upstairs had four-poster beds, cream carpets and restful views of the surrounding countryside. Sparrows and robins tweeted each morning and Marjorie had even seen a badger early one evening! It was wonderful here and the peace and quiet was a welcome retreat for her.

It was going to be a very quiet Christmas for just the three of them but Marjorie was quite happy about that too. The year had already had more than its fair share of troubles and excitement for everyone, as far as she was concerned. But if you'd asked her a year ago how she thought her year would pan out, she wouldn't have had an inkling that, by now, she'd have had more friends and adventures than she could count on one hand!

'I must say, Gracie, that was absolutely delicious,' Marjorie said putting her knife and fork together and patting her tummy after she'd finished her Christmas meal of sticky maple carrots and parsnips, Brussels sprouts (of course!) with cranberries and almonds, mashed and roast potatoes with plum jam gravy, perfect with their roast Norfolk turkey.

'Figgy pudding with vanilla custard *and* a dollop of cream, Marjorie? Your amazing daughter's handicraft, of course,' said Steven, grinning.

'Oh, gosh yes, please,' Marjorie had said.

Oh, it was grand to be spoiled rotten!

They'd already pulled the crackers and giggled over the contents and wore their silver paper crowns, when next came the gifts. They'd cleared the table and sat nursing coffees. Marjorie handed hers out first.

'Well, this is just what it looks like. It's a stack of vouchers, tied up in a bow! I had no idea what to get you both so I thought if I got this lot you could decide what to do with them. So there's lots of different ones, like Mothercare, for when the baby arrives and John Lewis and garden centre ones, so you can go have fun buying lots of different things for your new life together!'

'Oh, that's a wonderful idea, Marjorie. Thank you so much,'

Steven gushed, leaning forward to kiss both her cheeks. Gracie gave her mother a big hug and whispered, 'Thanks, Mum!'

'And because you told us about the spa treat you got for Dora, our Christmas gift to you is a three-day spa break at Ragdale for you and I, in March. It's a bit of mother and daughter time together before everything to do with babies, weddings and babysitting comes crashing down on us all!'

Marjorie burst into tears, at the thought of special time alone with Gracie, once again, but they were happy tears. 'Oh, Gracie, Steven, that's perfect, thank you so much! I'm really thrilled with that. It'll be lovely. Happy Christmas!'

Stacy had never cooked a turkey before. Fortunately, John had. So they'd cooked the turkey together, Tibs meowing gently between the two of them, welcoming any titbits that came his way.

This time, Stacy's mother and father knew Peter and Marvin were coming around for Christmas dinner and no words of detriment passed anyone's lips. Stacy's mother had asked them to go to theirs for Christmas but Stacy had privately balked at that idea. No way; not there. Not there, ever again, as far as she was concerned. She'd put old ghosts to rest and was done with the place. Too depressing and she was sure there'd be no background music or joy. Would there even be a tree? Nope, she'd wait until her parents moved into their new place before she graced their door with a happy-families visit. There was too much hurt wrapped up in the old place. She wanted to live her life, going forward, with brightness and laughter. So she'd invited them to hers, on the understanding that they were aware she'd invited Peter and Marvin. The boys were going to Bella's for Boxing Day.

And because Stacy had never had a big Christmassy family gathering before, John had bought her a huge tree and together they'd dressed it with hundreds of shiny baubles, tinsel, Christmassy bunting and draped it with coloured lanterns. Their theme for Christmas: a riot of colours and cinnamon smells to assault the senses! Christmas carols were serenading from an iPad in the background. John had got two extra chairs for her table and, once everyone had arrived – full of Christmas cheer – John handed pre-dinner drinks out. He asked to speak to Jerry privately before they all enthusiastically sat down, to tuck into their turkey roast.

'Wow this looks delish, sister-in-law-to-be!'

'Brussels or carrots anyone?' said Stacy's father. Marvin put his hand up and Jerry passed him the serving bowl with a smile. No cringing or scowling blighted his face these days, Stacy was relieved to note.

Stacy didn't recognise her father now. He'd even given her a long hug at the door and told her he loved her for bringing everyone together! Was that him talking or were those her mother's words? Her mother said she thought it was the casting off of his farm duties now it was up for sale.

'It's like he's opening his eyes to life and taking a step back to consider his actions for once. I think the farm got him down. But I feel as though I've got a new man! So our future certainly looks a lot rosier than it used to. I, for one, can't wait to move into a bright new home. I might even get Marvin to cast his eye over the one we finally settle on. We've already started looking at properties.'

After the pudding came the crackers, the paper hats and before each person handed out gifts and an outpouring of love and thanks for their meals, John stood up.

'Now I know Stacy and I haven't been together all that long, so thank you for welcoming me into your family enclave with complete acceptance and especially at Christmas – or are you frightened I'm going to book you for something later on, guys?'

Everybody giggled, nervously.

'So anyway, another reason I'm pleased you're all here today is because I'd like to ask for my wonderful girlfriend's hand in marriage, if I may, Stacy?' he said kneeling, taking a small velvet black box from his pocket, opening it and offering the solitaire diamond ring to Stacy.

Peter and Stacy gasped. Stacy's mother shot a glance at her husband. How would he react to this latest shock? Stacy's hand shot to her face in embarrassment, as Tibs curled round her ankles, meowing.

'Aye, well,' said Stacy's father. 'John asked me earlier if I'd be accepting of his proposal and I told him I'm totally accepting of it. She's a wonderful lass, our Stacy, as you all know here. She's woken us all up and put our family back together again and for that I think we're all very grateful. And I want to apologise to my children, on behalf of my wife and myself, for upsetting the applecart back in the day. We gave the farm more importance than the two of you. I'm sincerely sorry about that. But we're very proud of you both and your accomplishments. And I'm, er, I'm okay now about the forthcoming marriage of my boy to his young man, too. I'd like to come to the wedding if I may and I'm sorry for all the arguments I've caused, in that respect, too.'

'Wow! Thanks, man,' said Marvin, hoarsely, taking hold of Peter's hand under the table. 'That means a lot to us.'

Jerry glanced back at John and Stacy.

'So yes, John, I'm happy for you to be marrying my daughter, if she's happy to be accepting of your proposal. God bless you both.'

Stacy could not speak. Tears clouded her vision whilst she was trying to digest what was going on around her. And her father's amazing speech? She realised those were his own words, since no one – least of all her – had had an inkling about John's proposal! Oh, but her parents' final acceptance and acknowledgement of both herself and Peter was like a breath of fresh air into her soul. Peter was looking down, she noticed, sniffing back tears? He'd only ever wanted his own acceptance, too, of course. And now they'd been given it. It was simply too much to take in ...

But now John was taking the diamond solitaire out of the tiny black box and holding it out in front of her.

'So, Stacy Ann-Marie Phillips, would you do me the honour of becoming my wife?'

Simon held his glass, full of red wine, high in front of them.
'A toast!'

There was one of those small faux Christmas trees on the unit by the television with some red flashing lights and they'd just finished their crown of beef with carrots and mashed potatoes. Mince pies were waiting to be eaten on a plate in the middle of Simon's table. There were no crackers, no tinsel, no background music.

'So, Dad. Here's to our second Christmas without Mum. But we have our memories, don't we. Please don't cry, Dad. I'm sad too. But she wouldn't want us to be unhappy, would she.'

Raymond wiped his eyes. 'N-no she wouldn't, son. Well, okay then. Cheers to Mum! And thanks for having me for Christmas.'

They knocked their remaining wine back in large gulps and put the glasses down on the table. Simon offered his father another glass. Raymond shook his head and glanced at his son. He didn't look his normal cheerful self. His flat was also in a state of disarray, with clothes everywhere and unwashed crockery in the sink. The crown of beef had come out of a box and the mashed potatoes had been powdered. Their Christmas wouldn't have been like this if Dianne had still been alive.

'Simon, how're things with you these days? I mean, how's

work? And have you met anyone else yet, after the last one? You seem a bit low is all.'

Simon sighed and started to clear the table. 'Well, to be honest, I don't really know what to do about things now, Dad. You see, when Jo moved out and I sold up to split the proceeds when the divorce came through, I had to rent this flat because there wasn't enough money left over for me to buy another property. And it's been tight finding the rent because, well, there isn't as much work at the post office as there used to be and I've, um, I've recently been put on part-time—'

'So you're struggling?'

Simon nodded. 'But I don't want you to worry because I'm thinking about moving away and looking for work someplace else, Dad. I've been around these parts all my life. Perhaps it's time for me to try something else, now my girls are self-sufficient and my grandkids mainly do their own thing these days. I mean look at how your life has turned around since you started going to the community centre. Something like that might be just what I need to lift my own spirits.'

'Hmm. Right, for one thing, I don't want you to leave, son. I've already lost your mother so there's no way you're leaving the area. Look, now it's just an idea this, but why don't you move in with me for a while? It might be just what you need whilst you find a new job or get some money behind you. And then you can make a new start in your own good time. I'm sure we can work this out between us, Simon, can't we? I mean, you're always helping me out and I'd like to help you.

Plus it would give me a bit of company, too. You know I'm lonely living in the bungalow by myself. At least have a think about it, before you up sticks and leave. What do you say?'

Simon mulled that thought over. 'I remember you saying that was working out for your friend Marjorie and Dora?'

'Yes, it worked well for them. Dora had fallen on some challenging times, too. Friends and family help each other out like that, don't they? And, if it makes you feel any better, you can call it my Christmas gift to you, being as I haven't had time to get you anything yet.'

Simon nodded slowly. 'Well, I wouldn't want to impose, Dad. I mean we've both got our own lives. But, you know, I think I'd like to do that for a few months. It would definitely help me out. So, yes, Dad. That's a great idea. Thanks!'

It felt so strange to Dora. But it was a *nice* kind of strange!

Even though she'd been spending a lot of time with Lauren, as much time as she could with her amazing *daughter* she did not expect to be invited to Christmas lunch with her once-upon-a-time family that she had long thought would never happen. She was pleased her brother had been very sympathetic about her wanting to be with Lauren, this year, and missing out on their own usual Christmas family gathering, even though Yvonne was miffed about Dora's intentions.

'It's understandable,' said Stuart. 'And think how amazing next year's Christmas will be when all of our families collide for the same meal somewhere else!'

'Well, I'm hoping that the *somewhere else* you're referring to will be *my* new pad, when Marjorie has helped me kit it out, if you all fancy that?'

Stuart had nodded his approval and hugged his sister. 'Have a great Christmas, sis. Ignore our dragon mother! You deserve this.'

Grandma Pat's terraced house was a cosy home, festooned with streamers, a huge real tree with red and gold baubles, background Christmas jingles and moving white sparkly deer outside on the tiny lawn. It was like a magical grotto. She'd done it every year for them, apparently. She clearly adored her little family.

'Come in. Come in,' she'd welcomed when Dora arrived with a bottle of Champagne and gifts for all the family. They hugged on the doorstep. Lauren came whizzing up to them.

'Mum! Mum, come and see what I've got this year! Oh, you've got us presents and we've got lots of presents for you, too!'

A few days previously Dora had met with Andy in a café and they'd had a long, heartfelt chat about the whole situation. Dora hadn't been pleased with the way he'd duped their family into believing that she'd been the one to stray, which had resulted in making it near impossible to meet up with Lauren, before now. But she'd come halfway into understanding why he'd done it – so they could move on and look after Lauren whilst her mother was elsewhere. Their conversation hadn't entirely settled Dora's anxieties about other aspects of their relationship, either. But they'd agreed that the only thing that counted now was the way forward with Lauren.

Andy had offered to pick Dora up, and drop them at his mother's house for their Christmas meal with Lauren, and Dora had accepted. It was a chilly, crisp morning when Andy knocked on Aunt Philippa's door to collect Dora. And they drove in an awkward silence for the first half hour or so. But in the car, on the way to Grandma Pat's, Andy had suddenly pulled into a layby.

'I don't know why you're stopping,' Dora said, her arms crossed, defensively. 'There's nothing else I want to say to you, Andy. We said what we needed to say. But I have to say I still can't forgive you for lying to your mum and Lauren about me in that way. You completely screwed everything up, big time, you know.'

He'd taken hold of her hand.

'I know that. But, Dee, you played your part too—'

'Christ, where has this come from? How did I play *any* part in your cheating?'

'Look, Dee, I don't want to keep going over old ground, here, but you were depressed and clingy *before* the postnatal depression set in and I needed space. Now, like I keep saying, I was happy enough when you fell pregnant with Lauren and I was happy about us staying together for her. But because you were at home all day and didn't interact with anyone else apart from Jodie, you just wanted me all to yourself when I came home from work.'

'What? Isn't that what a relationship is all about? Adults, at the end of the day, talking and being close to each other? And, yes, even living in each other's pockets?'

'It probably is, I've since learned. But back then, one of the reasons I originally left Kent to go travelling was because my last girlfriend was clingy. And what I liked about you was that you'd told me you needed that sort of space, too. To get away from your parents and *their* constraints, you told me. So I thought we were a match made in heaven! But when we got back to Kent you became clingier and I needed space to breathe. And, I'm sorry to say, when your postnatal depression was doing its absolute worst I felt rubbish and trapped. So – I'm sorry – but I did what I did.'

'So you shagged someone because *I* was depressed and *you* needed space to breathe? What crap! I'd've understood it if you'd've just stormed off somewhere, rather than done that.'

Andy shook his head. 'I guess it's what men sometimes do.'

Dora studied him then. She'd doted on him – God! She'd loved and *adored* him. He was one of those men everyone fell for and he probably knew that. Some people emitted that kind of persona. But perhaps he didn't view *himself* in that guise? It was clear to Dora he'd had his own insecurities that prevented him from having fulfilling relationships. Maybe that's what had really ruined everything for them. There was clearly some issue with him forming deep, meaningful, loving relationships because Lauren had told her he'd never married anyone.

348

Dora shook her head and looked out the window at the wintry scene; there was no snow on the ground but it was icy underfoot.

Before all this, though, she'd long held secret fantasies of someday meeting up with him again and either taking her frustration out on him by battering him or dragging him back to bed for one last session, just to see if she was truly over him. She'd never met anyone who'd rocked her boat quite the way *he'd* rocked her boat, despite everything.

'So have you found anyone else you can love and care for in the way you *need* to, then?'

'No. I've had girlfriends, of course. You met Dariana that time. But you were the only one I thought I'd love being in love with and that's why I was happy to go back to Kent when you got pregnant – to give us a try. Lauren and I still live there, as you know, but I have a bigger house now and I have my own estate agency business, too. But there's currently no one in my life, apart from our girl. What about you?'

'Well, sure, I met plenty of other men after you. But I couldn't settle for anyone less than you. So I've actually been single for a very long time, too. But the best thing that's happened to me of late is being reacquainted with our daughter. Before that the best thing that happened to me was that I made a whole squadron of new friends through the Afternoon Tea Club I've joined. Plus I've just bought a flat. So I've been learning about putting down proper roots for the first time in my life. And, I'm really happy about all of that. I've also just recently secured a part-time job doing managerial cover in a small hotel chain, which is perfect for me. So I can actually say I've finally found my place in life. But are you – do you feel *complete*, now, Andy, living the life you do?'

'I wouldn't say I actually feel complete, yet. No.'

He looked down and was quiet for a beat.

When he looked up he searched her features, as if trying to read the depths behind her eyes. Her heart started racing. She knew that look and she knew she would not be able to refuse him if he tried to kiss her; it was what she'd been dreaming about for oh so long. He was her missing piece; it had always been him. No one else had come close. Her imposed bravado about not needing anyone had prevented anyone from guessing the truth.

And then, suddenly, he reached out for her and he did kiss her and she melted against him. But the ferocity of her bridled feelings flew to the surface, overflowing as a deep moan. Andy pulled back, his eyes travelling over her face in awe. She couldn't retract what she'd just felt. She didn't want to; she'd wanted this for far too long, despite everything. Yes, she was still mad at him for what had happened but she'd always wanted him ...

And then they made love in a frenzy of fumbling hands and urgent passion, in the back of his car, sweeping them to unadulterated highs that no drug had ever done; tearing the need and want from them both, like a tussle in an alley. And when it was done, when the feverish pitch had ebbed and died and they rested breathlessly in each other's arms, Dora had known. She'd known she could love no one else – no matter what the future held for them; no matter whether Andy wanted her or not. For her there would only ever be him.

So she turned to him and risked everything because, no matter what had happened between them in the past – unfinished or otherwise – she had so much more now than she'd ever had in her life before; she had her wonderful new friends and, most importantly, her beloved daughter. And all that made her feel fuzzy-warm inside, which was more than enough to Dora. So whether she won him back or lost him forever, she knew she was finally living life on her own terms.

'You're like a drug to me; you always were. I love you deeply, Andy, despite everything. And we will always be connected because of Lauren. Second chances don't usually come along and they rarely work out. Some people change; most of us stay the same. So I'll understand if you feel our time came and went all those years ago. On the other hand, if you want us to try again – if you want us to work towards trying to put some of the wrongs right, now we're a lot older and hopefully a lot wiser – I'm all for it. But I'd want to keep it secret and then see where it takes us. I don't want Lauren getting her hopes up about us and then it not working out again. And then if it doesn't work out for us, at least we'll have had our second chance and Lauren will be none the wiser, either way. And – truthfully – I'd be happy whichever way it swung. So what do you think? I've told you what I want. But what do *you* want for us now, Andy?'

Chapter 36

Eileen had rung and emailed the four of them. And so they'd turned up as requested on a grey damp January morning, three days before the first Afternoon Tea Club meeting of the New Year, sitting in the canteen drinking hot chocolate and coffees, gabbling away about their Christmases and New Years, like a flock of spared geese!

When asked about Stacy's Christmas, all she'd done was present her left hand and its sparkling diamond, which answered that question.

'Oh, darling,' Marjorie had cried, hugging her. 'I'm so pleased for you. Oh, I think that's the best thing that could've happened to you, sweetheart.'

'You finally found your knight in shining armour,' Raymond said grinning. 'Happy for you.'

'Well, he found me, I suppose. But I'm very pleased he found me because I was floundering.'

'You were, sweetheart. But you got there in the end,' said Dora, giving her a big hug too.

'I did but it's been a funny old year, hasn't it?'

'Yes, I'll drink to that,' said Dora. 'So how was your Christmas, Raymond?'

Raymond sighed pensively. 'Oh it was very quiet with just me and our Simon – our second Christmas without my wife. Nothing like the spread Dianne would've put on for all of us. His immediate family do their own thing every second year, so he wasn't included this year and he misses them terribly. Anyway, we had a good talk and made a decision – I'm moving him in with me for a few months as he's been struggling. It'll give me a bit of company and we can put him back together before he decides which direction he wants to go in life, again. A bit like you and Marjorie did. So how'd your flat move go, Dora?'

'Well, I'm in and loving it. And me and Marj have been out furniture shopping and Lauren has chosen which bedding and wallpaper she wants in her room. So that's really great. And Lauren and I spent the whole Christmas and New Year together, which has been pretty fantastic. I've told her she can come stay with me whenever she wants because she's got her own room now, which'll be marvellous for us both. It's wonderful getting the chance to be a mum again at fifty – ha, ha! But it's better now because I'm much more settled than I was and much happier. And she's a clever girl. She's an undergraduate at Bournemouth University, you know, doing a BA Honours degree in Accounting and Business studies.'

'A-ha!' spat a familiar voice approaching their table. 'So I can see yet another family business in the making. Small boutique hotel run by mother and daughter, no less, hey Dora? How ironic!'

Dora nearly choked on her coffee. 'What the hell are you doing here, Mommy dearest?'

Marjorie laughed at that reference. She could see that some peace had been restored between Yvonne and Dora. *Some!* But they were as typical a couple as that portrayed by Bette Davis and Joan Crawford in the film *Whatever Happened to Baby Jane?* According to Dora their New Year's get-together with the whole family at Philippa's place had gone swimmingly. Clearly Philippa had given strict instructions to Yvonne about getting over herself for the sake of smooth family relationships. But Dora and Yvonne would probably always have the occasional spat. It was in their blood.

'Well, you lot aren't the only ones in Eileen's address book! I think she even said Jodie was coming. Stacy's beau is coming – well quite a few of us have been invited, darling. Doesn't she want us for a group photo shoot or something?'

'Oh yes,' said Marjorie. 'They've set up a new website about the Afternoon Tea Club and they want to include all the success stories – you know – people meeting up with long-lost friends, people making new friends, long-lost families and that sort of thing, as well as the activities they provide. They're billing it as the best place in town to come and make friends and have some fun. I think it's a pretty neat idea.'

'It's a great idea,' said Raymond.

'So we're all going to be famous now,' added Stacy.

Suddenly more people started arriving. Jodie, who ran up to Dora and threw her arms around her. Steven and Gracie appeared, much to Marjorie's delight and surprise, and she set about introducing them to all her new friends, especially Raymond. Raymond's son, Simon, came up to him and shook his hand.

'Wow, Pops! It's quite a turnout. Yeah, I'll have a hot chocolate, thanks. Although I don't think that machine's gonna cope with all our demands.'

Eileen and her sons and Taynor arrived, and Stacy's face was a picture as her mother and father and Peter and Marvin arrived with John.

'Yay!' she squeaked at them as she ran up to each of them and showered them with hugs. 'Come meet all my new friends!'

Andy and Lauren came in with Pat, searching the crowd for Dora.

'Hi, Mum!' said Lauren, giving her mother a hug and, spotting Grandma Yvonne, Lauren slipped away to say 'hi' to her.

'Hello, Pat. Good to see you again,' said Marjorie. 'I think they've given up with the drinks machine. Or it's given up with us. Someone's opening the canteen, in a minute. So they'll serve you with whatever you fancy drinking.'

Marjorie noticed the way Andy brushed Dora's cheek with

his hand and how Dora looked at him. He followed Lauren to say hello to Yvonne and Philippa.

'You didn't tell me about, um, *this* ...?' Marjorie said provocatively, as she approached Dora.

'I didn't know there was a *this* until just recently,' Dora said with a wicked smile. 'In fact, it's quite a big *this* now actually, I'm thrilled to say! But I'll tell you *everything* when you come over to mine, next week. Oh and can you make it earlier? About 6.30 p.m.? I start work at my new job the next day. It's so exciting!'

'Yes, sure. Gosh it's all happening for you, isn't it? Your family storylines are better than *EastEnders*, I must say! Oh, and would you look at *that.*'

It looked as though members of a film crew were arriving. There were eight men and women dressed in black T-shirts and jeans making a clattering entrance with microphones, sound and recording equipment.

Eileen stood in front of the chattering crowd. 'Okay, everyone! Hello there! Can you all hear me?'

No one really took any notice of Eileen until Yvonne did a piercing wolf whistle, which made everyone stop but then start laughing.

'Quiet, people! This lady is trying to talk to you!' Yvonne said.

That did the trick. Dora looked embarrassed. Lauren put her arm around her mother's waist and nestled her head against her shoulder.

'Thank you, Yvonne. Well, everybody. Hopefully you've all

met up with each other and had a nice hot drink or two and a jolly good natter. Like I said in the email, this get-together is for our new website, so what we're going to do is make our way into the main hall and have a collective photo. Afterwards, some of you are going to be interviewed regarding your amazing stories because of the Afternoon Tea Club. Right, so if you're ready? Come this way,' Eileen said, leading everybody next door into the main hall.

She started positioning everybody with the tallest at the back and she found a chair for Taynor to sit on. Michael was wheeled next to Taynor with Eileen's mother in her wheelchair on the other side. Then she went back to the camera crew to give them instructions. Dora sighed and moved to the front of the gathering.

'Well, this is not working for me, people,' she stated, pacing.

Everybody started looking at one another.

'What's not working?' said Yvonne, folding her arms.

'Well, if this photo is going to represent the Afternoon Tea Club in the guise of "the best place in town to make friends *and have some fun*", then a photo of a sombre group of people with weird grins on their faces is not going to cut it. Wouldn't make me rush to sign up, is what I'm saying!'

'So what do you have in mind, Dora?' said Raymond.

'Well, it needs more drama; more action. Happy, engaging faces. Or something more impactful or creative. Hmm. Not sure what. I'll be back in a second,' she said, walking out of the hall.

'She's nuts, that one,' muttered Yvonne.

The camera crew moved their equipment into the hall and started setting up. Dora came back and started talking to them in a hushed voice. Eileen was watching her. Then Dora left again. When she returned she had a large bowl of what was most probably water, judging by the laboured way she was walking with it. She gave it to one of the crew members and then hurried back into the midst of the crowd.

'Right, I think that should do it,' she told everybody.

She found Andy and Lauren and stood between them with her arms around their waists. Andy kissed her cheek, as the opportunity presented itself, and Dora hugged her daughter. Yvonne and Philippa linked arms next to Lauren, with Grandma Pat next to Andy. Dora felt blessed to have her wonderful family all around her, as did everybody, that day.

'Wait for it!' She grinned at them both, holding them tight.

'Right, so are we ready now?' said Eileen.

'Yes, we are,' said Dora. 'So come on. Get in here with the rest of us, Eileen!'

The camera crew member winked at his mates and then shouted, 'On the count of three I'm going to chuck this bowl of ice-cold water over the lot of you and then we're gonna snap your response!'

Everybody jumped nervously.

'W-what?' said Eileen.

'They're doing *what?*' said Raymond, looking nervous.

'Ooh! No wait! My new frock!' yelped someone else.

But the crewman didn't wait for the audience to compose themselves nor did he give them the chance to bottle it and run off.

'One, two, *three*!'

The cold water formed an arc of droplets as it left the crewman's hands and splashed down onto the heads of the astonished assembly in Borough Community Centre.

There was a moment's silence as the dripping water slopped over them and then a cacophony of cries as the icy water soaked into their clothes.

'Aargh! Nooo!' yelped the crowd, collectively; mouths open, raised eyebrows, hands grasping, faces cringing ...

But Dora was right.

The result made one hell of a stunning photograph on the new Afternoon Tea Club website.

Acknowledgements

A book finding its way into publication via various media – audiobooks, ebooks, paperbacks – is not just about the person behind the writing. True, the author has honed their skill and written the tale. But behind them are those other skilled producers; the editors, the marketing unit, the bloggers, the writing community – all of whom are like one big family forever guiding the book forward; as well as one's own family and relatives, who are supportive of the author's talent.

So my heartfelt thanks goes to my brilliant Commissioning Editor, Katie Loughnane, for her continued passion, encouragement and dedication; Helena Newton, copy editor, with her eye for detail; the inspiring Sabah Khan, Head of PR; Ellie Pilcher, Marketing Manager, and the amazing team that is Avon, HarperCollins.

Thanks also to my friends who loved my debut novel. *The Woman Who Kept Everything.* So **BIG** thanks to, Sue Harness, Suzanne, Vanda, Sue H, Susan, Pippa, Bella, Bev Z, Jenny, Maxine and Jordanne, Jorge and Lis, Sue P, Andrew and Kathleen, Glyn and Jackie, Eileen, Anna and Gisela, Julie,

Jorge and Lis, and my wider family Lee, Anne, Ben, Charlotte and cousins Janet, Paul, Colin, Nikki, Auntie Joyce for her inspiring knowledge, my primary teacher Beryl Crabtree and English teacher in secondary school, Mr Philpot, whose enthusiasm and praise carries me along, as well as the occasional glass of wine!

And finally a big **THANK YOU** to all my readers. If I have brightened someone's day, I have, at least, done my job well.

Get ready to meet 79-year-old Gloria
in Jane Gilley's debut novel . . .

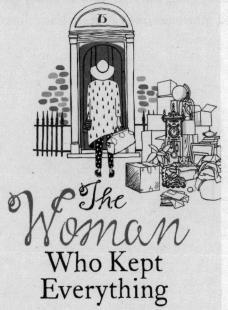

JANE GILLEY

The
Woman
Who Kept
Everything

An uplifting, funny and moving novel that
will warm your heart.

Out now!